LOST IN TIME

A SPLIT-SECOND TIME TRAVEL STORY

KEN JOHNS

To Shelly, Carrie, Thomas,
+ Downarcen

Thanks for your support

Ken Johns

Cover & eBook design by Crystal Clear Solutions

Cover images licensed from shutterstock.com

Author photo by Doug Buchan Photography

To Big Lar

CHAPTER ONE

July 9, 2017

Mila just couldn't force herself to enter her parents' house. Her home, really—she'd lived there for the first twenty years of her life. She stood close to the door as though it were about to open and she would step through. But she was actually standing that close to avoid the sight lines through the glass windows that bordered it. The closer she stood, the less likely she'd be spotted from within.

For the seventh time, her finger drifted to the doorbell without pressing it. She glanced at her phone. Where was her sister? Jess should have been here by now. They were supposed to go in and present their anniversary gift together. A corner of the envelope poked at her skin from the back pocket of her jeans. She reached down and pulled it out. The paper had begun to curve, and she flattened it out on her thigh.

Mila glanced up and down the street. What if her old neighbors spotted her through their sheers and wondered why she was standing outside instead of going in? Old

Mrs. Robinson would probably come out of her house and walk across the road just to ask if everything was okay. Mila wished it were winter, just for a second. Not because she liked the cold, but because the days were shorter and at least she would have the cover of darkness while she waited.

Why didn't she just go in? How bad could it be? They were her parents, for Christ's sake. She took a deep breath. Sandra would hug her and, with a strained look on her face, hold her at arm's length, studying her face for any signs of stress or fatigue or whatever it was moms looked for. John would give her a giant bear hug and pull away quickly with minimal eye contact. They would talk about the weather and uncomfortable silence would follow while John figured out a way to swing the conversation toward her. Had she landed any roles? Did she have a new boyfriend? Did she need any money? It never changed. So she was fine waiting outside. It was too bad she'd taken transit. If she had a car, she could have waited in it like a normal person.

The throaty rumble of a well-tuned engine pulled into the driveway next door. Mr. Clark's '67 GTO crept slowly up his driveway and eased to a stop on the far side of John's pickup. Had he seen her? *Shit.* He'd saunter over, scuffing his heels, and try to strike up a conversation. *Hey, Mila, it's been so long. How ya doin'.* His eyes, though hidden by mirrored glasses, would inevitably lose their grip on her face and ease down her torso. *Ugh.* He'd done that since she was thirteen.

His door opened, and his cowboy boots hit the ground.

Mila glanced around her yard. There was nothing close enough to hide behind. Inside with her parents, for better or worse, was her only escape. She pressed the doorbell. No ding-dong. *Shit.*

Mr. Clark stood up. His head came into view above the hood of John's pickup. The brim of his Mariners baseball cap covered the graying hair on his neck. His door clunked shut.

She rang the bell again. Still nothing. Was it even working?

"Hey, Mila!" Clark bawled across the lawn. "It's great to see ya."

Pretending not to hear him, she grabbed the handle and tried it. It turned. She stepped inside and closed the door behind her. She blew out a long breath and pasted a smile on her face. "Happy anniversary!"

"Hi, Mila!" Sandra walked out of the kitchen with her hands up behind her shoulder blades. Adjusting her bra? She combed her fingers through her hair as she came down the hall.

Mila hugged her and tried not to visualize the activities her parents had been up to that might have necessitated the adjustments Sandra needed to make under her sweater.

Sandra released her and slid her hands down the back of Mila's arms. "Here. Let me look at you."

The double-handhold once-over was imminent. Mila lifted her arms out of Sandra's hands. "That won't be necessary."

Mila stepped around Sandra to where John waited to give her a hug. "Hi, John."

"Hi, Mila." He leaned down and wrapped his enormous arms around her back.

She sucked in a breath and braced for the squeeze. He didn't quite lift her off the ground, but it was close.

When he stepped back, he said, "Can I get you a glass of wine?"

"Sure," she said.

He walked back to the kitchen.

"How are you?" Sandra said.

"I'm great." Mila smiled, following her into the kitchen.

John handed her a glass of wine. He leaned down and planted a kiss on Sandra's neck then returned to the stove to stir something.

Her parents had been married for twenty-five years, but they still found the energy to act like teenagers on their anniversary. Mila didn't know if she should be impressed or disgusted. She sipped her wine and pulled out her phone. She texted Jess: *Save me. The love parade is in full swing! ETA?* She put her phone back in her pocket. "Can I help?"

"No, everything's ready," Sandra said. "Your dad's been cooking all afternoon. He's on leave."

Mila inhaled the scent of sautéed garlic that permeated the kitchen. "Smells amazing."

"Let's take our wine into the living room while we wait for your sister." John gestured toward the comfy chairs with his wineglass, keeping his other hand on the small of Sandra's back.

Mila followed them to the couch and quickly sat down next to Sandra, ensuring that there was no room between them for John. She caught the smirk on his face as he crossed the room and took the easy chair by the TV.

Mila's phone chirped with a text. *Be there in 10. 5 if I use the siren.* Mila sighed her relief and texted, *Do it.*

"Was that Jess?" Sandra leaned over to read Mila's phone.

Mila slid the phone back in her pocket, nodding. "Mm hm."

"She's been working long hours lately," said John.

And there it was, the segue to the inquisition about work.

"Have you had any callbacks recently?" asked Sandra.

"Nope."

"Auditions?" asked John.

"No."

"Do you need some money?" Sandra smiled weakly, raising her eyebrows.

Every time. Mila took a slow breath in. "I'm fine."

"We worry, that's all." John held her gaze from across the room.

Mila read his look of concern that barely masked the underlying disappointment.

"Don't." She said it out loud for both of them. To him as an answer, and to herself as a warning. If she engaged, it would ruin the evening. But every fucking time they got her alone, it came up. When were they going to just let her live? She stifled the urge to check the time on her phone. Instead she glanced across the room and found the LED of the VCR, still working long after the format had become obsolete. John refused to let it die.

"Maybe if you had a steady income..." he continued.

"Enough!" Mila cut him off. "Don't you ever get tired of this?"

Sandra put her hand on Mila's knee and squeezed gently. "It's all right, Mila. We're only trying to help."

No, you're meddling. She wanted to scream it but instead she lifted her mother's hand off her knee and said, "I don't need your help."

The front door opened and Jess called from the hallway. "Happy anniversary!"

John raced into the hall to greet Jess. *Typical.* Sandra stood and followed him.

"Hi, Daddy," Jess squealed as she gave John a hug. She was almost as tall as he was, and in her Kevlar vest, their upper bodies were the same girth. She slapped his back as Sandra stepped in.

"I'm going to put supper on the table." John headed for the kitchen.

"Hi, Mom." Jess bent at the knees and air-hugged Sandra. "Sorry, that's all I can do right now. A real hug will Velcro your sweater permanently to my vest."

When Sandra stepped back she put a hand on Jess's cheek. "I'm glad you're here. Do you want some wine?"

Jess nodded. "Definitely."

"Coming right up." Sandra followed John into the kitchen.

Jess opened her arms again, but Mila held up a hand and pointed at Jess's gear. "I'll wait."

"Yeah, sorry. I had to come straight over." Jess rolled her eyes and then crooked her head to one side in her best vacuous-blonde imitation. "Obviously."

Jess hung her tac vest in the hall closet and put her holstered gun up on the top shelf, next to John's.

"You're just in time," Mila whispered.

"Oh, did I miss it?" Jess sounded disappointed.

"You did. But there were no waterworks. I nipped it in the bud."

"Well done." Jess leaned in for a hug. "It's good to see you."

"You too." Mila held Jess and whispered in her ear. "I

got the tickets!"

"Awesome." Jess pulled back. "Can I see?"

Mila handed her the envelope and grabbed a ballpoint pen off the hall table. "Here, sign the card while you're looking."

Jess read the anniversary card and smiled, but spent more time staring at the four tickets inside it. "I can't believe we're really doing this."

"We still have to convince them." Mila nodded toward the kitchen.

"Don't worry. They'll come." Jess sounded more confident than Mila felt.

"Okay, I can't wait any longer. Let's do it." Mila led her big sister into the kitchen. John took off his oven mitts as Sandra handed Jess a glass of wine.

Jess held up the wine. "A toast." She had to wait while the rest of them retrieved their glasses from the living room. "To our favorite parents. Your love inspires us. Hell, it spawned us. May you have another twenty-five years as good—or better—than the first ones."

They all took a sip.

Mila handed John the envelope. "Happy anniversary. From both of us."

"Thank you." John handed it to Sandra, then stood behind her to read over her shoulder.

Sandra read the front of the card and held the tickets out of the way while they finished reading the inside. She smiled. "Aww. Thank you."

When Sandra stepped toward Jess for another hug, Mila pointed at Sandra's hand. "Finish reading the rest."

"Oh, I'm sorry." Sandra held up the tickets and started to read. She seemed to take too long reading, as though it wasn't plain English. Then her worry wrinkles began to grow in her forehead. Finally, she held the tickets out to John, and Mila could have sworn she saw Sandra's chin quiver.

"Wow," said John. He finished reading. "Thanks very much. That's great."

Clearly, John wasn't picking up Sandra's vibe. Mila glanced at Jess.

"Mom," said Jess, "what's wrong?"

"Nothing." Sandra downed the last half of her wine. "You really shouldn't have. You know your father and I don't want you guys spending your money on us."

"Stop it." Mila forced herself to keep it light. "Did you count the tickets?"

John fanned the tickets, revealing four. "Hey look, Sandy. We can take the Taylors with us."

"Funny," Mila deadpanned. Then, with as much enthusiasm as she could muster, she said, "When was the last time we enjoyed a family holiday? We're all going."

"It's going to be great," said Jess with her infectious smile.

"I can't wait," said John.

Sandra elbowed him. "Do you even know where we're going?"

"I can read." John looked confused.

"Can you?" Sandra pointed at the tickets.

"It says, *Canterbury in England*." John didn't read where she pointed. "I think it's a wonderful idea."

Sandra pulled the tickets back. "It says, and I quote, 'The Split-Second *Time Travel* Company invites you to visit Canterbury. Follow in the steps of Chaucer's pilgrims and see Rochester Castle and Canterbury Cathedral in the year of our lord 1341.'"

Sandra let her hand fall to her side.

"John, it's time travel." Mila couldn't stay silent. She had to take control before Sandra's panic snowballed. "You know, like Aunt Beth and Uncle Jack did last summer?"

"You guys have talked about it for years," added Jess.

"Yeah," said John, "but I thought it was prohibitively expensive."

"It was, back when it was first discovered, but that was twenty years ago. I think the patents ran out or something, because the price has come way down," said Jess.

"There are all kinds of companies offering it now. I found a great deal online." Mila smiled outwardly, but inside she knew that if they didn't convince Sandra that night, they never would. "We're going to see castles and cathedrals in use and fully standing. Before they became the ruins they are today."

"Tapestries, minstrels, jugglers, and original stained glass," added Jess.

"And a tournament." Mila said this to John. If she could keep him on board, Sandra would follow his lead. "Jousting, melee—you know, grown men kicking each other's asses for sport."

"Are you sure it's safe?" John asked.

"You can check their safety records online," said Jess. "I did. The SSTTC has never had a problem."

John nodded slowly. "What do you think?"

"I think we should have dinner." Sandra moved to the table and sat down. "Your father prepared all this wonderful food, and it's sitting here getting cold."

"Fine." Mila sat down next to Sandra and plated a

large slice of lasagna for herself. "So, are we going, or what?"

Sandra frowned as she loaded tossed salad into her bowl.

Jess and John were both looking at her, literally hanging on her reply.

"Well?" said Mila.

Sandra blew a wisp of black hair off her forehead and smiled. "Yes. If Beth did it, I sure as hell can."

CHAPTER TWO

April 5, 2018

Mila banged on the door to Jess's hotel room. Again. "Come on. John and Sandra are already in the lobby."

"Coming," said Jess, her singsong voice muffled through the door.

When the door finally swung open, Jess stepped out wearing jeans and a sweatshirt, but she glowed. Mila had long since learned to quell her envy. Some people were just happy all the time, and her sister was one of them. Mila didn't smile before noon, as a rule, unless there was coffee or a camera. "You look good. Is that why it took so long?"

Jess smiled. "Oh, no. I jumped out of bed when you knocked on the door."

"Bullshit." Mila knew it took Jess at least an hour to do her makeup and hair.

Jess snickered as she lifted her phone and started texting as they walked toward the elevator.

"You can't bring that." Mila stopped walking.

"What?"

Mila pointed at the phone.

"Oh, shit, I forgot." Jess ran back to her room and disappeared inside.

Mila waited for a minute before she rolled her eyes and walked back to Jess's open door. "What's taking so long?"

Jess had the cabinet open under the TV. "I can't decide what pass code to use for the safe."

"Just use your birthday."

"Are you serious? Do you know how many people use their birthday as a password? That's like saying, 'Here, take my stuff.'"

"Will you just pick a number? You know the longer we leave Sandra alone, the more time she'll have to think of a reason to back out."

Jess shook her head. "She's not going to back out. Why fly to New York? If she was going to back out, she would have done it at home."

"I hope you're right." Mila checked the time on the clock by Jess's bed. Sandra's "decisions" were fluid at best. "Still, I'd feel a lot better if we were down there holding her hand."

"Fine." The safe beeped and Jess stood up. "Let's go."

Mila followed her out to the elevator. "So what number did you wind up using?"

Jess's mouth bent up at one side with the tiniest smile. "*Your* birthday."

"Bitch." Mila giggled as she stepped into the elevator.

When the doors opened, Sandra and John were standing right there. "What took you so long?" John asked Mila.

"Don't even start." Mila held a palm up to her father as she walked past him toward the hotel's main entrance.

"It wasn't her," said Jess.

"Oh," said John.

Mila didn't expect an apology. She was used to it. She stepped out onto West Forty-Fourth Street and held the door for her family. The crisp April air cut through her sweater, but if she suggested a cab, Jess would counter-suggest walking, and John would side with Jess. So she didn't.

"Which way?" said Sandra.

"Ten blocks," said John, pointing up the street. Holding Sandra's hand, he moved into the stream of pedestrians, and a gap opened around him. He had that effect on people.

Mila had no interest in occupying that space at the moment, so she let a clump of people pass before slipping into the flow of humanity with her sister. She needed some room. Who knew what cramped quarters they might have to occupy in the days to come? She'd better enjoy these moments while she could. She wasn't worried about losing sight of John. His head and shoulders stood above the average height of the crowd, and she and Jess had both inherited that genetic trait.

"You okay?" Jess said in her ear.

"No." Mila sucked in a breath through her mouth and let it out slowly through her nose.

"Anything I can do?"

"Remind me why we're doing this," Mila said.

"Seriously?" Jess put her arm around Mila's shoulders. "I think you felt nostalgic for a past family vacation that may or may not have ever really happened and you thought, *hey, wouldn't this be cool.*"

Mila rolled her eyes, but she did manage a smile as they walked. "Thanks, Doctor. Next time I decide I want to spend a long time in close proximity to John, just slap me, okay?"

"Done." Jess smirked.

Mila studied her sister's face for a moment. "You would, too, wouldn't you?"

"With love," said Jess, drawing back one open palm. "Like this."

"Don't." Mila pointed a single finger in Jess's direction.

Jess giggled as she lowered her hand.

They walked in silence until John led Sandra through the crowd to a building on their left and opened a door. "We're here."

Mila stopped and read the unobtrusive brass engraving next to the door. *Split-Second Time Travel Co. – Welcome To The World That Was.*

"Are you coming?" John held the door. Sandra and Jess were already inside.

"Yeah." She stepped past him. "Thanks."

The door closed behind them with a long, metallic echo. Mila jumped and stared at the offending door. It resembled every other heavy glass door. "That was creepy."

"What did you say, sweetie?" asked Sandra.

"Nothing." Mila smiled quickly, turning to face her mother. That was the last thing she needed. If she wasn't careful, her comments could set Sandra off.

White marble lined the cavernous lobby. A wraparound desk on a dais the size of a flatbed stood at least fifty meters away. A small head, just visible above the desk, bobbed to some unheard beat. John led them down the long room toward the movement. The receptionist sat with her back to them, leaning over an open file drawer.

"Good morning," called John.

No response. The bopping continued.

"Hello!" Mila offered.

Jess climbed up onto the dais, stepped around the desk, reached over, and tapped one rocking shoulder.

"Fuck!" the receptionist growled. She whipped her wide-eyed face toward the offending finger, wielding her stapler in a defensive sweep.

Jess pointed at her own ear.

"Oh!" The receptionist pulled out her ear buds and added more quietly, "I forgot I had these in." No trace of the cornered beast remained. She placed the stapler on her desk and picked up an iPad. "Do you have a reservation?"

"We're the McLeods," John said.

"Your orientation will begin shortly. Please follow me." The receptionist walked down the two steps from the dais and led them to a frosted glass wall behind the desk. She slid open one panel and held it while they all entered the anteroom.

Mila turned to thank her, but she was already climbing back up to her desk as the door closed on its own with a creepy hiss. Mila slumped down on a leather sofa just inside the door. Jess joined her. Sandra sank into the easy chair and John stood in the middle of the room in a position he called "parade rest," facing the only other door. Would he be able to relax at all on this vacation? "There's plenty of room." Mila pointed to the space between her and Jess.

"No, I'm good." John returned his focus to the door.

Mila let her eyes wander to the framed posters that extolled the excitement of the tours offered by the Split-Second Time Travel Company. *Ancient Rome under Hadrian's Rule* showed the iconic Colosseum in its pristine state, not broken and shored up like it was nowadays. *Jerusalem in the Time of Christ* showed a beautiful marble temple that Mila didn't recognize. *The Birth of Democracy in Ancient Athens* displayed a columned building trimmed in gold and blue. It kind of looked like the Parthenon, but Mila wasn't sure. All of the pictures were glossy and enticing.

The door in front of John opened, and a man in a lab coat stepped through. He wore a name tag sticker that said *My name is_____*, and in the blank he'd written *Bob*.

Mila rolled her eyes when he opened with, "My name is Bob. I'll be your guide for the orientation today."

Bob passed them each a clipboard with a single page and an attached pen. "These are your release forms. Please read and sign them. I'll be back in a few minutes."

Bob left, and Mila skimmed the fine print. Before she'd gotten halfway down the page, she heard Jess scrawl her signature. Mila raised an eyebrow. "Seriously?"

"What?" said Jess. "It's just a formality. You know if anything goes wrong, I'm suing their asses. This single page won't mean shit in court."

John and Sandra were busy reading every word. Mila returned to her own document. It started with the usual indemnities. Then came a set of rules designed to limit the participant's impact on the past and therefore the future. That's where it got interesting.

"Did you even read this part?" Mila pointed.

Jess lifted her own clipboard and started reading out

loud. "'One: the participant will share no information with any inhabitants of the time period visited. Two: when speaking with inhabitants, it is recommended to keep the subject matter related to food or weather. If this cannot be accomplished, then not speaking at all is recommended. Three: at no time should any participant touch or have any physical contact with the inhabitants. This is for the safety of both the participant and the inhabitants. Four: your SSTTC guide will do their best to avoid situations where conflict might arise between inhabitants or between participants and inhabitants. If you find yourself in an unforeseen or unavoidable conflict situation with an inhabitant, do not fight. Your best course of action is to run. Fighting will only result in potential harm to the inhabitant and therefore to the integrity of the timeline. Five: any participant caught breaking any of these rules will be sent home immediately and prosecuted to the full extent of the law.'" Jess stopped reading. "Okay, so the guide is also a babysitter."

"You still think it's just a formality?" Sandra said. "They seem pretty concerned about this stuff. Don't talk to them, don't touch them, don't fight back. What's that all about?"

"It means you could change history if you tell somebody about the future, even by accident," said Mila.

"Or if you hurt somebody," added John.

"But it says not to even touch them," Sandra frowned.

"That's probably about disease," said Mila.

"What kind of disease?" Sandra's eyes popped wide. "Plague?"

"It can't be the plague," Mila said quickly. "I read somewhere that this tour is taken before the plague came to England." She smiled. "It seems like they've done their homework."

"It could also be us bringing modern diseases into the past," said Jess.

Mila signed her release in a show of confidence she didn't really feel, but she had no reason to distrust the SSTTC. "So, are we good?"

John signed his form and put a hand on Sandra's shoulder. "How are you doing?"

"I'm not sure." Sandra put her hand over his.

Bob came back in. "Is everybody ready?"

They all watched Sandra. She glanced at each of them, then huffed and signed her form.

"Yay!" said Jess with a little clap.

They all handed Bob their clipboards, and he glanced at each one. "Next, I will lead you to the change rooms. There you will be provided a locker for your personal belongings and a set of SSTTC JumpGear to change into. The ladies' JumpGear is a woolen robe, much like a housecoat. The gentleman's JumpGear is like a set of wool pajamas."

"What about underwear?" asked Mila. Wool could be so itchy.

"Including underwear," said Bob. "Nothing from the present can travel back in time to before its date of invention. Bras and panties had not been invented in the fourteenth century."

"What?" said Jess. "They had to wear something."

Bob shook his head. "It's history. I don't make the rules. The period undergarment was a chemise, which will be provided along with your full costume upon arrival. The JumpGear has been designed for ease of movement and speedy removal, so that you may change quickly into your period clothing. Our company guide will meet you with a carriage that serves as a rolling wardrobe and a changing room."

"Cool," said Mila. "Will there be any choices? Style? Color?"

Bob scowled. "It's the fourteenth century. Your costumes have been designed to blend in, not stand out. We do not wish to draw any attention while we are visitors. You must remain as anonymous as possible."

"Fine," Mila sighed. "Just asking, Bob."

"Are there any more questions?" Nobody said anything, so Bob led them to the change rooms.

———

MILA CAME OUT OF THE CHANGE ROOM FIRST AND stood waiting for the rest of her family. She twisted her neck and rolled her shoulders in a futile attempt to ease the itchiness. The sooner they got there and changed, the happier she'd be.

John came out of the men's change room and stood next to her. "All set?"

Mila nodded. "Mm hm."

John smiled. He seemed pretty happy, standing there in his JumpGear pj's.

Jess and Sandra finally joined them, but before they could say anything, Bob appeared at the end of the hall.

"Please follow me." Bob led them through a reinforced steel door. They shuffled into a dimly lit room lined with computer racks. The hum of cooling fans negated any conversation, so Mila kept quiet. Bob motioned to a black sliding door at the end of the racks. They moved through it into an elevator-sized room. Once they were all inside, Bob slid the door closed, cutting off the hum. "Let me introduce you to the MCV."

Bob pointed to the baseball-sized globe sitting on a waist-high plastic column in the center of the room. They'd all had to step around it when they entered. Now they stood in a loose circle facing it.

"This is the Miniature Chrono Vehicle." He smiled. "Or MCV."

Mila furrowed her brows. Why was Bob so stoked about such an obvious acronym?

The MCV seemed to be made of the same white plastic as the pedestal. But when Bob reached out to it, it assumed the color of his fingers.

"As you can see, it's camo enhanced." Bob swiped right across the surface of the ball and a holographic display appeared above it. "And it has a touch screen interface and the holo-display you see here." He actually pointed. Mila threw a puzzled look at Jess, who shrugged and smiled back at her.

Bob returned his hand to the ball and said something that sounded like "little big horn" as he began to type. What the hell was that about? The date *April 27, 1341, 9:00 a.m.* appeared in translucent red characters in the air between their faces.

"You must all touch the MCV together in order to travel to the same time and place. There is a flash of light during the jump, so I suggest once you have placed your hands on the MCV, you close your eyes." He pointed to the sliding door. "I will be monitoring from the computer room."

The sliding black door was in fact heavily tinted glass, and they had a dim view out to the computer room. Why was it so dark?

"When I leave the room, I will start the sixty-second countdown." Bob pointed to a small LED clock in the corner near the door. He raised his eyebrows. "Are there any questions?"

Mila had a question, but she didn't want to ask it in front of Sandra. Thankfully, Sandra asked it for her.

"Does it hurt?"

"Does what hurt?"

"Time travel," said Sandra.

Bob shook his head. "It is almost instantaneous. Some people have reported a slight feeling of euphoria."

Reported? So Bob had never done it. That wasn't very comforting.

"Any other questions?" he asked.

Mila had some, but Bob apparently didn't have any answers that hadn't been prepared for him, so she kept them to herself.

"Then please place your hands on the MCV, and have a nice trip." Bob opened the door. The wall of computer noise slammed them until he slid the door closed. He stepped to a console across from the door. The countdown began.

"Wow," said Mila as she watched the little clock counting down. "He's not wasting any time."

CHAPTER THREE

April 5, 2018

John tore his eyes off the countdown clock. The girls smiled with anticipation but Sandra fussed with the belt of her JumpGear. He put his arm around her shoulders. "Hang in there." He smiled. "Hard part's almost over."

Sandra blew a wisp of black hair from her eyes. "How do *you* know? You've never done this before either."

"What, time travel? No, but I can read a clock." He nodded at the clock that showed thirty seconds to go.

"Shit." Sandra huffed.

A hissing drifted up through the grate beneath their feet.

"Please place one hand on the MCV, Mrs. McLeod." Bob stood just outside the glass with a wireless mic in his hand. He pointed at the ball. As if she couldn't see it. John smirked. This guy was a prize.

"It's okay, Mom," Jess said. "We'll be fine. I'll see you when we get there."

Sandra gave Jess a weak smile but to John she said, "I don't want to do this anymore."

He gave her a squeeze. "Are you sure? T-minus twenty is a helluva time to back out."

"Mom!" Mila glared at Sandra. "Quit whining and put your hand on the MCV."

"I'm sorry." Sandra drew in a quick breath. "I don't think I can do it."

"Fifteen seconds on the clock, ladies. What's it going to be?" John took his own hand off the MCV.

"Wouldn't you like to go to Venice instead?" Sandra grinned. "My treat?"

Mila rolled her eyes and sighed. "Mom. I'll make it really simple. I'm going." She glanced at Jess.

"Well I can't let her go alone." Jess shrugged. "I guess I'm going too."

That was no surprise. Ever since they were kids, Jess had always backed Mila's play. Even though they were both adults, they were still his daughters. John didn't want either of them going without him. Ten seconds. Surely Sandra felt the same way. If she didn't, he'd have to step in and somehow stop them from going. Even when it was her panic attack, he would have to be the asshole.

Sandra huffed once and put her hand on the MCV. "Put your hand on the damn ball, Sergeant. They're not going alone."

He smiled as he put his hand on the MCV next to hers. "I hoped you might say that."

The launch room vanished.

CHAPTER FOUR

April 27, 1341
John's lungs refused to expand. Something collapsed his chest like a fist to the diaphragm. The air pressure pasted his wool shirt to his abs, his back, and his sides, as if he were free-falling. He couldn't breathe, and he couldn't see. Cave black had swallowed them. Hadn't Bob said there was a flash of light? And this was the longest "instantaneous" he had ever had to wait through.

The world erupted with light.

Shit. John's eyes closed instinctively, but the purest white shone through his eyelids. Even with his face buried in the crook of his elbow, it diminished only to a brilliant orange. He waited while it faded to a bearable level and wondered if this was normal or if he should start to worry. The pressure dropped away from his shirt and he gasped.

Broken earth poked his feet through the thin leather JumpGear slippers. He opened his eyes. *Bluebells?* They weren't in New York anymore.

The sea of flowers sloped away, covering a meadow

about two hundred meters across. A giant oak stood alone in the center, where a cart track circled it and led away into the woods. A narrow path led down from where they stood and ended near the tree. Their guide with his carriage should have been parked right there, in the trampled patch around the oak.

But he wasn't.

The retch of vomiting pierced the silence. John spun to see Sandra, on all fours, heaving up her breakfast in the field of blue. "You okay, babe?"

Sandra wiped the foul drool on her sleeve before she nodded.

Mila groaned and glared at Jess. "Aren't you feeling it?"

"It wasn't that bad." Jess spread her legs a shoulder-width apart and bent at the hips to stretch.

"Yeah, right." Mila cradled her stomach.

"Come on. Just take a few deep breaths." Jess straightened up, gathered her long blonde hair, and tied it in a bun. Her hair immediately began to loosen, and she shook it out and tried again. "I don't know what I'm going to do without hair elastics." Jess put a hand on Mila's shoulder.

"Stop it." Mila brushed the hand away and vomited.

Jess snapped her hand away, avoiding the deluge, but John leaned over Mila. "Are you all right?"

"Everybody just back off. I'll be fine, okay?" Mila said.

John let her be. If Mila said she would be fine, she would be fine. Like most fathers, he'd been slow to realize his babies had become grown women who did not want or appreciate his constant concern. Jess had had the good sense to wait until she actually was an adult before gently suggesting his attention might be more appreciated elsewhere. Mila had been her own woman by the age of seven.

Sandra stood up and undid her JumpGear housecoat. She held it open at the front as she smoothed the sides toward the center. The view was magnificent. The fact that the SSTTC had not provided undergarments was an added bonus. At the age of fifty, she still held a power over him that was as strong as it had been when they were in high school. Sandra's fitness regimen would put most of his recruits to shame, and the result was the hard body of a woman half her age.

"Mom." Mila's eyebrows climbed up under her bangs. "Why don't you just take the whole thing off and prance around the meadow?"

"Okay." Sandra let the garment slip down off her shoulders.

"Mom!" Mila and Jess shouted in unison.

John laughed. Sandra never tired of teasing her girls. They were still in denial that parents could be sexual beings.

Sandra pulled the dress back up. "There's no one here."

That snapped him back into the moment. "The guide was supposed to meet us when we arrived." He scanned the forest edge again. "Where is this guy?"

"It's only been five minutes," said Jess. "Give him a chance."

"We're too exposed out here." John pointed behind them. "Let's move up to the woods while we wait."

"You're spoiling it for everyone." Mila turned her back and adjusted her dress. "This is supposed to be a holiday, not a maneuver."

Sandra touched his arm. "Will you calm down if we move into the trees?"

He tried not to show the true level of his concern, but the training was a part of him. He stifled the urge to order them and smiled instead, hoping they would indulge him so he wouldn't have to insist.

"Dad, you're so paranoid." Jess started up the slope toward the forest.

At least she *got it*. As a member of the RCMP, Jess could understand his concern. Now he just had to convince the other two. He put his arms on their shoulders and nodded after Jess. "Shall we?"

Sandra and Mila followed her, but only after registering their protests with a sigh and an eye roll.

John took one last look around the meadow before following his family up the hill. He took a deep breath through his nose while he walked. He smiled at Sandra, who seemed to have completely forgotten about her panic before the jump. It was still a beautiful day. They climbed through a breathtaking field of wildflowers, but, oddly, there was no aroma. Shouldn't it have been more noticeable with so many flowers? Jess had reached the forest edge and sat down on a fallen log. Mila and Sandra were halfway there when the searing pain in his thigh ripped the smile off his face.

CHAPTER FIVE

April 25, 1341

A strong wind kept the clouds away as the sun baked the cathedral late in the afternoon. Fingers of light pointed through the dust in yellow and red shafts, illuminating the confessional in stained-glass fire.

Bishop Edward Deville sat naked in the darkened booth. His robes hung next to him, blocking the penitents' view through the lattice. The heat on his skin reminded him of his last journey to Rome. This was his favorite place in all of England. Here in the enveloping warmth of the confessional, he felt closest to God. From here he listened to his children and grew to know them, intimately. He could guide them to a deeper relationship with God, cajole them when they resisted, and scold them if they refused. Here he was in control. Here *he* was supreme.

Except today he was not. The penitents had ruined his mood. Today, like so many days recently, he seemed to be losing his grip.

First, the tanner asked why his wife questioned him at

every turn. This seemed innocent enough, and Edward recommended a sound thrashing. The tanner accepted the advice and went on his way.

The miller asked why he must go with the baron to France. Edward pointed out that the miller lived on the lord's lands, and military service was a condition of that tenancy. The man understood the argument but not the reason for it. Edward told the miller that he need not understand the reasoning as long as he followed the rule.

When a villager's wife asked why she could not leave the village, he told her she would become an outlaw and she should know better.

A series of merchants asked why God did not answer their prayers. Edward told them God had no interest in their profits. Yet the very asking was heresy. The last merchant asked why he had to pay the church tax. Unbelievable!

A rivulet of sweat dripped off Edward's chin and splashed onto his thigh. The heat did not usually affect him like this. He held his robes away from the latticework so he could breathe the fresh air that wafted in with the next penitent. He waited next to the opening to catch a glimpse of who it would be.

The door to his own side began to swing open and he grabbed it and slammed it closed. "Other side, please, my child." Did they see in? Would he have to explain his nakedness? *It brings me closer to God. After all, were Adam and Eve not naked in the Garden of Eden?* He had prepared the story so long ago, he had forgotten when. It sounded convincing—it always did—but he had never had to say it out loud. No, the door had only come open three inches, six inches at most. His secret was safe.

"Forgive me, Your Grace," came an unfamiliar feminine voice, courtly yet somehow foreign.

He had missed his chance to glimpse her face. He waited for her to continue. The silence was too long. She should already have begun the litany. "Do you not know the words, my child?"

"Oh, I am sorry, Your Grace. I have nothing to confess. I just wanted to see the inside of your confessional. Have you suggested it to the council? I do hope the church adopts it. It is an excellent idea." Her door creaked open and she stepped out.

Edward peeked through the lattice but only caught a glimpse of white robes as she disappeared. Who was this woman who dared to enter the confessional with no intention to confess and then left without permission? Outrageous. He stood and pulled his golden robe over his head. It had barely fallen into place when he rushed out and stormed down the aisle. He swung open the cathedral door and stepped into the wind.

A few villagers walked past. "Good day, Your Grace."

He raised a hand in acknowledgment. The woman in white was not among them, nor was she across the square. She should have been easy to spot, rushing away along any of the roads that led from the square. But he saw nothing so bright, just the brown village dirt, silvering wood, tan thatching, and green weeds. Everything dull. The woman had vanished.

Edward lifted his gaze to the castle on the hill, where the baron's presence always dominated the landscape. He gathered his robes, leaned into the wind, and hurried up the narrow road that led to the castle. He had to find a way to regain control of the villagers. If he could find the source of the heresy, perhaps it was not too late to stamp it out. If he could only find some way to show the hand of God at work, the people would come back to him. The Bible was a tool, a textbook of fear. He only had to use it properly to restore order. Show them somehow... scare them.

Edward found a crowd blocking his way. A man at the back turned to see who had joined him. It was the miller, and when he recognized Edward, he bowed his head and hurried away.

The crowd surrounded a horse-drawn carriage. It was not the first time Edward had seen it parked in the village. Who owned such a large carriage? Surely not the king—it had no ornamentation. The driver sat up on his bench, but curtains concealed the occupants below. The villagers seemed to speak with those within. An arm appeared and handed out a small parcel. Edward caught a glimpse of white sleeve. *The mysterious woman!*

He pushed his way between two villagers and started toward the carriage. As he passed each villager, they recognized his robe and suddenly seemed to have somewhere else to be.

"Sorry, Your Grace." A man bowed and moved away from the back of the crowd.

"Forgive me, Your Grace." A woman ushered her daughter toward a nearby alley.

The crowd grew smaller and smaller the closer he got to the center. When he finally reached the carriage, Edward stood alone.

A hand appeared and offered a parcel. He took it and examined its contents. The two pieces of soft bread with warm ground meat and sliced onions between them, dripping with melted cheese, smelled heavenly. He threw it to the ground.

"You there!" Edward addressed the driver. "Whose carriage is this?"

The man whipped his horses.

"Stop!"

The carriage started to roll.

"Stop! In the name of God, I command thee!"

The carriage accelerated down the road, turned a corner, and disappeared from sight. No one ignored him. Unbelievable.

CHAPTER SIX

April 25, 1341

Chad whipped the horses again. They responded with another surge as if changing gears. The carriage bucked and rocked as the horses dragged it out of the valley. The hard bench beneath him jarred his spine with every bump and reminded him how wonderful modern suspension would be when it was invented. He glanced behind, half expecting to see a charge of fully armored knights. Obviously, the bishop wouldn't be able to organize any kind of response that quickly, but still.

The outskirts of the village fell away as Chad raced through the fields. He let the horses have their heads as they entered the forest. The two-rut track led into the woods and joined one of the old Roman roads that scarred the countryside. Now all he had to do was watch for the turnoff to his farmstead.

The Turners and the Wilsons were jumping home tonight. That was just as well. He could use his day off to find out if the bishop was still looking for him. Damn the abbess. He should never have agreed to let her come, let alone leave the carriage and go into the cathedral. But he couldn't say no to a holy woman. Now the whole operation was in danger. If the bishop still hunted him, he'd have to abandon the farm and move to a new location. Some place far away from Rochester, perhaps closer to Canterbury. The move would be expensive and time consuming. He did not relish the idea of explaining to his supervisor that their cover was blown and their investment lost.

Chad pulled the reins to the left and eased the horses off the road. The horses threaded their way around a giant stand of oaks that masked the trail to his farm.

———

"Is everybody ready to go?" Chad spoke in the general direction of the stairs. The Wilsons had changed out of their period costumes and stood out by the carriage in their wool JumpGear. The Turners still hadn't come down.

Margaret, his local assistant, wrapped the rest of the cheeseburgers in a cloth sack. She pulled the drawstring and handed him the bag. "Thanks," said Chad. "Can you go upstairs and see what's keeping the Turners?"

"It's her." She stood there staring at him as though that was explanation enough.

"Well, please go and ask them to come down."

Margaret pushed past him and started up the stairs.

Chad stood a moment, mesmerized by the gentle sway of her hips as she climbed. Why was she angry now? The answer eluded him, as it always did, so he went out to the carriage.

Mr. Wilson stood waiting for him. "Can I ride up top with you this time?"

"Sure. If you can get yourself up there." Chad wasn't willing to bet either way. Wilson was as round as he was tall. If he could climb up to the driver's bench on his own, then he'd have earned the view. Chad went inside the carriage and placed the food under one of the benches. The carriage rocked and leaned as Wilson started his climb. Chad backed out, and Mrs. Wilson brushed past him to take her seat inside.

"Thanks for a wonderful trip, Chad." Mrs. Wilson smiled at him.

Damn, she was hot. He could never figure out why all the gorgeous women were married to fat guys. Wilson seemed like an okay dude, but she was way out of his league. Wilson must be rich or hung like a horse, but staring into Mrs. Wilson's bottomless cleavage wasn't likely to get him the answer. Chad forced his eyes up to her face. "Ah, you're welcome."

If he could just get the Turners loaded up, he could get them all to the staging meadow and be back before dark.

Margaret came outside without the Turners and shrugged.

Chad stomped into the cottage. A chair scraped the floor above his head. He moved toward the stairs, but Mrs. Turner appeared at the top, so he stepped out of the way. She rocked from side to side as she placed both feet on each stair. She could only lead with her left, because she had a bad right knee, as she'd told him about a hundred times. It was painful to watch.

"Thank you, Chad darling." Mrs. Turner had reached the bottom of the stairs. She took a deep breath and began to lurch toward the door. "I only wish I could have brought a camera."

"Please take your seat in the carriage, Mrs. Turner. We do need to get going."

Mr. Turner came down off the stairs behind her. "Sorry for the delay, Chad. She does love to chat."

"No problem." Turner had the cadaverous look of a man who had resigned himself to the life of a permanent caregiver.

"It's been a wonderful vacation, son. Thanks for everything." Turner patted him on the back.

"You're welcome, sir." After watching Turner help his wife out the door, he headed for the stairs.

The abbess stood there lacing on her white traveling cloak. "Hello, Chad. I have been speaking with Mrs. Turner. She does have such wonderful stories." Her infectious smile snuck up on him and he almost forgot he was pissed.

She flowed down the stairs. "I would very much like to come with you and see them away."

That would be just perfect. How was he supposed to deal with a local who had witnessed the time jump? Let alone an abbess. They hadn't covered *that* in the training sessions.

"No," Chad said. She'd shown up at the cottage that morning. He had no idea how she'd found it; they weren't on the main road. She'd asked to come in and he'd had no choice. You couldn't tell the clergy to bugger off, not without raising suspicions. She'd ingratiated herself with his guests and they had invited her along on their last carriage ride. He should have just said no right then.

"My goodness, Chad. Why ever not?"

"It's complicated. I'm sorry, I have to get going. I'll try

to explain when I get back." Chad walked outside before she could reply. He went around to the far side of the carriage to climb up beside Wilson.

Margaret was waiting for him by the step. She threw her arms around his neck. "Hurry back, Chaddy. I don't want to be left alone with the abbess."

"Why?"

Margaret stared at him, and gave him a long, wet kiss. "Oh, you are a daft one, Chaddy."

Now he didn't want to leave. Could he justify delaying their departure for fifteen minutes while he took Margaret inside for an *important matter*? No, the abbess was still here, and the Turners and Wilsons would never stay put on the carriage that long. He pulled himself away from her and climbed up to the driver's bench.

The cold reins chafed in his hand as he urged the horses in a tight circle. They began the climb out of the little glen toward the forest.

Mrs. Wilson and Mrs. Turner whispered and giggled beneath him. What were they on about? At least he wouldn't have to worry about entertaining them on the long ride to the meadow. When the horses reached the Roman road, they hesitated, and Chad pulled them to the left. The carriage lurched up onto the flat stones.

"So how long have you been here?"

Great. Now Wilson wanted to chitchat. "About six months." Six months that had started out crappy but turned out pretty awesome. Uncle Abe had bought the rights to the time travel technology when its patent had ended. He started the SSTTC and offered Chad the guide job on the medieval tour because he remembered Chad had had a poster of a castle on his bedroom wall.

When he was twelve. But Chad had said sure. It beat the hell out of working at the Supercenter in Austin.

"Still like it?"

Margaret's wet kiss still cooled his lips.

"More than ever," Chad said.

Mr. Wilson nodded behind them. "I can see why."

Chad shrugged. "Well, you know. A man's got to live, right?"

"Are you sure that's wise?"

"There's no harm. We're both adults."

"Well, *we* all had to sign an armload of waivers that said we wouldn't even *speak* to the locals before we were allowed to come."

Chad had forgotten Wilson was a lawyer. He shifted on the bench. If Wilson told the SSTTC, he could be in deep shit.

But Wilson pressed on. "You see where I'm going with this, don't you? How can it be okay for you to have intimate contact, when your company thought it prudent for us to have no contact whatsoever?"

"Look, I get it, man." Chad twitched the reins. He'd been good at first. For months he'd lived like a monk. Then he'd started experimenting. He'd chatted with the villagers a bit and they were friendly enough. He'd started going to the local alehouse on his days off. That was where he'd met Margaret. She'd been an alewife. She'd lost her husband and she barely made enough to feed herself. He'd asked her if she wanted to come and work with him. She'd said yes, and since then she'd said yes to pretty much everything he'd ever asked her.

"Isn't this the kind of thing that will corrupt the timeline?" asked Wilson. "Maybe not now, but eventually? What if Margaret was supposed to meet somebody else, but she won't because she lives with you?"

"Look, dude, did you notice anything changing in the future before you came back?"

"No, but..."

"Well, there you go." Chad cut him off. "Margaret and I have been together for two months now. Doesn't that prove it's safe?" Chad smiled at him and hoped Wilson would drop it.

But Wilson had the scent. "Not really," he said.

"Dude, there's a fail-safe in place, but you're not supposed to know about it." Chad couldn't talk about the APR, but he had to tell Wilson something just to shut him up.

"Why not?"

"It's bad for business."

"Hell, you've got *my* money already. So, why not tell me?"

Chad lowered his voice and leaned toward Wilson. "The plague," he said.

"The plague?" Wilson's head whipped around, searching the forest.

"Shh. Keep it down, man. What are you looking for?"

"I don't know." Wilson returned his attention to Chad. "How is the plague a fail-safe?"

When the black plague struck Europe in the mid-fourteenth century, there had been, on average, a fifty-percent mortality rate. As with every average, there had been highs and lows. In this particular town the death toll had been one hundred percent. That fact alone had brought the SSTTC here to stage their Medieval Canterbury tour. It was the perfect fail-safe. If any of the time travelers were to have significant contact with the locals, it wouldn't matter in the long run, because they would all be dead inside seven years. But that didn't read very well from a PR standpoint, so it was a company secret.

Chad whipped the reins. "I can't talk about it."

CHAPTER SEVEN

A *pril 25, 1341*

A green log snapped, sending a comet of sparks spiraling toward the four wolfhounds asleep on the hearth in the great hall. Baron Reginald Fitzdumay, constable of Sussbury Castle, pushed the offending log deeper into the fireplace with the iron poker. "You are not making any sense, Edward. I still do not see any reason to start a manhunt at vespers."

Edward clasped his hands and shut his eyes. *Lord, grant me the patience to convert this witless man into your holy instrument.* He opened his eyes as Reginald returned from the fire. "Let me try again, my lord. I am sure I can rephrase my incoherent ramblings in a way that will make perfect sense to you."

"If you insist." Reginald heaved himself into a chair by his dogs. "But be quick about it. I have problems of my own." He tilted his head toward the table, where his ledgers lay unattended.

"Yes, my lord." Edward plucked an apple from the

bowl on the sideboard. He sat down in a chair across from Reginald. The wolfhounds growled.

"Shut it!" Reginald lingered on the last word.

The wolfhounds whimpered and put their heads down on the hearthstones.

Edward took a bite. The sweet white meat cleansed his teeth while it pleased his tongue. The apple had such an unfortunate reputation for something so delicious. It was all Eve's fault. He let his gaze drift over the ledgers on the table, always a little surprised that Reginald could even read. "What is the nature of your problems, my lord?"

"They are *my* problems."

"I do not mean to pry, my lord, but I thought the problems might be related." *If I could describe my problems in terms of your problems, they would be our problems, do you not see? You ass.* He waited to see if Reginald would reveal anything.

"My earnings are down this season." Reginald nodded to his ledgers. "Yet I thought we had exceptionally good weather this year. Chamberlain said when we finish paying for the tournament and the wedding, we will hardly have enough to keep us through the winter. I have been through the ledgers to confirm it, and there is no mistake. Can you explain to me how my share of an exceptional year can be less than that of a normal year?"

"I do believe I can, my lord." Edward took another bite of apple. "The villagers have begun to complain. They complain about their labors. They complain about their wives, their feudal obligations, and even the church tithe. For weeks I have heard nothing but heresy during confession. They are changing."

"How?"

"They are... thinking."

"Of course they are." Reginald dismissed this statement with a wave.

"The people are thinking more... independently." Edward had to find a way to put it so this cretin could understand the danger. "They question everything. It is as though they have awoken from a long sleep and are no longer satisfied with their lot. I cannot placate them."

"But why? Have I not been fair?" Reginald raised his voice. "Have I not been tolerant?"

"Yes. Of course you have." Edward glanced around the great hall to make certain none of the servants could overhear him. "I believe the people are bewitched."

"Come now, Edward." Reginald shook his head. "I do not believe in witches any more than you do."

"Ordinarily no, but this is new. Until today I had no idea who or what could have visited this evil into the hearts of an entire village. I was on my way here to discuss it with you when I came across a carriage surrounded by the villagers. When I drew near, I was handed a parcel of food so intoxicating I was forced to drop it, lest I devour it on the spot." He searched Reginald's face for some spark of recognition or even intelligence.

"What does the heresy in confession have to do with good food? Have you lost your wits?"

Edward pressed on. "Moments before, a strange woman had entered the confessional with no intention of confessing. I tried to find her outside the cathedral to ask her why, but she had vanished."

Reginald threw up his hands. "I am lost."

"She was one of the occupants of the carriage. Do you not see?" Edward willed Reginald to understand. "Today

I realized these impenitent strangers entice our villagers with exotic foods, and while the unsuspecting fools stand around eating, they talk to them and put these heresies into their ears. I tried to question the driver, but he drove away, refusing to obey my commands."

Reginald stared into the fire and, finally turning, he said, "What reason could they have for disturbing my peace?"

"You must find this carriage and its occupants. They alone can provide the answers. I believe they are spreading Satan's word into our land to test our faith." But to make sure this simpleton baron did not miss the point, Edward added, "They test the people's fealty itself."

"It sounds like revolution. Captain Henri!" Reginald bellowed in the general direction of the door.

Edward sighed. *That took longer than it should have.*

CHAPTER EIGHT

April 25, 1341

A The abbess sat in the back of the carriage and peeked out through the curtains. Chad had stopped in the meadow and asked the Turners and the Wilsons to leave the carriage. Mrs. Turner had whispered goodbye to her as they stepped out into the meadow. The abbess had managed to stay hidden, watching Chad lead them up the slope. He said goodbye to them as they climbed, but there was no village nearby and no other path out of the meadow. They stopped a short distance away, and she strained to hear more of what he said.

Chad handed them an orb. They each placed a hand on it. Chad backed away and took a piece of cloth out of his pocket. He placed it over his head, like an executioner's hood. Surely, he was not sending them to meet their maker. It could not be. She held the curtain open to get a better look, but Chad had no visible weapon. It appeared to be a ceremony of some kind, but she could not discern its meaning.

The meadow erupted in a light so brilliant she fell

back onto her seat in the carriage. She ran her fingertips across her eyelids just to see if they were closed. The carriage rocked beneath her. Chad climbed into the driver's seat. She opened her eyes and lunged for the curtain. She looked back up the slope to the spot where Mrs. Turner and the others had been. She searched, hoping she might see a movement or something in the bluebells that would give a clue as to what had happened. The carriage rolled in a circle and she lost sight of the spot.

She stuck her head out the window to look up at Chad. "What have you done?"

Chad spun around. "How did you get here?"

"Where is Mrs. Turner?"

"Home."

"Do not lie to me, you monster." She pointed at his face. "I saw you kindle them."

"Look, you don't understand." He reined in the horses and began to climb down.

Did he intend to send her home? She held the door closed from the inside. "What are you doing?"

"I came to help you up onto the driver's bench so we can talk," he said.

"I am quite comfortable here, thank you." She tightened her grip on the door.

"We need to get moving. If you want to hear the explanation, you need to sit up with me. I don't feel like yelling as I drive."

"How can I trust you?"

"Look, I'm going back up. If you want answers, you'll have to join me."

The carriage rocked as he climbed. She opened the door and stepped out into the meadow. Chad stared down at her. He was just a man. She sensed no animosity from him, just a mild anger. Or was it fear?

"Last chance." Chad picked up the reins.

She needed to hear what he had to say but she had no desire to be that close to him. She started climbing. There had never really been a choice, and besides, she had her dagger. If he pulled out his little hood, it would be the last thing he ever pulled out.

————

CHAD DROVE IN SILENCE THROUGH THE DARKENING forest. The horses knew the way, which allowed him to focus on what to tell the abbess. No one was supposed to know about the time travel station or the process. Now he had to tell her everything just so she didn't think he'd killed her newfound friends. That would make her an extreme liability. If his uncle found out, he was totally getting fired. He had to contain this.

The abbess sat watching him. "I am waiting."

"I know." Chad urged the horses. "I'm trying to think of the best way to put this."

"I find the truth to be of value in a case like this." She raised an eyebrow as if daring him to lie.

"I don't know whether you could understand the truth." He hadn't decided how much he could really tell her.

"Are you suggesting I am daft?" Her eyebrows threatened to disappear up inside her coif.

"No, no," Chad said quickly, but it was too late.

"I spent ten years at the Abbey of St. Mary." The abbess was on a roll. "My Latin is impeccable; my French is better. I have translated the Bible from beginning to end."

"Okay, okay, I get it. You're a genius."

Confusion spread across her face. She pulled her hand from the folds of her robe, revealing a dagger. "I am not a spirit, I assure you."

"Smart. I meant smart." Chad leaned as far away as he could.

"Smart?" She waved the dagger. "This will smart if you make me use it."

He'd forgotten to use the simplest word available. The damn language barrier would get him killed if he wasn't careful. Usually if he spoke slowly and pretended to be four, the words he chose were recognizable enough for the Middle English villagers to understand him.

"Clever?" he offered.

"Clever I can accept." She lowered the dagger.

Chad sighed and straightened up. The abbess stared at him. He had to tell her something. He could start with the truth and see where that led. If she didn't take it well, he could change his story.

"I didn't 'kindle' the guests. They're not dead. They've been sent back to the future."

She did not speak, so he continued.

"The light you saw was just the release of energy that occurs on arrival and departure."

"Where is *the future?*"

"The future is not a place, it's a time." Her face remained blank so he added, "Where did you think they were from?"

"I found their accents rather charming and their ideas progressive, but I had not tried to guess where they were from."

"Well I'm sure it probably looks like magic to you, but they... *we* are from the future. Approximately nine hundred years from now some clever chick—I mean woman—invents the ability to travel back in time. The people you met have enjoyed a vacation here, in your village, in what they think of as *the past*. Do you understand?"

She let her gaze drift to the horses. Chad began to wonder if she had heard him.

Her jaw dropped open. "No."

"Okay, let's try it like this. Do you remember what you did yesterday?"

"Yes. Of course I do. I am not a fool."

"Of course not." *Jeez.* She was sure touchy about her intelligence. "What would you say if I told you I could send you back to yesterday, where you could stand next to yourself and watch yourself doing all the things you did yesterday?"

"I would say *what a bloody waste of time.*"

"Yes, yes. But the idea that you could physically visit any day from your past. Do you understand the idea?"

"Why did you put on the executioner's hood?"

Chad laughed. "It's not a hood. It's more of a sock, really. It covers my eyes so I don't have the momentary blindness when the MCV fires up."

"Em-see-vee? Is this the orb you used in the ceremony?"

"Yeah. Miniature Chrono Vehicle. MCV. Get it?" He smiled, but she did not.

The abbess faced him but she wasn't looking at him. She was far away. And then she was back. "*Any* day?" she said.

"Yes."

He expected a follow-up question, but she sat quietly. He paid attention to the horses for a while and left her to deal with it. They ambled along the flat road, their hindquarters rising and falling rhythmically, reminding him of Margaret. That was distracting.

He shook off the image. "Okay, now it's your turn to be honest. Are you going to tell anybody what you saw?"

"Of course not, Chad." She smiled at him.

Damn, that smile was like a weapon. The abbess pulled off her coif and shook out her long black hair. She was gorgeous. If only she wasn't an abbess, she could have any man she wanted. Chad realized he'd been staring and looked away.

She touched his arm and said, "I will need one small favor."

Oh, here it comes. "What?"

"I would like you to send me to *the past*."

"No." *Crap.* "Ask for something else."

"But that is all I desire." She smiled again.

He tore his eyes away from her face and found the strength to say, "No. I can't do it." But he knew he could do it. It would just be complicated.

The road took a bend, and Annie's inn came into view.

As they passed the inn the abbess said, "Please stop the cart. I have lodging here."

Chad reined in the horses. Disappointment washed over him. The urge to change his mind and offer her the trip just to keep her in the seat next to him was overwhelming.

"Did you know your chin wiggles when you lie?" she said as she climbed down.

He didn't know how to answer that.

As she walked down the short path to the inn, there was a sway in her hips that hadn't been there before. She turned and caught him staring. There was definitely a gleam in her eye. She said, "I will visit you tomorrow so we may continue our discussion," and disappeared into the inn.

Chad frowned. There was no discussion. He'd already said no. There was no way she could convince him to take her back in time. But he did wonder what kind of leverage she would bring to her argument. That smile and that wiggle? *She's an abbess, jackass! She's not going to seduce you.* But he couldn't help thinking about what she might have hidden under her habit.

CHAPTER NINE

April 26, 1341

Captain Henri led his guards out of the fog at the forest's edge. He stopped his horse where the village path met the Roman road. The moist air sapped the heat from his body, and he pulled at the neck of his chain mail to ease the rings away from his chin. Across the valley, the castle seemed to float in a sea of fog, and he pictured the baron's dogs sleeping on the warm hearthstones of the great hall. The dogs had it better than the men. But here they were, out in the brisk air just after lauds.

"Jean-Pierre."

His tracker hurried over to stand near Henri's horse. *"Oui, capitaine?"*

The man could speak a little English, but Henri preferred to stick to French so that nuance was not lost and the English guards were not privy to their conversations. "Can we still see the trail?"

"The tracks are clear until they reach the main road," Jean-Pierre said. "Then the carriage is lifted up out of the mud, and they are gone." He pointed to where the tracks disappeared.

"It sounds like we just need to follow the road until we see where the tracks leave it. Yes?"

"Yes, but if we miss them, we could wind up in Canterbury."

"Please do not miss them. I have no desire to go to Canterbury today or any day."

"*Oui, capitaine.* It is a dangerous place." Jean-Pierre smiled as he started along the road.

The last time Henri had been to Canterbury, he'd had to save Jean-Pierre from a pilgrim's wife. The fact that the pilgrim had been an enthusiastic participant was of no consequence. The pilgrim's wife had been surprisingly adept at the sword, and Henri had had his hands full extricating his friend.

Henri signaled his squad to follow Jean-Pierre and waited as they marched past him. He dismounted and led his horse up onto the road. Warmer now that he was moving, he settled in to the slow but steady pace his men had set.

Around prime, Jean-Pierre left the road and disappeared behind a copse of oaks.

"Hold." The squad stopped at Henri's command.

When Jean-Pierre reappeared, he smiled. "We will not be going to Canterbury today."

CHAPTER TEN

April 27, 1341

John's leg collapsed. Sometimes being right hurt like a son of a bitch.

"Get down," he shouted from the ground.

Mila and Sandra spun around.

"What happened to you?" Sandra asked.

"Run!" John pointed up the hill.

"What is wrong with you? Why are you shouting?" Mila's said.

"I'm shot." John lifted his hand off his thigh. It was drenched in blood. "Now run before they shoot you too."

The bolt had penetrated his thigh from behind as he walked upslope. He glanced down the meadow. There was no sign of the threat. He had to assume uphill was safe. Unless the bolt had been meant to drive them into a trap. He gave his head a shake. *Stop overthinking it.* He rolled onto his stomach and started to commando-crawl up the slope. The bolt in his leg stabbed him every time it caught in the dirt. He twisted on his side to keep it elevated and dragged himself with only his arms.

"Dad, come on!" yelled Mila.

He tried to speed up, but he couldn't go any faster. He'd been shot before, but those bullets now seemed like beestings compared to this tree trunk that tore his leg open further with every movement. He wanted to stop and cradle the wound, but that was not an option.

"Come on, Sergeant." Sandra was suddenly above him with Jess. They grabbed his arms, hoisting him to his feet. John hopped on his good leg as they half-carried, half-dragged him up the hill.

Mila kicked away some rocks and broken sticks, clearing a spot on the ground behind the log. "Here." She pointed, and they sat John down with his back to the log, shielding them from the meadow.

Mila and Jess crouched on each side of John.

Sandra tore his pants to expose the injury. "Let's take a look at that leg."

He snuck a peek over the log behind him, and Mila followed his example. Three knights in plate armor walked their horses onto the meadow. Four foot soldiers followed them. Each man wore a long chain mail shirt with a sword belted at his side. The bastard with the crossbow at his shoulder must have been the one who shot him. The men moved cautiously, and he was thankful they weren't in more of a hurry. Who were they, what did they want, and why would they attack without warning?

"Ah!" John spun back, grabbing Sandra's hand to stop her from wiggling the bolt. "A little warning next time?"

"Sorry." Sandra gently touched the sides of his leg near the wound. "Can you lift it?"

He bent his knee so Sandra could examine the entrance wound on the back of his thigh.

"Okay." Sandra sat back. "It wiggles, so it's not in the

bone. And it's not gushing, so it's probably not in the artery. I say we take it out and tourniquet your leg."

"Do it," said Mila. "Hurry."

He couldn't run. And they needed to run. Fast. The tail on the short bolt had disappeared into the back of his leg. He wrapped his hands around the tip, took a deep breath, and held it as he pulled. The bolt slid up a few inches, grinding on his femur. Pain swamped his leg. He let go and breathed out. Three inches were still buried in his leg. He leaned back against the log to catch his breath and let the pain subside.

"Faster." Mila kept her eyes glued to the knights. "They're not resting, we're not resting."

Sandra straddled his leg, pinning it to the ground with her thighs. "Jess, put his left arm around you. Mila, you take his right."

"Hang on. What are you thinking?" He knew a little knowledge could be more dangerous than complete ignorance. Sandra was no medic. She was the certified first aid attendant in the law office where she worked.

"Quit whining, Sergeant, I'm all you've got. Now shut your eyes and give your girls a hug."

He held his daughters but he did not take his eyes off Sandra.

"Three..." Sandra yanked the bolt out of his leg.

"Ahhh! Ah ha ha haaa!" He took a huge breath and clenched his teeth. "What the hell was the counting for?"

Mila pointed at the approaching knights. "Can we go now?"

Sandra tucked the bolt into her waistband. She tore off the bottom of his ripped pant leg and tied it around the wound. He winced when she tightened it in place.

"Now what?" Sandra's voice cracked. Her wide eyes

and trembling chin told him the adrenaline that had allowed her to focus on his leg in spite of the danger was gone.

He reached out and squeezed Sandra's hand. "Nice job. Thanks." He tested his leg then glanced over the log. The knights and soldiers were halfway up the meadow. He ducked back behind the log and faced them. His leg reminded him he was far from combat ready, but the three most important people in his world needed him. Now.

"We need to move."

"Really?" Mila's jaw dropped open. "Thanks, Captain Obvious."

John ignored her and rolled onto his hands and knees, slowly crawling behind a tree. Once he was sure he couldn't be seen, he stood up. His right leg poked him, but he forced himself not to limp. He had to keep their morale up. If the girls thought he wasn't going to be up to the job, they might panic. Fear had to be managed.

"Okay, crawl over behind this tree and follow me into the forest. But stay down and stay quiet. Let's go."

———

HENRI STOPPED HIS HORSE AT THE EDGE OF THE TREE line where the trails of trampled bluebells ended. "Hubert, take a look."

The man-at-arms drew his sword and crept into the forest. A few moments later he returned. "Captain. The heretics are gone. They will be moving slowly. The big one is bleeding."

"Henri," said the baron. "Collect our prize. We want them alive. The bishop and I are returning to the castle."

"Yes, my lord." Henri watched the two armored men wheel their mounts and trot down the slope. Typical. When the danger level was unknown, the lords moved to the rear. But of course, there was some merit in their choice. These heretics were still a mystery. No one knew what they were capable of.

"Hubert, take your men and find them." Henri tried to ignore the similarity to what Reginald had just done. "Jean-Pierre and I will follow."

The three men-at-arms raced into the forest.

"Henri, why do we not hunt with Hubert and his men?" Jean-Pierre unloaded his crossbow and slung it across his back.

Henri dismounted. Jean-Pierre would never question his courage, but Henri found himself feeling guilty. It was a valid question. He knew they were a more cohesive fighting unit when they were together, and so did Jean-Pierre.

"Why do you think the baron and bishop have left us?"

"They do not like to sweat?"

Henri smiled at Jean-Pierre's insolence. "That may also be true, but they have retreated because the danger is unknown."

"And now we do the same?"

His tracker always spoke his mind. Henri had to remind himself that was why he held him in such high regard. He stifled the urge to reprimand him. "Let that be the end of it. We must be cautious, that is all. We will follow at a distance." Henri led his horse into the forest as the men-at-arms disappeared from view.

CHAPTER ELEVEN

April 27, 1341

Mila followed John up the forested hillside. He was moving far too slowly for her. John's face told the story of his pain. With each step he grimaced, and while he forced himself not to limp, he couldn't go any faster. She wanted to sprint until she couldn't breathe. There was no way they could put any distance between themselves and their attackers at this pace. It was only a matter of time before they caught up. And then what?

Mila had once taken a stage-fighting class, and John had questioned its relevance. When he'd suggested a real self-defense course, she'd told him he knew nothing about acting. He'd backed off. Now she kind of wished he'd insisted. Jess was RCMP, so she could defend herself. But these guys had swords. How useful would John's hand-to-hand combat training and Jess's suspect arrest and control skills be against these men?

And on top of all that, they weren't supposed to fight anyone here. That was the tricky part. How were they supposed to defend themselves against people who obviously meant them harm without fighting back? They had all signed the waivers before departure.

And where the hell was their guide? So much for keeping them out of conflict. Thanks, SSTTC. *Fuck.*

"Do you trust me?" John climbed over a log and held a low branch out of the way.

"Of course," said Jess as she stepped past him.

"Sure," said Mila.

"Why?" asked Sandra.

"We need to switch to a military model." He took a ragged breath and continued up the hill. "I need you to follow my orders without question or hesitation. It's the surest way for us to survive. Can we do that?"

"Yeah," said Jess. "You're the expert."

"It'll be just like when we were little," said Mila.

"Except I need you to really listen to me." John looked her in the eye. "Not like when you were little. Can you handle that?"

"Why are you singling me out?" Mila scowled.

"You know why. You're the independent thinker. You're the one who always has to try things your own way."

"John, take it easy." Sandra touched his arm.

"I can't. She needs to understand." He pointed at his bleeding leg. "This is real. These guys aren't fucking around. When they catch up to us, I need to take them out with non-lethal force. Can you think of a way to do that?"

"I have a couple of ideas," said Mila. "Do you want to hear them?"

"No."

"John!"

"Sandra, stay out of it. This is exactly my point. By now I should have already told you my plan, but I'm still trying to convince Mila that having one person in charge is the best way to survive."

"Ah, Dad?" Jess said, pointing.

"What?"

"There's movement in the trees."

Three of the foot soldiers emerged from behind a stand of beech trees a hundred meters down the slope. There was no sign of the crossbowman or the knights.

"We need to divide their group." John started up the hill again. "That means we need to split up."

"I don't like that idea," Sandra said. She wrapped her arms around her chest as she climbed.

"We don't have a choice," said John. "See? This is what I mean about not questioning me."

"I don't want to split up. That's all I'm saying."

"Okay. Thank you. Noted." John must have known she was scared, but he just kept climbing. "We still have to split up, so Jess, when I say the word, you and Mila run to our right for a hundred meters then cut left and find your way to the top of this hill. When they see us split up, they'll send at least one man after you. Keep him following you, but don't engage him. Once you reach the top of the hill, lead him back down toward your mother and me. By that time, I'll have taken out the other two and be ready for your guy. Any questions?"

"What about your leg?" said Jess. "Are you sure you're up for this?"

"My leg is fine," he snapped.

Clearly not fine, but Mila kept her thoughts to herself.

He wanted them to take orders, and she was fine with that. Besides, she'd been wanting to run for the last hour. The run would clear her head and relieve the knot in her chest.

"I think Mom and Mila should be the bait and I should stay with you." Apparently, Jess was not quite ready to give in. "I have the most to offer in a fight."

"Agreed, but you and your sister are the fastest runners. You're young and agile. I don't want your mother slipping and falling and getting caught."

"Thanks, asshole," said Sandra.

Nice one. Mila smiled.

"You know what I mean," he said.

"Dad, these guys have swords." Jess offered her standard insightful reality check. "When's the last time you fought a guy with a sword?"

"Don't worry about it. A sword is like a long bayonet. I'll figure something out." John looked at Mila. "Anybody else?"

Mila shook her head and kept climbing. There was no way she was getting into it.

"All right, how close are they?" said John.

Jess glanced behind them. "Seventy meters."

"When they hit fifty, you go. Got it?"

"Got it," said Jess.

They continued to climb at John's pace, placing each foot carefully to avoid slipping in the damp underbrush. The rocks on the forest floor provided traction, but a simple twisted ankle could be their undoing. At one point, John bent and picked up a hunk of wood the size of a baseball bat. Good idea. Mila started looking for something similar as she climbed.

"They're at fifty," said Jess. "Let's go." She took off across the hillside.

"See ya later," Mila said and rushed after Jess.

They ran around the bend of the hill. When Jess started climbing up, Mila glanced behind them. She couldn't see John and Sandra anymore, but apparently two of the foot soldiers had chosen to follow Jess and her, not one like John had predicted. *Thanks, John.*

When the ground flattened out, Jess stopped. Mila came up behind her and stopped. They were still surrounded by trees, but clearly they couldn't climb any higher. The ground sloped away in every direction. The two guards climbing up through the trees had slowed to a walk, so Mila squatted down on her ankles and leaned her back against a tree.

"Are you serious?" Jess stood with her fists on her hips.

"What?"

"Sitting? Don't you think that might be a little cocky?" Jess glanced at the men. "Are you okay?"

"I'm fine." Mila sighed.

"Bullshit." Jess frowned at her sister. "You haven't said a word since Dad lit into you."

"Exactly. He wanted us to listen and take orders without question. But the first thing you and Sandra did was interrupt with questions. I'm the only one who did what he asked, but do you think he noticed? Hell, no." Mila took a breath.

"Okay, okay, I get it." Jess stood next to Mila. The soldiers had halved the distance to the top. "I think right now we need to focus on leading these bastards into Dad's trap, right?"

"Yeah, yeah." Mila dragged herself to her feet.

"Hey." Jess put a hand on Mila's shoulder. "Can we talk about this later?"

"Why bother?" Mila shrugged. "You know he'll never change."

"Yup." Jess nodded.

One of the guards was cutting across the hill face to their right while the other one continued directly toward them.

"That's not good. They're splitting up. Let's go." Jess sprinted across the top of the hill. Mila bolted after her.

"Down this way." Jess veered left, jumping down between two trees. The closer man rushed to intercept them. "Faster. It's going to be close."

"You go faster," Mila said between breaths. "I'm right on your ass."

"I'm trying!" Jess jumped over a root and accelerated.

Mila wasn't applying any braking force, just letting gravity pull her down the hill. She focused on finding safe places to put her feet. The terrain was rocky and riddled with trees, roots, and underbrush. The slightest misstep would lead to a skin-grating fall. She glanced at the soldier, who was closing in.

"He's going to be right on us when we go by," Mila yelled.

"What's he doing now?"

"Keep going," Mila shouted. "He's running parallel, about ten meters. But he's drifting in as he goes."

Jess snuck a glance at the soldier. "Shit."

Mila risked a longer look. The man's knees were hampered by his chain mail shirt. He couldn't take a full stride. At that moment, he tore off his helmet to lose some excess weight. The man's long hair was pasted to his skull with sweat. Mila refocused on her path down the hill and smiled.

"Okay, ease up a bit," Mila yelled to Jess.

"Why?"

"He's done." Mila and Jess had both run middle distance in high school. Their coach had been an Olympian, and when they had showed promise, he'd taken their training to the next level. That had included studying the stride of their opponents to know when their tank was empty and when to make a move. Who would have thought she would come to the fourteenth century to find a use for that particular skill?

The soldier ran out of gas as he converged with their path. He slid in behind them and followed them down the hill.

Mila and Jess raced by an oak tree on their left.

John stood in its shadow, giving them a thumbs-up with one hand and holding a sword in the other. He must have relieved the third guard of it. When the guard chasing them ran past John's position, he stepped out and clotheslined him.

Mila and Jess tried to decelerate gradually without falling.

Sandra came out of hiding and held out her arms to Jess. "I've got you."

Jess skidded into Sandra's embrace, and they both caught Mila. She and Jess bent over with their hands on their knees to catch their breath.

Sandra stood between them with a hand on each of their backs. "Are you all right?"

Mila straightened up and, without trying to interrupt her heavy breathing, just nodded. Jess stood and walked back toward John.

"Where's the third one?" John limped away from the guard lying on the dirt. Before either of them could answer, the undergrowth crunched behind him and he spun around. The last guard leaped over his fallen comrade and dove at John, leading with his sword.

CHAPTER TWELVE

April 27, 1341

Sandra stopped breathing and stared. There was nothing John could do. Just before his face was split open, he lifted his own sword. He deflected the incoming blade, but the guard crashed into him. John grabbed a fistful of chain mail, bent his knees, and let the man's momentum push him down. He landed hard on his back and kicked out with both legs into the man's hips, lifting him into the air.

The man flew, inverted, down the hill.

Jess had to dive out of the way.

The back of the soldier's head caught on a tree root and snapped forward with a sickening crunch. He landed awkwardly, and didn't get up.

They all converged on the unmoving form. The man lay on his back, but his head was bent so that his ear touched his shoulder. His eyes found each of their faces, but nothing else moved. There was no rise and fall to his chest.

"Shit. His neck is busted." John said. "I'm sorry."

The man's eyes drifted away from them and settled on the sky. He was gone.

John shook his head. "I shouldn't have thrown him. I should have held on and controlled his descent. I know better than that." He sat down hard. He ran his hands through his hair slowly, undid his tourniquet, and started to tighten it again.

"Here, let me do that." Sandra knelt beside him.

"Ladies, please strip these two men of all armor and weapons while we're waiting," said John to the girls.

"Eww," said Mila, but she walked up the slope toward the other soldier.

"Mila, I would feel more comfortable if you would take the corpse. If that guy wakes up, I'm sure Jess can put him out again."

"Forget it. I'm not touching the dead guy." Mila bent over and started stripping the unconscious man.

Jess bent over the corpse.

"What have you done?" Sandra hissed at John while she retied his tourniquet. She had stuff she needed to say, and he was going to hear it. "You said *non-lethal*. The waiver said, if we kill someone in the past, we can't go home. You knew that. You yelled at Mila."

"Sandra—" said John.

She ignored him. "What were you thinking? We're going to be stuck here forever." Sandra jerked the ends of the bandage.

"Sandra." John grabbed her hands and gently but firmly pulled them off the bandage.

"What?" She let herself look up into his eyes.

"I'm sorry."

She took a breath and glanced at the corpse. She knew she should feel something for this man, but she couldn't stop thinking about the damned waiver. "What's going to happen to us?"

John took too long to answer. "I don't know, but we're alive, right?"

She nodded.

"I'm going to keep us that way." He touched her cheek. "I promise."

"Are you going to get us home?"

"I'm trying," said John.

That didn't exactly fill Sandra with confidence, but she knew it was about all she was going to get at the moment.

John stood up and tested his leg. He walked over to the pile of armor and weapons that Jess had taken off the corpse. He pulled on the man's chain mail shirt and the padding that went under it. "Sandra, you should put on the other set."

"What?" Sandra screwed up her face. Why the hell would she need to put on medieval armor?

"Just do it," snapped John. Then he said, "I'm sorry. We talked about this. Following orders? Please. Trust me."

Sandra glared at him. John had never given her orders before, and she couldn't say that she liked it very much. That definitely needed to come to an end as soon as possible. She walked over to where Mila had just finished undressing the other soldier, picked up the under padding, and sniffed it. "It stinks."

"I know. But we need to blend in." said John. "Okay?"

Sandra huffed, then removed her dress and threw it at John.

He caught it and tucked it into his newly acquired sword belt. Everything he wore was a little tight. He picked up the sword he'd been fighting with and handed it to Jess. That made Sandra wonder why he wasn't dressing Jess in the armor. She knew it made more sense to prepare Jess for fighting, but she kept it to herself. She forced herself to trust John. As hard as that was, she had to give him the benefit of the doubt. He was a trained soldier—he had to have a plan.

"Was there any kind of a view from the hilltop?" John asked the girls.

"I didn't really notice." Mila shrugged.

———

Henri and Jean-Pierre stood over Hubert as he opened his eyes.

"How do you feeling?" asked Jean-Pierre in his best English.

Hubert lay there for a moment, touching his nose. His hand came away bloody. "Like I have just been through a battle."

"*C'est bon,* no?" said Jean-Pierre. "You do alive." He offered him a hand up.

"But why?" Henri scanned the woods around them. "They had your sword. Why would they leave you alive?"

"I know not, my lord, but I am thankful for it."

"Can you keep up?"

"Of course, my lord."

Henri mounted and nosed his horse up the hill. Jean-Pierre followed, helping Hubert. A short distance up the hill, Henri stopped his horse near Robert's body. His dead eyes stared at the gray sky.

"You were right, Henri," Jean-Pierre said in French as

he bent over Robert's body. "The heretics are more dangerous than I thought."

Henri dismounted. Being right was no consolation when it came at the cost of the life of one of his men. If only Reginald had given him the ten men he had requested, maybe Robert would still be alive. But Reginald had insisted he needed the men to continue preparing for the tournament.

Henri drew his sword and turned it tip down in front of him so the hilt formed a cross. He lowered himself on one knee and bowed his head. "Lord, we pray you will accept Robert unto your glorious realm. Please forgive his sins. Amen."

"Amen." Jean-Pierre and Hubert crossed themselves.

Henri paused for a moment of silent prayer, but it was time to move on. The living needed him. He stood and sheathed his sword. "Put Robert on the horse."

Jean-Pierre and Hubert wrestled the body onto the animal's back. They tied the hands and feet together under its belly.

A groan came from up the hill. Jean-Pierre spun toward the sound and drew his sword. Stephen sat up from the undergrowth.

"Stephen, *mon Dieu!*" Jean-Pierre slapped his sword back in its scabbard. "I could have kill you," he added in English.

"You would have been doing me a favor." Stephen touched the side of his head. He stood and stumbled toward them.

"How did this happen?" Henri pointed at Robert.

Stephen saw the body and stopped. "Is he dead?"

Henri nodded. "Tell me what happened."

Stephen stared up through the forest and told the

story of how they had tracked the two women up the hill. Then when they tried to take them, the women had outrun them and led them back into a trap set by the other two strangers. Stephen's gaze returned to Robert's body. "Damn heretics," said Stephen.

Henri would have to warn his men about the speed of their quarry. It was strange indeed when a woman could outrun a man. He checked the sky. It had to be getting close to none. They could no longer continue the search and still find their way out of the forest by nightfall.

"Our day is done. We will spend the night at Annie's and tomorrow take Robert back to the castle." To Jean-Pierre he said, "I'm sorry, my friend, but you must stay and track these witches. Get word to me when you find out where they are headed."

"*Oui, Capitaine.*" Jean-Pierre ran up the slope.

"We go." Henri led the horse away.

CHAPTER THIRTEEN

A*pril 27, 1341*
Mila, Jess, and Sandra stood on the hilltop watching John as he walked from tree to tree. The forest thinned out at the summit, but there was no clear view of the countryside. John said they needed to know the lay of the land, the proximity of settlements, and where they might hide or find help.

He limped back to them. "Jess, can you climb one of these trees and try to get a look around?"

"I'll do it." Mila said. She walked over and started climbing the nearest tree. Its trunk was the size of a minivan, but she had no trouble getting started.

"Okay." John watched her for a moment. "You two keep an eye out. Find a tree or something to hide behind that will give you a clear view down the hill. I'll try to catch Mila if she slips."

"*Try?* Where's your commitment, Sergeant? If she slips, you *will* catch her." Sandra stood, fists on hips, glaring. "Is that clear?"

Mila smiled as she climbed.

"Yup. That's what I meant," said John sheepishly.

"Good." Sandra wandered over to an elm tree and stood behind it, looking down the slope.

And then Mila was at the top. The sky was endless, and the green of England reached to the horizon in every direction. To the north there seemed to be a gray or a light blue that drew a line between the green and the sky. That had to be the sea. To the south a small hill grew out of the green, and on one side of it was a cream-colored square. It was too far away to make out any more detail, but it was too square to be anything but a building.

Mila climbed down to the lowest branch and dropped to the ground. "Trees. Everywhere. It's like being lost in the middle of a national park."

"I get it." John grimaced and added, "Anything of interest?"

She pointed behind John. "That way is the ocean." She motioned behind her. "This way there's a big building on a hill. I'm guessing a castle, but I can't make out any detail at this distance."

"Okay, let's move," John said to Sandra and Jess. He took a few strides then stopped. To Mila he said, "You're on point. Take us toward your castle. Jess, you're with Mila. Stay low, stay quiet, and stay alert."

Wow. Mila tried not to smile. Had John just given her a responsibility? She started off in the direction of the castle and let the smile spread across her face once John was behind her.

"Eyes peeled, ladies," he said.

Sandra walked beside John. "Do you really think she knows what 'point' is?"

Mila rolled her eyes as she eavesdropped.

"Pretty sure," said John, then louder he said, "Mila?"

"What?" she growled.

"Your mother wants to know if you know what 'point' is."

"Tell her she's an idiot." Mila smirked.

John said, "You got it."

Sandra said, "How's the leg, asshole?"

"Hurts like a son of a bitch. And you?"

"All right, I guess."

"Really?"

There was a long silence, and Mila thought they would finally shut up. Even she knew they had to be quiet in the woods.

But then John said, "Spit it out."

"It's nothing."

"Dammit. Just say it."

"You've shut me out."

That was all Sandra said. Again, Mila thought they were done.

But then Sandra started up again, and it was like an open floodgate. "What's your plan? What are you thinking? You haven't told me why we're going toward this damn castle instead of away from it. The way I figure it, the closer we get, the more likely we'll run into more guards."

Mila and Jess stopped and glared at Sandra.

John laced his fingers into her hand.

"What?" Her voice was sharp. She pulled her hand away and crossed her arms under her chest.

"We have a boatload of problems," John said. "Not least of which are food, water, and shelter. But the highest priority is finding out what happened to the guide. Without him to send us home, we're fucked. We need to find people we can talk to who aren't trying to kill us.

Then maybe we'll meet somebody who can help us find the guide."

"And you think there'll be people like that at the castle?" she asked hopefully.

"Where there's a castle, there's usually a village or a town. If the castle Mila saw is the same one that's on the SSTTC website, there's a village. I remember the drawings."

"Thanks for including me." Sandra unclenched her body and reached for John's hand.

"You've got to understand that in the heat of battle—"

"I get it. You're in charge, baby." She gave him a kiss on the cheek. "Enjoy it while it lasts."

"Are you going to be quiet now?" asked Jess.

Sandra scowled but nodded.

"Good," said Mila.

About twenty minutes later, Mila stopped behind a giant beech tree and held up her hand in a fist.

Jess stopped next to her. "Nice one," she whispered. "What movie is it from?"

Mila smiled. "Duh. All of them."

John and Sandra came up behind them. John whispered, "Why are we stopped?"

Mila pointed ahead where the forest thinned out. "There's a road over there, and I saw movement."

As she pointed, a knight led his horse along a flat stone road about fifty meters ahead of them. A naked man hung over the saddle and two men walked behind, one naked, one not. It could only be the group that had been after them.

John sat down slowly and cradled his leg while he motioned for the others to join him on the ground. "We need to let them get well ahead of us. Then we'll follow."

"Where are the crossbowman and the other two knights?" Jess sat next to him, keeping her eyes on the road.

"The crossbowman's probably tracking us," John said. "It's likely he's watching us already."

Mila glanced behind them. Jess and Sandra did the same.

"Easy now." John smiled. "Don't let on you know he's out there."

They all stopped looking that way and tried to look nonchalant about it. Sandra suddenly had to fix her hair, Jess had an urgent need to stretch her back, and Mila giggled quietly when she squatted as though she was taking a piss.

"Eee-ew," hissed Jess. "Really?"

"What?" Mila smiled angelically.

John almost laughed. "Nice one, but I don't think you'll see him unless he wants you to. He probably has orders not to shoot, so don't get too excited."

"How can you be sure?" Sandra's eyes drifted behind them as she continued to scan the forest.

"I can't. But it's what I would do. If more than half my unit was injured or killed, I'd try to keep the enemy in sight while I waited for reinforcements."

"Do we try and lose him?" Jess asked.

Mila knew that wouldn't happen. Not while John couldn't run.

"After dark there could be another option," said John.

The knight and his men disappeared over a crest in the road. John pushed himself up. "Okay, ladies, time to move. Besides the crossbowman, we still have two other knights unaccounted for. They could be ahead, they could be behind, but they're probably on the road."

"Why?" Sandra always had questions. Mila rolled her eyes. When was she going to get with the program?

"They're too loud," John said with more patience than Mila could have managed. "A fully armored horse carrying a knight is not meant for stealth. It's the fourteenth-century equivalent of a tank."

"It's just a question." Sandra glared at Mila. "I don't know why you're getting so angry."

"Just stop asking so many questions," said Mila. "Okay?"

John stepped between them, eclipsing Mila's view of Sandra. To Jess and Mila he said, "I want you two to stay in the trees at the side of the road. Move from tree to tree. Stay low. Keep your eyes open. Take turns. One of you moves ahead to a tree and stops, looks all around, and signals for the other to follow if it's clear. Then you switch and the other one leads. Got it?"

They nodded and headed out.

Mila and Jess took turns following the knight and his injured men. It wasn't difficult to keep them in sight because the road rarely turned. It was mostly straight and paved with stones, so Mila guessed it was probably one of the roads built by the Romans.

As the light faded, it became harder to see the knight, so Mila and Jess risked getting a bit closer. And then the road took one of its rare bends and they lost sight of the knight. Mila took off at a run to get to the bend and reestablish a visual with their target. She came around the corner and stopped.

When the rest of her family caught up to her, John said, "Why are we stopped?"

"They've gone over there." Mila pointed to a pair of wooden buildings barely visible in the fading light. "The knight went inside the big hut. The other two took the horse around back."

The buildings stood in a small clearing. Smoke wafted out of a gap in the thatched roof of the two-story hut. A warm light spilled through the open door into the yard. The building around the back had a fence for a door: probably a stable.

"Somebody might spot us if we go past on the road, so let's cut into the forest here." John pointed to their right. "We'll go two hundred meters in, take a left, and go half a click parallel to the road before we take another left and come back out."

Mila rolled her eyes at Jess while John went blabbing on with his plan.

"Ah, Dad?" Jess interrupted. "Mila has something to say."

"Speak up," said John.

"Well." Mila continued to glare at Jess. "I didn't know if we were entertaining questions from the audience at this time."

"Cut the bullshit, and get on with it," said John.

"I'm hungry," said Mila.

"I'm thirsty," echoed Jess.

"We can't go in there." John swallowed hard. "I thought that was obvious."

"We can't go in there *now*." Mila raised her eyebrows. "But what if we wait until the knight leaves and then go in?"

"I like your idea," said John.

"What?" Mila's mouth fell open. She had been preparing to defend herself and justify her opinion.

"But we need to take care of the crossbowman first," John continued. "We'll still move into the forest two hundred meters. You guys will turn and continue the half click. I'll stay behind and greet our shadow. Then I'll come and find you. Clear?"

"Are you up to it?" Jess nodded at his leg. "You're looking pretty gray."

"Don't worry about it!" John snapped. "Sorry, Jess," he added more quietly. He looked at Sandra and Mila. "Any other ideas or concerns?"

They shook their heads.

"Okay, let's move."

———

"HELLO, ANNIE." HENRI STOOD IN THE MAIN ROOM of Annie's inn and grinned as he spotted the tray of ales she carried.

"Hello, Captain." Annie held up the tray.

"You are a sight for sore eyes." He took an ale.

"Will you be staying the night?"

"Can you board the three of us?" he asked.

Annie smiled. "I can, but you will be down here. The abbess has the upstairs room to herself."

"It is no matter." Henri furrowed his brow. "What is the abbess doing so far away from the abbey?"

Annie glanced up the stairs then lowered her voice. "She has been here for days. She goes out on long walks then comes back to her room at night."

Strange. There was nothing within walking distance of the inn... except the heretic's cottage. "Is the abbess here now? I would speak with her."

Annie shrugged. "I do not know. She leaves early and returns late. Sometimes I do not see her at all."

CHAPTER FOURTEEN

April 27, 1341

It was too dark. The forest canopy and the overcast sky blocked even the starlight from reaching the ground. John leaned against a tree swallowed by the darkness. As Sandra and the girls felt their way through the forest, the crunching of underbrush receded. It was risky to move around in the forest at night. They could trip on a loose stone, rake their faces on an unseen branch or impale themselves if they fell on a pointed stick. Maybe it wasn't such a good idea to send them off by themselves. He was about to call out to them when a faint rustle interrupted his thoughts—or woke him up. He wasn't sure which.

There it was again, a crunch in the underbrush, too slow and too deliberate but closer. Then nothing. The crossbowman had to be close.

John bent his knees and silently lowered himself. His leg complained. A dull thud struck the tree where his face had been. A man cried out and John lunged up toward the sound. The man must have staggered back, because John came up into empty air.

"Merde," whispered the man.

John swung his good leg in a roundhouse aimed at the voice. His kick connected with the side of the man's head. He lowered his leg and tensed for the expected counter, but the only thing that emerged from the dark was the sound of a body collapsing in the undergrowth. That was lucky.

He grabbed his injured leg. The move had cost him. Blood trickled out of the wound, but he had no time. The downed man was his priority. He bent toward the ground, reaching out in front of him. When he touched the ground, it was soft and inviting. It felt better to sit. He could find the collapsed man just as easily from a sitting position. He reached out in ever widening circles. Leaves brushed against his cheek as his head neared the forest floor. He lowered his chest to the ground and thought he might close his eyes. Just for a moment. Maybe he would remember what he was looking for...

———

JESS PICKED HER WAY BACK TOWARD THE TREE WHERE they'd left her dad. They'd waited for over an hour for him to find them. Her mom's agitation had grown to the point where Jess and Mila had agreed to disobey his orders and go and look for him instead of staying put. It was so dark Jess sensed, more than saw, the trees in front of her. She stopped moving to listen.

"Why are we stopping?" Mila whispered.

Mila's hand rested on her back, and she had to assume her mom was still behind Mila. After a few collisions with blunt objects, they had formed a chain of sorts and now moved as one.

"Shh!" Jess said. "I'm trying to listen. I think we might be here."

"What are you, a bat?" said Mila. "I can't see fuck-all."

"Are you done?" Jess rolled her eyes in the dark. When Mila didn't answer, Jess turned her head to offer new sounds to her ears. The steady hiss of the wind in the leaves overhead wasn't helping. The occasional rustle on the forest floor had to be rodents or birds. This was England. They didn't have poisonous reptiles or giant insects, right? *Stop it.* She shook her head. *Just find Dad.*

She took a step forward, tripped on a clump of undergrowth, and went down. She put her hands out to break her fall but they landed on... chain mail?

"Dad?" She felt along the body until she found a face. The throat had a pulse, but it also had a beard. "Shit."

"What's going on?" Mila said.

"I just fell on an unconscious guy, *and it's not Dad.* Quick, help me tie and gag him." Jess held her hand out toward Mila. She waved it around a bit until she found Mila's hand seeking hers. She guided Mila to the ground beside her.

Jess ran her hands down the unconscious man's chest and crossed a strap. She followed the strap around to his back and found it attached to a quiver of arrows. A little lower, she found a sword belt. They used that to tie one of his boots into his mouth and tied his hands and feet together in front of him with the strap from the quiver.

"Where's Mom?" said Jess.

"I don't know."

"I thought she was behind you." Jess tried to look

around, but the different shades of black did not reveal her mother.

"She was, but when I started helping you—"

"I'm here, honey." Her mom spoke from a couple of meters away.

"What are you doing?"

"I'm just retying your father's dressing."

"You found him? Dad! Why didn't you answer me?"

"He can't hear you right now, Jess."

"What's wrong? Is he okay?" Mila asked.

"He's just sleeping." Mom sounded almost whimsical.

"Mom, you're scaring me. Is he alive?" Jess sucked in a breath.

Her mother didn't answer. She wanted to reach out and throttle her. Why was she stalling? *Just answer the question.* Please. "Mom!"

"Yes, he's fine. I was just taking his pulse again."

"Thanks for the heart failure, Mom," Mila said. "Can you say *bad timing*?"

"I know, right?" Jess's heart pounded in her throat.

"I'm coming toward you," said Mila. She started moving in the dark. "Hold out your hand in my direction, so I don't step on you."

Jess took a long, controlled breath and let it out slowly, washing away the adrenaline buzz. She was spent. They all needed sleep. But what would Dad do? A watch, yeah, that was it. "Okay, guys, we need to take turns sleeping and keeping watch."

"It's pitch black. What are we going to watch?"

Jess rolled her eyes. Mila's sarcasm was a sure indicator that she was feeling better. "We need to know when the knight leaves the inn, genius. I'll go first, then

Mom, then you. Whoever sees the knight leave wakes the others. Plan?"

"Plan," said Mila.

"That sounds fine, Jess," said Mom.

Jess shivered as the chill of the night penetrated her dress. That was all right. The cold would keep her awake and vigilant. But Mila had on the same flimsy JumpGear traveling dress. "Mila, you should cuddle with Mom. It's the only way you'll stay warm enough."

"Thanks, Constable Obvious. We're using her dress as a blanket."

"Oh, good idea." She had forgotten that Dad had stuck it in his belt when Mom threw it at him. *Never discard anything,* his voice advised in her head. *You never know when you might need it.* He was still looking out for them, even when he was unconscious. That made her smile.

CHAPTER FIFTEEN

April 28, 1341

A Mila stood shivering in the cold. The black of night had grayed and now verged on light blue as the new day arrived. She kept her eyes on the inn, just visible through the trees. Fingers of white smoke reached out through the gap in the thatching. Someone inside had started their day.

It wasn't long before the knight appeared, leading his horse onto the road. He set out in the direction of the castle, his men hurrying to catch up.

Mila walked back to their little camp and shook Jess and Sandra. They stirred and stood to stretch. The crossbowman was already awake and watching them.

Jess stepped toward him. "I'm going to ask you some questions. Nod if you understand me."

The man did nothing.

"*Je vais vous poser quelques questions. Hocher la tête si vous me comprenez.*"

The man nodded.

Jess leaned over and removed the makeshift gag from his mouth. "*Quel est votre nom?*"

"*Jean-Pierre.*" He smiled up at her.

"*Bonjour, Jean-Pierre. Ou est l'arbalète?*"

"*C'est derriere l'arbre.*" He pointed at the nearest tree with his tied hands.

"Mila, translate for me," Sandra said. "I want to know what he says."

"Jess asked him where his crossbow was, and he said it was behind this tree." Mila walked around the tree, and there it was. She picked it up and felt its weight. A bit heavier than the modern crossbow she'd held as a teenager. She wandered back around the tree to show Jess.

Jess nodded.

"Why did you attack us?" she continued in French.

"We were sent to capture the witches." He shrugged.

"Who told you we were witches?"

"I have seen it with my own eyes. You appeared instantly, like a miracle." Jean-Pierre glanced at John. "He fights well-armed, battle-hardened guards with only his hands... He sees in the dark like a devil."

"Okay, I get the picture. Why are you being so cooperative?"

"I have seen what you can do."

Jess stepped away and turned a full circle, scanning the forest.

"What are you looking for?" asked Mila.

"Just maintaining my situational awareness. I didn't want to stay focused on JP here in case he was intentionally trying to distract me."

"Makes sense," said Mila. She did a three-sixty of her own and didn't see anyone.

Jess knelt in front of Jean-Pierre. "Who sent you to capture the witches?"

"The bishop."

Mila wondered why the hell the bishop would think they were witches. They'd never been there before.

"Do you know why?" said Jess.

"They do not tell me why."

"I can't think of any other questions right now," said Jess. "You?"

Mila and Sandra both shook their heads.

"We need to strip him of his armor and weapons," said Jess.

"How are you going to do that while he's tied up?" Mila pointed at his bindings.

"Do you know how to use that thing?"

Mila dropped the business end of the crossbow to the ground and put her foot in the foot loop. She bent her knees and grasped the drawstring with both hands. Keeping her back and arms straight, she straightened her legs and strained the drawstring up onto its locking peg. It was a lot harder than she thought it would be. She grabbed a bolt from the pile they had dumped out of the quiver and slid it in place. She aimed at Jean-Pierre's head. "*Ma soeur va prendre vos vêtements. Reste assis. Si tu bouges, tu meurs. Comprendre?*"

He nodded.

"What did you say to him?" Sandra asked.

"She said if he moves he's dead." Jess undid the quiver belt from his hands and legs.

He sat untied on the ground. If he was going to try something, this would be the moment, but Mila edged closer.

Jean-Pierre's eyes flashed from Jess, to Mila, to the

crossbow. He quietly slipped his chain mail over his head and handed it to Jess.

"Shirt, pants, and boots." Jess pointed at the rest of his clothes. When he had removed them, they could see a pouch attached to a leather thong around his waist. Jess reached down and pulled it off. The jingle of metal revealed its contents.

"Have you got him?" asked Jess.

"I've got him." Mila's aim hadn't wavered.

"Okay, I'm going to put this stuff on. You can have the next set."

"Be my guest." Mila wrinkled her nose. "I can smell them from here."

Jess slipped off her dress and handed it to Sandra. "You can use this to make some more bandages for Dad, but save me a couple of long ones to retie this guy."

"And now you're just showing off." Mila shook her head.

Jess glanced up. Jean-Pierre's mouth hung open as his eyes roamed her naked body. "*Détourner le regard connard, ou je vais te botter le cul.*"

He dropped his eyes.

After Jess was dressed, Sandra handed her a couple of long strips of cloth, and she retied Jean-Pierre.

"Should I ask?" Jess said.

"What?" Mila picked up the quiver and knelt to put the rest of the crossbow bolts back in it.

"How you became proficient in the handling of a crossbow?"

"Remember Pete?" Mila stood and slung the quiver over her shoulder.

Jess shook her head. "Is Pete one of the fallen?"

"Yeah." Mila smiled. Jess had long since lost track of

the number of boyfriends Mila had gone through in high school and then college. She seemed to have a new one on her arm at every family function. Jess used to joke that she would dump them just before their birthdays so she wouldn't have to buy them anything. "We used to shoot targets behind his barn after school."

"Is that all you did behind his barn?" Sandra said as she put a fresh bandage on John's leg.

"Don't ask questions you don't really want the answers to." Mila smirked. "But if you must know—"

"No," Jess said, shaking her head. "We're good."

"Well, as it turns out, he had this huge—"

"Mila!" Jess stopped her.

"Bruise on his ass where I kicked it." Mila stood there, smiling back at her.

Jess sighed and chuckled. "Some guys don't understand *no*."

"He understood," Mila laughed.

"What are you laughing about?" John opened his eyes and sat up.

"Dad?" Jess knelt next to him. "How do you feel?"

"Never mind that. What's our situation? What did I miss?"

"Answer the question, John," Sandra said. "You lost command of this unit when you passed out."

John faced her. "I feel tired, thirsty, and hungry. But I'm going to ignore those things and try to focus on what's important. Now, will you tell me what's going on?"

Sandra glared at him.

"Dad, we're doing fine." Jess touched his arm. "We tied up your crossbowman, took his stuff, and got some information out of him. The knight left the inn about a half hour ago. If you can stand, let's try to get something to eat." She jingled the money pouch.

"Thanks, Jess." John smiled up at her. "I knew I could count on you."

"Are you serious?" Mila couldn't believe he was pulling this shit. Here. Now. "Like Sandra and I are on fucking holiday!"

"Mila. Let it go. He's not himself."

Mila glared at Sandra. "Really? Cause if you ask me, *he's himself*."

"Hey, I'm sorry."

John's feeble apology rang hollow in her ears. "Forget it. Let's just get something to eat."

Mila reached down to give John a hand up. He gripped her right hand and started to transfer his weight onto his legs, but he wasn't coming up. Jess grabbed his left hand, and between the two of them they dragged his ass up.

"Thanks, guys," he said.

He looked at Jess when he said it, but Mila kept her comments to herself.

John adjusted his sword belt so that the sword hung at his side with the hilt easily accessible. "Like this," he said to Jess and Sandra. They were wearing their swords hung at the front. They slid them around to the side.

"You grip the sheath with your left. And pull the sword out with your right." He demonstrated. "If it's not around at your side when you start, you run out of arm before the blade clears the sheath. Practice that a couple of times."

While Sandra and Jess were trying what he'd shown them, John turned his attention to Mila. She still had on the JumpGear dress, so there was no way he could find fault with that. She'd put the quiver over her head and draped it down her back above her left shoulder.

"Do you really know how to use that?" John sounded skeptical.

"Yes." Mila kept her answer toneless. She really didn't feel like arguing with him.

"Do you pull the trigger with your left?" asked John.

Mila knew immediately what she'd done wrong. "Shit." Why did *he* have to notice before she did? She would have known the first time she went to draw an arrow that the quiver was hanging on the wrong shoulder. She pulled the trigger with her right, so the quiver should have been on her right shoulder. She slipped it off and adjusted it to the other side.

"Better to figure these things out now," he said, as though he'd been reading her thoughts. "You don't want to wait until speed might matter."

"I know," Mila said. "You're right." Two of the hardest words she'd ever say.

"What's this for?" Jess was holding a leather strap with a metal hook on the end of it. It was attached to the front of her belt and dangled into her crotch.

Mila was working on sexual innuendo, but before she could come up with anything decent John said, "It's to cock the string on the crossbow."

That made perfect sense. Faster. Easier. You could lift with your legs and take the strain off your hands. "I want it," said Mila. "Does it come off?"

Jess checked the top of the strap where it was fastened to the sword belt. She found a buckle and undid it, handing the device to Mila.

"Cool. Thanks," said Mila. She looped it around the belt of her JumpGear and buckled it in place.

"You're gonna wanna double-knot that belt," said John. "Or it'll just come undone when you put any kind of force on it."

"I got it," said Mila. She had been in the process of double-knotting it when John had said it.

John's eyes went up to her hair. "Is there anything we can do about this hair?"

"What's wrong with my hair?" Mila snapped.

"Nothing," said John quickly. "Do we have anything to tie it up with? Not just yours." He motioned to Sandra and Jess.

Sandra handed out some strips from Jess's dress. They all tied up their hair as best they could.

John stood back and studied them. A smile appeared on his face. "You guys look fierce. I wish I had a camera."

"Can we try to find some breakfast now?" said Mila.

"Let's go see what they have." John led them out of the woods toward the inn.

CHAPTER SIXTEEN

April 28, 1341
        As they approached the door to the inn, Sandra spotted a woman rushing out from behind the building. Her simple shift was torn open from her neck to her waist, and she held it closed with one hand. She moved like a hunted animal and it was clear by the leaves matted in her hair that she'd slept in the forest. She slowed to a walk and glanced around the clearing as she approached them.

The woman stopped and offered a weak smile. "Ah need yer hilp." She sounded Texan.

Sandra pulled out one of the extra strips from Jess's dress. She stepped closer to the woman and held it out. She demonstrated by wrapping it around her waist and sliding it up under her breasts. "You can use this to tie your dress closed."

The woman took the cloth and copied what Sandra had shown her, but when she cinched it, she winced. Sandra moved the woman's hands. The gouges that ran down into her cleavage were freshly scabbed. They couldn't have been much more than a day old.

"What's your name?" Sandra gently tied the cloth off.

"Margaret."

"Why don't you tell us what happened, Margaret?"

"They have my Chaddy." Her Texan accent had disappeared.

"Who does? Who's Chaddy?" said John.

"She doesn't need your questions right now."

"Well that may be, but we need—"

"Back off." Sandra touched his chest. "I'll handle it," she added more quietly.

John sat down with his back to the door of the inn. Sandra, Jess, and Mila stood in a loose circle around Margaret as she told her story of how the castle guards had come for them two days ago...

A hollow thump of something heavy hitting their wooden door awakened them. Chaddy rolled off the bed and rushed to the chest in the corner. He grabbed his em-see-vee and called to Margaret.

She rolled over slowly. "What is it, Chaddy?"

Another crash came from downstairs, and the door splintered.

"Come here." Chaddy motioned toward himself. "Quickly."

Margaret stumbled out of the bed and rushed to his side. He hugged her for a moment and handed her the em-see-vee. "Do you remember what I told you?"

She was still half-asleep, but she nodded. He held the chest open, and she folded herself inside to the sound of boots rushing up the stairs.

Chaddy closed the lid on her as the guards stomped into the room.

She stayed in the chest until she was sure they had left. When she came out, Chaddy was gone and so were the guards. Margaret knew they would take him to the castle, so she got dressed and walked into the village.

She went first to the cathedral to seek the bishop's help. She took a bag of Chaddy's silver, he had so much of it. She was sure the bishop would help her if she offered him the coins.

At first the bishop seemed pleased to see her. He escorted her to the castle. He said he would take her straight to Chaddy. It wasn't until she arrived at the castle that she began to realize she had made a mistake. The bishop took her down the stairs, then suddenly grabbed her arm and forced her into a cell. He gagged her, chained her, and slammed the door, leaving her alone.

A few hours later he returned, dragging her out of the cell and down the hall. A door stood open at the end of the hall. When the bishop led her into the room, her heart nearly stopped. The baron stood just inside the door, watching her Chaddy, who was tied to the rack.

The bishop shoved Margaret across the stone floor. She stumbled but stayed on her feet, steadying herself on the side of the rack. Chaddy stared at her. She was too ashamed to look at him because she had ignored his instructions and been captured instead.

"Do you know this woman?" The bishop grabbed her chin and twisted her face toward Chaddy.

Chaddy didn't answer.

"Do you know her?" The bishop squeezed her chin.

"A bit," said Chaddy.

"How?"

"She has visited the carriage and received food from the travelers."

"Is that all?" The bishop snickered.

"Yes," Chaddy said.

"I think not." The bishop shoved Margaret toward the wall behind her. He threw the chain holding her manacles over a hook mounted high on the wall, forcing her arms above her head. She winced behind her gag.

"What are you doing?" Chaddy twisted his head around, trying to keep Margaret and the bishop in sight. The bishop moved to the table and studied the rows of tools. They all appeared sharp and painful, and Margaret shuddered at the thought of their uses. The bishop's hand slid across the short knives and caressed the curved hooks before it came to rest on a tiny rake. He picked it up and slid his finger along one of its tines. A small drop of blood appeared, and he kissed it off his finger before placing the rake into the brazier that stood in the corner of the room.

The bishop returned to Margaret and placed his hands inside the neck of her dress. With one jerk he tore it open, revealing her breasts.

"Such a shame." The bishop cupped one of her breasts. Margaret tried to squirm away, but he squeezed it. She cried out from the shock and the shame of it.

"She doesn't know anything!" Chaddy struggled, pulling on the straps around his wrists, but that only proved how helpless he was.

The bishop walked back to the brazier and carefully turned the rake over as if tending to a meal. He returned to Chaddy's side. "You were saying?"

"What are you going to do? She doesn't know anything."

"Is there anything you would like to tell me?" One side of the bishop's mouth curled into a smile.

"Yes," said Chaddy. "But only if you let her go."

Chaddy lay back, and his eyes fell on the baron leaning by the door. "Please, I'll pay you anything you want."

"Pay me?" *The baron stood straight, suddenly very attentive.*

"Name your price!"

"You hardly look like you could afford my price," *said the baron, but he did wander toward the rack.*

"Try me. I have more money than you think."

"Do you indeed?" *The baron crossed his arms on his chest.*

The bishop glided over to the brazier and picked up the rake. He held it up, examining the faint red glow before he walked back toward Margaret.

When the bishop held the red-hot claws level with Margaret's breasts, Chaddy whipped his head back toward the baron. "Quickly, or the deal's off."

The baron held Chaddy's gaze and then raised a hand. "Hold a moment, Edward. I want to hear what he is offering."

The bishop sneered. "My lord, surely you do not believe this man should be allowed to buy his freedom."

"Any man has the right to negotiate," *said the baron.*

"But my lord, what of his heresy?" *The bishop inched the hot metal toward Margaret.*

"If you fucking touch her, I will not say another word!"

"Edward! Stay your hand," *said the baron.* "I believe him."

"Why do you feel so strongly about a girl that you only know a bit?" *The bishop smiled gleefully.* "Why did she present herself at the cathedral this morning and beg for your release, promising to do... anything?"

"I don't know." *To the baron, Chaddy said,* "Please, my lord. Name your price for my—the lady's—freedom."

The baron studied Margaret and let out a sigh. "This is no lady. You can hardly afford to clothe her, let alone buy her freedom." His eyes lifted to the bishop. "Edward, I have heard enough." He strode from the room.

"Wait," yelled Chaddy. "I can pay. I have a chest filled with silver!"

But the baron did not return.

"Now," the bishop said as he returned his attention to Margaret.

"Tomorrow," said Chaddy, "I can prove I was telling the truth about the travelers from the future."

The bishop held the red-hot iron so close to Margaret's breasts that they were sweating despite the cold.

"I'm listening," said the bishop.

"Tomorrow a new group of travelers is coming. If you see them arrive, you will be convinced. They will instantly appear. One minute they will not be there, and the next they will be standing in front of you. Poof. Like magic, except not. It's science."

"Where is this place?"

"In the valley beyond the blue hill, past Annie's inn. There is a meadow with a single oak tree." Chaddy closed his eyes. "Now will you let her go?"

"Of course." The bishop carelessly let the tool drop from his grasp. Its red-hot claws raked down Margaret's breasts and snagged in her dress, igniting it.

She screamed behind her gag as she writhed, desperately trying to get the deadly iron to fall free of her dress.

"You bastard!" shouted Chaddy.

The bishop signaled the guards as he walked from the room. They tightened the winch, and the ropes lifted Chaddy off the rack's netting and held him taut. There was *a horrible tearing sound, like boning chicken, and Chaddy fainted. Margaret was dragged from the room and set free in front of the castle...*

Margaret paused for the first time since starting her tale. "I'm so sorry."

Sandra put a hand on her shoulder. "Then what happened?"

"I came into the forest to try and warn you. Yesterday, when the bishop and the baron galloped past me on their way back to the castle, I ran off the road to hide. I knew it was too late to get to the meadow, so I hid behind the inn to see if Captain Henri had captured anybody. When he and his men left without prisoners, I hoped you might still be alive, so I waited."

"Who is Chad?" John said from behind them.

"Chad's our tour guide, and Margaret's his lover," said Mila.

"Oh," said John.

"What was the plan that you and Chad had prepared?" Sandra said.

"I was to hide, then meet you and send you home."

"Well, that's great." John said. "Let's get going."

"John! We're not leaving." Sandra sounded angry.

John huffed. He sat there with his eyes closed for a long time. Then he mumbled something that sounded like, "Why not?"

"She needs us to rescue Chad—" Sandra lunged toward John as his head went limp. She caught his left arm just as his slack body fell into the void behind him when the door was pulled open.

A short woman stood in the doorway, wiping her hands on her apron as she gaped down at John. "What is the matter with him?"

Sandra ignored her and gently patted John's cheek. He did not respond.

"Don't just stand there gawking, Annie," Margaret said.

"Margaret?" Annie studied Margaret. "I didn't recognize you. You haven't been this dirty since before you took up with that foreigner. And how is our Chad?"

"Annie, stop prattling and give us a hand." Margaret knelt beside Sandra and put her hands under John's knees. Jess grabbed John's other arm, and the three of them dragged him into the inn. Annie pushed a table out of the way, and they lowered him to the dirt floor.

Mila came in last. The three of them had things under control, so she took up a lookout stance by the door. With one eye on the road, she watched Sandra tend to John.

Sandra undid John's tourniquet. She seemed to like what she saw, because she rewrapped it with the same dressing.

"Can we have some water, please?" asked Mila.

"You don't want the water." Annie smirked. "You'd better stick with me ale."

Margaret nodded. "No one drinks the water."

"Okay. Thank you." Sandra shrugged. "Ale would be fine."

Annie did not move.

"Annie!" Margaret said. "Bring the ale."

"We don't just give it away." Annie stood with her arms folded across her chest.

"How much will this buy?" Jess held out the money pouch.

Annie made to reach for it, but Margaret smacked her hand away and took the pouch from Jess. She dumped the glittering silver coins into her hand. "You could buy the inn with this."

"It's not for sale." Annie sounded concerned.

"Bring us ale and bread." Margaret handed her a single coin. "And be quick about it!"

Annie examined the coin with wide eyes and scurried through a door at the back of the room.

Margaret poured the rest of the coins back into the pouch and returned it to Jess.

Movement outside caught Mila's attention, and she focused on the road. "Here comes Jean-Pierre." She took the crossbow off her back and cocked it with her new accessory. *Nice. Way easier.* She slipped a bolt into the groove.

"Already? I thought he was tied up." Sandra glanced at Jess, who just shrugged her eyebrows.

The room they were in offered no place to hide. Stairs led up to a second floor. Sandra pointed to the door Annie had used. "What's through there?"

Jess ran to the door. "It's a kitchen, I guess. But there's a door out the back."

"Grab his arms." Sandra and Jess each took an arm and dragged John toward the door. Margaret lifted his legs and helped them carry him through the kitchen.

Mila came through behind them and grabbed the tray Annie had prepared. "We'll take this to go." She caught Annie's eye. "If you tell that guard where to find us, I will shoot him as he steps through this door. Are we clear?"

Annie nodded.

They moved across the clearing behind the inn and found a place to crouch in the trees. Mila aimed her crossbow at the back door. For a moment she thought she saw movement in the window above the door, from one side of the room to the other. But by the time Mila pulled her focus up to the window, it was gone. She didn't believe in ghosts, but she could have sworn whoever it was had been dressed in white. No other color would have caught her eye in such a dark room. Mila pulled her focus back to the door. The real threat was Jean-Pierre. She would just have to hope that whoever was upstairs in the inn would mind their own business.

"Do you want me to cover the door, so you can eat?" Jess asked as she put her hand out for the crossbow. Jess chewed as she spoke, and Mila shuddered.

"No." Mila touched her gut. "I can't."

"You need to eat." Jess pushed a hunk of bread toward Mila.

"Later."

"This might be the only chance we get."

"I don't feel like it." Mila took one hand off the crossbow and pushed the bread out of her face.

"Come on, Mila."

"Back off, okay?" Mila raised her voice. Having a type A older sister meant living your life with three parents. Jess meant well, but Mila could only take so much before she had to snap at her to shut her up.

"Ladies," Sandra said, trying to sound like John and failing miserably.

Mila stifled a smile. When John said *ladies*, you listened, or you paid the consequences. John was a big believer in consequences. That was the reason she no longer called her parents *Dad* or *Mom* or any other affectionate moniker.

It had been one afternoon when Mila was about thirteen. John had been yelling about something she'd done, ordering her around like one of his trainees at the base. He refused to listen to reason. He refused to see her tears. He was always right and had no interest in anything or anyone that might question that. His yelling and her tears had become their permanent reality, and there was nothing she could do to change it. That day, she had decided there would be consequences. After that, she refused to call him *Daddy*, *Dad*, or *Father*. He was just John. And her mom became Sandra for her tacit acceptance of his treatment of her. Consequences.

Fucking hard-ass. He was supposed to be looking out for them, not the opposite. He was losing consciousness from loss of blood, and that should have been Jess's focus.

"Go help John." Mila returned to watching the back of the inn.

Sandra stood up. "We need someplace to hide, so John can heal. Then he can make a plan to get your Chad back."

"Chaddy's cottage," Margaret said, as though there was no other choice.

"Won't they be watching it?" Jess asked.

"I had not thought of that, but everything you need is there. Food, water, weapons and the em-see-vee that you people use to come and go."

"Well, I guess we're going to Chad's, then," Jess said.

"Hang on," Sandra said. "What if somebody is watching it?"

"We don't have a choice. We need the MCV. We'll just have to take a look and make a plan based on what we find," said Jess. "How long will it take to get there if we stay off the roads?"

"Half the day," said Margaret.

"Even if we're carrying John?" Mila kept her eyes on the inn.

"Good point. Are there any horses in that stable?" Jess asked.

"Just one," Margaret said.

Mila glanced over at the stable off to their right in the trees. Jean-Pierre led the horse out the door. Jess sprinted toward him.

"Just get him clear of the horse!" Mila ran after her.

Jean-Pierre must have heard her shout, because he spun toward the horse. He lifted his foot up to the stirrup, presenting Jess with a perfect target. She field-goaled his dangling testicles. He fell back from the horse and collapsed, cradling his balls. Jess took the reins of the horse as Mila stopped next to him and aimed the crossbow at his head. This bastard had caused them enough trouble for one day.

"You don't have to kill him," Jess said. "We'll just tie him up again. We'll be long gone by the time he gets loose."

"Do you think Annie will just leave a castle guard tied up in her back yard?" Mila didn't take her eyes off him.

"Probably not."

"Exactly. She'll untie him the minute we leave."

"But we can't kill him. We just need to slow him down so he's not a threat."

Mila lowered her aim, letting the sights trail down his body, pausing when she found his hands.

John lay motionless on the ground. He'd always taught her that actions had consequences. Well, this motherfucker was the reason they were cold, wet, and running for their lives. The hair on the back of Mila's neck stood up, and she began to shake as she slowly brought her eyes back to Jean-Pierre.

"*Non!*" he shouted.

She squeezed the release lever. The bolt pinned his hands to his groin and the dirt under them. The crossbowman's eyes rolled up into his head, and he passed out.

"Mila! I meant shoot him in the leg or something."

"I picked something." Mila's voice cracked.

Jess grabbed her shoulders and spun her around. "What's wrong with you?"

Mila let the tears run down her cheeks. "He shot Dad."

CHAPTER SEVENTEEN

April 28, 1341

A   Sandra rode behind John on the horse's rump. He was wedged into the saddle and had drifted in and out of consciousness. Right now, he was out. His chin rested on his chest, and it was all she could do to keep him centered in the saddle. Her elbows burned from the constant strain of keeping him balanced as he teetered from side to side.

Margaret led them through the forest. They had forded streams and climbed hills most of the morning. The low-hanging branches threatened constantly, but because John was in front of her, he absorbed the brunt of it with his chain mail. She felt a bit guilty about hiding behind his unconscious bulk, but even so, her forearms were raked raw.

"We are almost there," Margaret said as she stopped the horse and pointed down through the forest. "You cannot see it, but the cottage is at the bottom of this hill."

"Okay, I need a break." Sandra waved to her

daughters. "Come here." She let John slip toward them. "Watch his head."

They caught him and half-lowered, half-dropped his two-hundred-and-twenty-pound frame to the ground.

"Thanks. I don't know how much farther I could have gone." Sandra slid off the horse and massaged the inside of her elbows and biceps. "You and Mila go with Margaret and take a look around. Be careful and stay out of sight. We'll make a plan when you get back. Okay?"

"Yes, Sergeant." Jess gave her a mock salute. "You sound like Dad."

"Well, when you spend half your life with a guy, he tends to rub off on you." She stepped between her daughters and reached up to put her arms around their shoulders. She gave them a little squeeze. "Go on. Look out for each other."

"We will." Jess hugged her back and stepped away.

"Look after John," said Mila.

"I will." Sandra's chest tightened as she watched them pick their way down the slope. When they were out of sight, gruesome images of what could happen to her babies began to flood her mind. An overwhelming urge to yell their names and race down the hill swept through her. They needed her.

"Water?"

She spun around. John lay there, looking up at her.

"You bastard." The tears ran down her cheeks. "What the hell are you doing lying around on your ass?"

"I thought you said you weren't going to be emotional in front of the girls."

"I'm not." She took the jug off the horse and knelt beside him.

He took a drink. "That's not water."

"Apparently they don't drink the water around here."

"I'm okay with that." He took another long pull from the jug.

"You like that stuff? The girls think it tastes like piss."

"I've tasted worse." He handed the jug back to her. "Where are they?"

"You just rest. They'll be back soon." Sandra fixed her eyes on the place she'd last seen the girls disappear into the trees. She wiped her tears on the back of her hand. With John awake and smiling, maybe things would work out.

CHAPTER EIGHTEEN

A*pril 28, 1341*
        Jess crouched in the undergrowth at the north edge of Chad's secluded farmstead. The entire clearing was about the size of a soccer field. Three small paddocks surrounded a two-story cottage and barn. The nearest paddock held pigs. The one to the east, upwind, smelled like cow, and the one behind the barn seemed empty. On the south side of the buildings, the clearing narrowed to a point where a two-rut track disappeared into the forest and probably led to the main road.

There was something different about the place. The inn was well weathered and lived in. Here the wood hadn't silvered yet. The thatching still had a hint of green. Everything was new. How could the SSTTC have built all this and still hoped to keep its tours anonymous?

A carriage stood between the cottage and the barn. It had to be the one the guide was supposed to have brought to the meadow.

Three men emerged from the cottage. They wore the same style of chain mail as the soldiers that had attacked them yesterday. One carried a wooden chest, the next carried a bundle of swords and axes. The third man held the drawstrings of three cloth sacks over his shoulder. They threw everything in a pile next to the carriage. One soldier began loading everything into the carriage, while the other two returned to the cottage.

Why were the baron's men stealing all of Chad's stuff? Was he dead? Or was he just left to rot in the dungeon?

The underbrush rustled to Jess's left, and she glanced up as Mila rejoined her. "See anybody else?"

"Not that way," Mila said. "Where's Margaret?"

Jess scanned the forest edge to her right. She'd sent Margaret in the opposite direction, but she should have been back by now.

"What do you want to do?" Mila squatted beside her, resting one knee on the ground. "I think we should steal the carriage."

"Mom wants us to come back after we recon."

"I know. I just think we might be able to use some of the stuff they're putting in it, and it would be way easier to carry John."

"Good call. When Margaret gets back—"

"She's not coming back."

"How do you know?" Jess followed Mila's gaze across the farmyard. Margaret poked her head around the side of the barn. "What's she doing?"

Mila shrugged. "How would I know?"

The two guards emerged from the cottage with another chest between them. They set it down next to the pile and stood there talking until the third guard pointed them toward the barn.

Margaret ducked out of sight. Once the two had

entered the barn, she reappeared and continued watching the man loading the carriage. When he disappeared through its door, she ran and hid behind the vehicle. The man emerged and picked up the swords. When he climbed back inside, Margaret ran for the cottage.

The guards in the barn came out, leading a pair of horses. One of them started attaching the horses to the carriage, while the other walked into the cottage.

"Shit," said Mila.

Jess held her breath, hoping Margaret had heard him coming and was safely hidden. They hardly knew Margaret, and now her reckless behavior had put them all in danger. Jess breathed out slowly. *Dammit.* Whatever Margaret was up to, they had to help her. Margaret was the only person who knew where the MCV was. Without it, they could never go home.

"What's the plan?" said Mila. "They're getting ready to leave."

"I see that." Jess said, but she just continued to stare across the field. She had a sword, Mila had the crossbow, but neither of them really wanted to get in a fight with these guys. *If only Dad was here, he'd know what to do.*

"You know we don't have time to go back for Mom, right?" Mila rested her fingertips on the ground on either side of her knee, like she was getting into the blocks, ready to blast across the field and help Margaret.

"I get it," Jess said. Mila would just wade in swinging, but this wasn't a movie and Jess knew better. She had to come up with a plan. Margaret was trapped in the cottage and there were three men between...

"What are we going to do?" Mila poked her shoulder.

"Give me a minute." Jess glared at her.

"You don't have a minute!"

The guard came out holding a burning log with fireplace tongs. He threw the log and the tongs up on the roof. The thatching caught quickly, and the flames licked their way toward the peak. He stood near the door watching the fire spread.

Crap. Now Margaret was trapped in a *burning* cottage.

"We need a distraction," Jess said.

"I know. Like an explosion or something, right?"

Jess ignored Mila's excited contribution and worked the problem. If they could steal the carriage and get it going toward the road, that would certainly draw the soldiers away from the cottage. But if they had come on horseback, they'd be able to chase her down. "Did you see any other horses?"

"No." Mila shook her head. "Why?"

The flames ate away at the thatching. Jess's heart hammered in her chest. They needed to do something. Not sit here.

"Okay. You draw one of the guards toward you and shoot him in *the leg*," said Jess.

"Why am I the bait? What are you going to do?"

"I'm going to get Margaret and steal the carriage once that guy finishes attaching the horses."

"Why can't I steal the carriage?" Mila said.

"You've never been near a horse in your life."

Mila seemed to grasp the basic logic in the choice. "Fine. The leg. Then what?"

"When he cries out, the others will come running. I'll get Margaret, and we'll jump on the carriage. You sneak around the edge of the glen and meet us where that track heads into the forest." Jess pointed.

"Sounds good." Mila nodded. "But how do I get one of these bastards to come this way?"

"I don't know. They're men, right? Why don't you flash them?" Jess poked her in the boob.

Mila lifted her elbow to block the intruding finger. "Seriously?"

"It wouldn't be the first time."

"Fuck you. It was a dare."

Jess smiled, stood into a crouch, and raced away.

———

Mila kept her eye on the guy working on the horses. As soon as he stepped away, that would be her cue to create *a distraction*. And she wasn't going to be flashing anybody. She could just yell. That would work fine.

The guy attaching the horses to the carriage was taking his sweet time. Either that or he was an idiot. The fire had finished off the thatching and started in on the rafters. Margaret was running out of time. But Jess couldn't make a play for the carriage until this guy finished his job.

The rafters cracked and sagged as the fire devoured them, and the main beam collapsed into the cottage. Margaret screamed. The guy watching the cottage ran inside. The other guards moved closer to see what was going on.

Jess's plan was toast. She raced out of the forest toward the carriage. Mila stood up, but she didn't yell right away. There was nobody on her side of the cottage to hear her anyway. She ran toward the pig paddock and ducked by the fence. Jess reached the carriage and vaulted onto the driver's bench. She picked up the reins and the carriage started to roll. One horse let out a whinny.

Two guards appeared, and ran after the carriage. Jess grabbed the whip and snapped it at the horses. They started to trot. The men chased her up the track.

The third guard emerged from the cottage with Margaret's inert form draped over his shoulder. Well, at least Margaret was out of the fire. But then the asshole laid her on the ground on her back. Her dress had ridden up while he carried her, and now she lay there, half-conscious and half-naked. The guard glanced around the field and hiked up his chain mail shirt.

Mila stood up. "Hey, asshole!"

He froze. Mila's bolt leapt from her crossbow and sailed home. The man fell over backwards, screaming. Mila sprinted around the pig paddock toward Margaret.

The men chasing Jess heard their screaming comrade. They stopped and raced back toward him.

Mila helped Margaret to her feet. "Can you run?"

Margaret shook her head. Mila lifted Margaret's arm around her own shoulders and rushed toward the barn with Margaret limping beside her. When they reached the barn, Mila decided their best option was to keep right on going out the other end. They had almost reached the far door when two guards came racing in behind them.

"Mila, I'm coming," Jess yelled from somewhere outside.

One of the guards heard her and went back out the door. The other one kept coming.

They made it out the back door and Mila put Margaret down so she could reload her crossbow. She knelt about twenty feet from the mouth of the door and waited. Whoever came through would be ventilated.

————

Jess steered the carriage toward the barn. "Mila, I'm coming."

One of the men must have heard her, because he came out of the barn to investigate and charged the carriage. *Good, Mila only has one to deal with.* Jess steered the horses off the track into the field and aimed them to the left of the barn. Maybe if she circled the barn, she'd meet Mila and Margaret coming out the back.

The carriage rocked on the uneven ground and lost speed as its wheels rolled into the soft earth. She whipped the horses again. They pulled admirably, but the overloaded vehicle sank deeper and deeper into the field.

The soldier was two strides away when she ground to a halt.

"Get down!" The man stopped between her and the barn, blocking her path.

"No." She needed him to climb up after her, so she could jump down the other side and get a head start running. She snapped the whip toward his face.

He winced. A small cut appeared on his neck. He put his hand up to it, and it came away bloody.

She whipped him again.

He ducked and put his arm up. The blow glanced off his chain mail. She whipped him again. This guy was a slow learner. She needed to get him climbing.

The man stepped back out of range.

Great. Was he smart or scared? She took the whip and jumped down on the far side of the carriage.

He did not move.

Damn, smart after all. She would have to take the long way. *Let's see what you've got, smart guy.* She took off at a fast jog, past the horses and toward the back of the barn. No sense showing him top speed sooner than necessary. The soldier ran after her. She had about a ten-meter lead on him. As long as she could maintain that, she would be out of sword range.

The man started to close the gap.

She accelerated to keep her lead.

He matched her. *Damn. Fast and smart.* She put on a burst of speed as she rounded the corner to the back of the barn. Mila and Margaret stood outside the back door. Mila had her crossbow aimed at the opening.

"Behind me." Jess ran to her left, giving Mila a clear line of sight.

"Can't help you." Mila did not take her eyes off the opening.

"What?" Jess glanced behind her and saw Fast'n'smart come around the corner. She stopped and drew her sword.

He slowed to stop, drawing his own sword, and smiled as he came *en garde*.

Jess wouldn't last in a prolonged sword fight. She needed to close with him, neutralize the sword, and take him down quickly. She whipped him again.

"I've got a cagey one," Mila said. "He won't give me a target."

"Plenty of targets over here." Jess whipped Fast'n'smart again.

"I can't shoot your guy and reload in time. My guy will come busting out at me."

"Make a run for the forest. That will draw him out."

"Margaret can't run."

Fast'n'smart circled Jess, trying to go between her and Mila. "Dude, really?" She whipped him twice, driving him back. She needed to engage him, but she continued to delay the inevitable. She took a deep breath to calm herself. What was the worst that could happen? *This guy could come up with a sword move that I can't possibly anticipate, and I'll be bleeding my guts out, that's what.*

A rock pinged off his face. He put his arm up to protect himself. She whipped him. He tried to grab the end of the whip, but a piece of horse shit landed on his ear. Margaret was throwing anything and everything she could find.

"That's perfect, Margaret, keep it up. But work your way around behind me as you do."

Margaret limped her way behind Jess, throwing clumps of dirt, horse shit, and little rocks. Fast'n'smart huffed and grimaced. He was either going to rush her or retreat. Margaret continued to hurl debris at him. Some of it even found its target.

"Okay, Mila, back away from the door. We're heading for the forest. Are you with me?"

"Roger that, Constable." Mila backed away from the door, keeping her aim on the opening.

"Margaret, back toward the forest with us but keep throwing. Got it?"

"Gawdit." Margaret's Texan accent was back.

The three of them walked backwards in a row. Fast'n'smart followed at first, but he was continually struck by Margaret's projectiles. When they were halfway to the forest, Mila shifted her aim from the barn door to Fast'n'smart himself. That was when he must have decided he'd had enough, because he ran back to the barn.

———

THEY STOPPED WHEN THEY MADE THE TREE LINE, but Mila kept her aim in the general vicinity of the barn. There was no way she was going to let one of these assholes sneak out of the barn.

Jess pointed at Margaret's leg. The gouges bled from her knee to her ankle. "Sit down and let me take a look."

"No, I'm fine," said Margaret.

"No, you're bleeding. Please."

Margaret lowered herself slowly without bending her injured leg.

Jess pointed at the bottom of Mila's JumpGear dress. "I need to tear a few inches off the bottom of your dress to make a bandage."

"What?" Mila rolled her eyes. She huffed and handed her the crossbow. "Cover the barn and give me your sword."

Jess complied, and Mila cut the bottom three inches off her dress. It was now officially above the knee and unsuitable for professional dress codes everywhere, to say nothing of the fourteenth century. She handed Jess the bandage and sword and took back her crossbow.

When Jess finished wrapping the injured leg, she helped Margaret to her feet. "If it starts to throb, let me know and we'll loosen it."

Margaret took a few tentative steps. "Oh, that is better. Thank you."

"No problem." Jess crossed her arms. "Please tell me

it was worth it and you got what you wanted out of the cottage."

"I got it." Margaret smiled and held up the MCV.

"Good." Jess blew out a breath. "Next time tell me what you've got in mind before you go all lone-wolf on me, okay?"

"Lone wolf?" Margaret raised her eyebrows.

"Forget it." Jess smiled. "Are you far enough away to reload if they charge us?"

Mila shrugged. "Yeah, but my aim is shit at this distance."

"Okay. Do you want to make a play for the carriage or head back to Mom?"

The carriage was stuck in the soft field to the right of the barn, its wheels buried almost to the axles. Mila scowled. "I see you managed to get it nice and stuck."

"Yeah, well, I think if we threw some stuff out we could get it free."

"What about those two assholes in the barn?"

"They seem smart, not brave. I bet if we were down by the carriage and you kept guard, they'd leave us alone."

"Why would they do that?" said Mila.

"The only way they could get into sword range would be if they rushed us. One of them would wind up getting shot, and I don't think either of them would risk it. Do you?"

"My guy sure was a chickenshit." Mila smiled.

"And my guy was fast and smart. Fast'n'smart isn't going to take a bolt for Chickenshit."

Margaret burst out laughing. "Your names for them are good," she said.

"I don't know their real names," said Jess.

"I do, but yours are better."

"It's not magic," Mila said. "Where we come from, you learn to read men early."

"So you spend less time with creeps," Jess finished.

"It looks like we might not have to worry about them after all." Mila pointed at the guards lifting their fallen comrade. "They're helping Woody to his feet."

"Woody?" said Jess.

Mila scowled. "Yeah. I kind of shot him in the groin."

"What?"

"He deserved it. He was trying to have a go at Margaret while she was down."

"All right, then." Jess held up her hands. "How far away is the castle?"

"It takes half a day to walk from here," said Margaret.

The guards moved toward the track leading out of the glen, helping the injured man between them. Then Fast'n'smart took off, running ahead of the other two.

"Okay, we have a limited window. Chickenshit has Woody going as fast as he can. Fast'n'smart has gone ahead to get help." Mila did the mental math. If Fast'n'smart could run the whole way—and Jess said the guy had wheels, so he probably could—he would get there in half the time. If the help came back on horseback, that would halve the time again. "Worst case scenario, we have less than two hours to get the carriage free."

"Let's give it a shot." Jess jogged toward the carriage.

CHAPTER NINETEEN

A*pril 28, 1341*
    Baron Reginald Fitzdumay, constable of Sussbury Castle, strolled through the outer bailey. Bishop Edward Deville walked with him although Reginald had not invited him. Edward always seemed to be present when Reginald was busy tending to his duties. Reginald tried to focus on his steward, who held a drawing of the tournament grounds and pointed out where each of the knights would set up their pavilions for his tournament. Edward's constant questions were slowing down the entire process and growing quite tiresome. Reginald just wanted to have done with it. "Do I really need to know this?"

"No, my lord." The steward bowed his head. "I only thought you would be interested."

"I am not." Reginald stopped and pointed at the drawing. "Just make sure Wessex and Raymond are at opposite ends of the camp."

"Yes, my lord." The steward rolled up the parchment and scurried away.

Reginald sighed, glanced at Edward, and continued toward his new lists and tilts. He placed a hand on the topmost board of the fence. The work felt sturdy and serviceable. Now all he had to worry about was paying the carpenters.

Reginald could not remember why he had agreed to host the tournament. He glanced at Edward. Edward had said the king loved to joust and this would bring the barony into favor. But what did that even mean? Reginald had no ambition at court, and he could not think of a single thing the barony needed from the king other than to be left alone. He had enough trouble keeping his estates functioning smoothly and paying his ever-increasing taxes. Now he would be hard pressed to do either. Damn the bishop and his manipulations.

"Reginald," Edward said.

"Hmm?"

Edward pointed across the bailey. One of the guards ran toward them. The man's face was dirty and bleeding.

"My lord." The man stopped and bowed.

Reginald raised an eyebrow. He recognized the guard and thought his name might have been Eric. "Good news?"

"No, my lord," said Eric. "We were attacked at the heretic's cottage."

"Attacked?" asked Edward. "Who would have the gall to attack castle guards?"

When Eric did not answer straight away, Reginald asked, "Who were these men?"

Eric kept his eyes down at the ground and said, "They were not men."

"What then? Wolves? Boars?" Reginald wanted to ask about the silver, but now Eric had piqued his interest. "What kind of beast could do this to castle guards?"

"Women," said Eric.

Reginald wasn't quite sure he'd heard him correctly. He thought the man had said *women,* but that was absurd. "Speak up, man. I can hardly hear you."

Eric finally raised his face. "I'm sorry, my lord. It was women. Two strangers and the local girl, Margaret."

"The heretics from the meadow," said Edward.

"It is the only explanation." Reginald nodded. "And what of the silver?"

"My lord," said Eric, "Adrian has been shot. Paul is helping him walk back. But I fear if I do not return with horses immediately, he will not reach the barber in time."

"Eric." Reginald decided not to strike the impudent man. "I asked you a question."

"I am sorry, my lord. We did find a chest filled with silver. We also found food, weapons, armor, and fine dresses, but we lost everything when the heretics attacked."

"Damn." Reginald wanted to yell for Henri but Edward stood in his way. He could have stepped to the side to avoid yelling into the bishop's face, but he was not in the mood. "Henri! Attend me at once."

Captain Henri, who stood talking with the carpenters at the far end of the lists, rushed over.

If Reginald could get his hands on the heretic's silver, he might yet be able to salvage some remnant of dignity. He had no desire to borrow money. That was the surest way to lose everything.

Captain Henri arrived and bowed. "My lord."

"Eric has lost my treasure to the heretics. Please retrieve it for me. Take as many men as you need."

"Yes, my lord," said Henri.

Eric lingered. "But my lord, what of Adrian?"

Reginald stared at him. Why did he continue to harp about this wounded man? Could he not see the priority?

"Eric," said Henri. "Come. Do not waste the baron's time."

The annoying man bowed and scurried after Henri. Edward was right. The people were changing.

CHAPTER TWENTY

A *pril 28, 1341*
"Push!" Mila yelled.

She and Jess leaned into the back of the carriage with every bit of strength they could muster. Margaret whipped the horses from the driver's bench. Finally, the vehicle began to roll.

"Keep them moving," ordered Jess. "Don't let them stop until you reach the hard ground of the path."

Margaret drove the carriage around the barn and disappeared.

Mila and Jess searched the pile of loot the castle guards had loaded into the carriage.

"We should definitely take the money box," said Jess.

Mila opened a chest and saw the beautiful cloth from the dresses that Chad was supposed to have arrived with at the meadow. "I want these dresses."

"No," said Jess. "You should be looking for chain mail. In case you haven't noticed, the holiday is over."

"I know." Mila just wanted to feel clean. She started

opening other chests and looking in the cloth sacks. "Here, I found something that looks like bread."

"Food, we'll take," said Jess.

"I know. I'm not an idiot." Mila draped the sack of bread over her shoulder.

"Do you see any chain mail?"

"No." Mila stood up after she checked the last bag.

"We need to get going." Jess pointed at the money box. "Grab a handle."

Between them, they carried the money box toward the carriage. Margaret climbed down and opened the door. Once inside, Jess opened the lid. "Margaret?"

"Yes?" she poked her head in the door.

"I'd feel safer if we hid the MCV in this box."

Margaret nodded and handed it over. Jess dropped it in on top of the mound of silver, and it had turned silver by the time she closed the lid. "Okay, let's hit the trail."

Jess climbed up to the driver's bench, and Mila started to climb up the other side.

"Not you," said Jess. "It has to be Margaret."

"Why?" snapped Mila. "She has a sore leg, I'm sure she'd rather ride inside."

"Margaret's the only one who knows where we're going."

It was true. Margaret had said she could show them where to stop once they were on the Roman road. She knew the place where it would only be a short hike up the hill to where Sandra and John waited. Mila climbed inside the carriage. "Wake me up when we get there."

Mila never did fall asleep. Jess drove the horses hard. The carriage juddered along the stones of the ancient road. Mila's ass was bruised by the constant jarring. She could not get comfortable. When she tried to lay on the bench, her skull bounced on the wood like a basketball.

Finally, the bumping slowed and stopped. Mila poked her head out the door and climbed down to the mud. They were parked at the side of the road in the middle of the forest.

Margaret pointed. "Your mother waits just up this hillside."

"I think Margaret should stay with the carriage," said Jess as she climbed down. "She should rest that leg."

"Bad idea." Mila studied the forested hillside. She would be lost as soon as she was out of sight of the road. "Margaret's the only one who can find them."

"Okay, fine," said Jess.

"I'll go with Margaret." Mila knew she wouldn't be able to sleep anyway. Her ass was so bruised she could hardly sit. "You stay and guard the stuff."

Jess leaned in and gave Mila a hug. "Be safe."

"You too." Mila followed Margaret up the slope into the trees.

CHAPTER TWENTY-ONE

April 28, 1341

A Captain Henri galloped through the streets. Villagers lunged out of their way as the knights rode by. He always felt invincible with Marc and Luke at his side. Together they had survived Halidon Hill. They would have no problem retrieving this chest from three women. He had been surprised when the baron let him choose his own force, but it was misguided to think Sir Reginald was finally realizing the danger of the heretics. Eric had explained that silver had motivated the baron's change of heart.

They left the village behind and raced along the road that led across the fields to the forest. On two occasions they had to ride into the fields to avoid fully loaded carts headed for the village. Bloody foreigners. This was the baron's road. Henri could have demanded they give way to the guard, but he had no time. He wheeled his mount around the second cart and regained the road.

"There!" Eric pointed.

Paul staggered along the road with Adrian hung over his shoulder. Adrian's head and hands dangled behind Paul's back.

Henri reined in and dismounted. The look on Paul's face could only mean Adrian was dead. He lowered the body to the ground. The other knights dismounted and joined Henri next to Paul. They all bowed their heads and knelt by Adrian.

Although he had the right by rank, Henri let Marc offer the prayer. He was the most learned of his knights and would be far more eloquent.

"Lord, we pray you welcome Adrian into your house," Marc said. "He was a righteous man. Please forgive his sins and remember his many acts of bravery and selflessness. He will be long remembered for his good humor, his able sword, and his lust... for life. Amen."

"Amen." They crossed themselves and stood.

"My friends," said Henri. "We have failed in our attempt to save this man, but let us not waste the day. Since we are armored and ready for war, I offer a heretic hunt in honor of Adrian. Who will be at my side?"

"I will," they said as one.

The knights mounted.

"Paul, take Adrian's body and see it buried."

"Yes, my lord."

"Eric, you will come with us, but leave Paul your horse."

Eric mounted behind Marc and they galloped into the forest.

———

Flames overwhelmed the woodpile that had once been the heretic's cottage as Henri and his little band came down into the glen. Eric pointed around the barn and they rode in that direction. The heretic's possessions were piled in the field.

Henry stopped his horse and dismounted. "What does it mean?"

"They had to empty the carriage to free it from the mud, my lord." Eric pointed to a spot next to the pile. "It was stuck here when last I saw it."

Henri led his horse in that direction. He stopped next to the pile. A chest of lady's dresses, a sack of armor, three swords, a mace, and two spears were nearest. Two more chests stood together with a longbow and quiver of arrows leaning against them. "Do you see the chest of silver?"

"No, Captain." Eric shrugged. "The heretics must have stolen it."

Henri was not sure they had stolen it. After all, it had once belonged to them, but Lord Reginald had claimed it as his own, so that would be the end of it.

"We go." Henri remounted his horse and squeezed his spurs into its sweaty flanks. The animal thundered back up the track into the forest.

———

Henri spotted the carriage as they came around the bend. It was just pulling back onto the road, one man visible on the driver's bench. He pointed. "Our prize!" Marc and Luc spurred their mounts, and they raced away, gaining on the carriage. The driver snapped the whip and the carriage picked up speed. But it was far too late. The driver of the carriage could not possibly hope to outrun Henri's knights.

Luc caught the carriage first and passed on the left, and Marc came up on the right. Eric leaned from behind Marc as if to jump from the horse to the side of the carriage.

The carriage driver pulled hard to the right and drove the carriage toward Marc. Marc backed off to avoid getting his mount entangled in the wheels. But the right-side wheels of the vehicle dropped off the road into the mud and immediately slowed its progress.

The driver pulled to the left, but Luc came even with the carriage's horses. The driver tried to whip Luc, but the blow fell harmless on his armor. He leaned over, grabbed the closest horse by its bridle, and lowered its head. The horse slowed to a walk. Marc came alongside on the right, and the chase was over. Henri stopped his horse behind the carriage.

"Get down." Eric jumped off Marc's horse and faced the driver.

The driver made no move to comply, just sat there studying each of them. Only when she looked at him did Henri realize the driver was a woman.

"Heretic." Henri lifted his faceplate. "Two of my men are dead at your hands. I would be perfectly within my rights to kill you now and be done with it. However, the bishop wants you alive. I will give you one chance to surrender and live. If you choose otherwise, my men will kill you and enjoy the sport of it."

The woman did not move.

"Climb down," Henri said. "If you try to flee, Luc will run you down."

Luc lifted his faceplate, smiling with his three teeth.

The woman began to climb down. As she neared the ground, Eric put his hands on her ass. She spun loose and jumped to the ground, punching him in the face when she landed. He went down hard. She tried to run, but Luc was there. He lifted his boot clear of its stirrup and kicked her in the face. She dropped like a sack.

CHAPTER TWENTY-TWO

A*pril 28, 1341*

Mila walked next to the horse as Margaret led it down the hill. Sandra rode the horse's rump, trying to hold John in the saddle. The horse rocked from side to side as it stepped, and John's head matched the rhythm. Mila might have smiled if she hadn't been so stressed about getting back to meet up with Jess. As soon as she and Margaret had climbed into the forest, she'd regretted leaving Jess behind. They should have stayed together and just left the carriage. The Roman road came into view and Mila sped up, no longer needing Margaret to show her the way.

"What's wrong?" Sandra said.

Mila didn't answer. She hurried through the trees, searching as far along the road as the dense undergrowth would allow. Nothing. She checked the other direction. The carriage should be visible by now. Jess could have moved it, but that would be stupid, knowing the rest of them would be expecting to find it where they'd left it. She ran out on the road, her heart thumping in her ears.

She found the spot in the mud where it had been parked. But she saw no sign of it. A deep breath could not control the squeezing in her throat. Where would Jess have gone? There was no reason to move the carriage. Mila had no idea how to even begin to figure out where her sister could be. With John out of it, and Jess gone... She sucked in a breath. *Solve this. Just solve it.*

Margaret crunched out of the forest, leading the horse. John had his eyes shut as his head swayed... That was it. They had watched John Wayne westerns together when Mila was a kid. John had usually fallen asleep, but she had been fascinated by the movies. Wayne always had a Native American tracker with him and... Mila snapped her eyes down to the mud. The ruts left by the carriage wheels led back up onto the road in the direction of the inn and disappeared. Mila took off down the road.

"Mila! Wait!"

She ignored Sandra's pleas. Jess was all that mattered. Scanning the mud on both sides of the road as she ran, she slowed a bit to conserve energy and absorb more detail. She couldn't afford to miss any clues. And there. On her right. The tracks reappeared in the mud.

Mila stopped, bending over to catch her breath. The ruts sliced off the road and deepened where the carriage had stopped. Hoof prints dug up the surrounding mud. Unless Jess had detached the horses, which seemed unlikely, there were more than just the two carriage horses. There were too many horseshoe imprints outside the grooves cut by the wheels. She followed the two parallel slices that angled back up onto the road. She walked across the road and checked the mud on the other side. They reappeared in a semicircle, turning in the opposite direction.

Mila raced back to the others. She could usually run for miles with no pain, but today her chest burned. She focused on her breathing and tried to clear her head. Breathe in, three strides, breathe out, three strides. She had to think.

But she didn't think. She wasn't a thinker. She reacted. Maybe John knew her better than she wanted to admit.

Sandra and Margaret were kneeling next to him when she ran up. He lay on the ground near the horse. Mila slowed to a walk and stopped.

"Mila, don't rush off like that." Sandra stood to face her. With one hand on her chest she said, "You scared me."

"Well, that's about to get a lot worse. I think Jess has been captured."

"What?" Sandra's hands flew to her mouth. Tears welled in her eyes.

Mila slammed her eyes shut and sucked in a breath. She had to keep it together. Seeing your mom cry was the fastest way to lose your shit. She opened her eyes, facing Margaret. "The carriage tracks go around the bend and stop. There are at least two other horses standing around the carriage, and then it turns around and comes back this way. Where would they take her?"

"To the castle," Margaret said matter-of-factly.

Mila stared down the road in the direction of the castle. Her heart rate climbed. Jess needed help, and it wasn't coming from John or Sandra. Mila was Jess's only chance. "I guess I'm going to the castle."

"No one's going to the castle." Sandra wiped her nose on her sleeve.

"Somebody has to help Jess."

"No. I'm not losing you too." Sandra put her hands on Mila's triceps. "Let's take your father back to the future and get him fixed up. Then he can come back and get her."

Mila took a beat to process it. She hadn't considered it until that moment. "We can't."

"Why not?" Sandra's voice cracked.

"The MCV was in the carriage with Jess."

Sandra staggered back. Her legs must have given out, because she sat down hard and stared off into the forest.

Mila fought the urge to go to her. If she held her mother, she knew she'd lose it. Instead, she reached out and touched her shoulder.

"Don't worry. I'm going after Jess. I'll get her back."

"Are you joking?" Sandra chuckled bitterly. "What can you do? You're not a cop or a soldier."

Mila pulled her hand back as if she'd been slapped. She choked back the tears. Sandra was not herself, of course, but the words stung like hell. When she could speak without a quaver in her voice, she said to Margaret, "How can I get into the castle?"

"Invitation by the baron. It's the only way I know."

"What do you do to get an invitation?"

"Usually something quite good," Margaret said, shrugging, "or something quite bad."

"I'm sorry, Mila." Sandra got to her feet. "I don't know what you think you're planning, but—"

"Shut up! I don't want to hear it." To Margaret she said, "Please look after John."

Margaret nodded. "I will."

Mila started running but stopped after three strides. "How do I find you?"

Margaret thought for a moment. "In the village

square, there is an inn. It has a cock hung outside. Very easy to find."

"Thank you." She turned and ran.

"Mila!" Sandra's cry chased after her, but she did not look back.

Mila kept her pace easy. How far would she have to run? And what would she do if she caught up with the carriage? What *could* she do? She almost stopped then but forced herself to keep running. To work the problem.

The oaks and beeches that slid past in her periphery started to look the same. But she wasn't lost. It was mainly a straight road with some undulating hills but no forks. She couldn't possibly have made a wrong turn, because she hadn't made any turns. When the light started to fade, she glanced skyward. She had hoped to be out of the forest before dark, but it seemed to go on forever.

Margaret had said it was half a day from Annie's inn to Chad's, so it must have been around noon when they confronted the guards. She'd also said Fast'n'smart could walk to town from there in half a day. It had taken them the better part of an hour to get the carriage free, and then they had doubled back into the forest to get her parents. Her hike up the hill and back had cost at least an hour. So, all things considered, she was probably looking at a three-hour run. *Shit.* She'd never run a marathon. The longest she'd ever done was a 10k with her friends and Jess.

Jess.

Mila kept running.

She heard the horses before she saw them. She ran straight to the side of the road and hid in the trees. She struggled to control her breathing, but it was impossible. She just let herself breathe long and heavy, hoping she might have more control by the time the riders got close enough to hear her.

A pair of riders approached, one man and one woman. Mila caught glimpses of ruffles and lace peeking out from beneath long riding cloaks. They were wealthy. Behind them came a cart, well loaded and ridden by a man driving a single horse.

As Mila crouched in the undergrowth, her thighs started to cramp, and she stifled a scream. She desperately rubbed her quads to ease the pain. She'd had cramps before, but this was by far the worst. It was a sure sign of her dehydration. Only when the riders were well ahead was she able to stand and walk out the cramps.

Once the pain had receded to a bearable level, she tried to resume her running. But her legs were done. She needed water. She walked as fast as she could, hoping to hear a stream or brook near the road where she might get a drink. Instead she heard the unmistakable howl of a wolf. *Shit.*

She pulled the crossbow off her back and loaded it, but she could barely see into the forest. She'd failed to keep track of the fading light, and if it was anything like last night, the darkness would be complete.

She started running, forcing herself to push through the constant throbbing in her legs. But with the loaded crossbow in her arms, she was in danger of dropping the bolt or, worse, shooting it into the forest by accidentally hitting the release lever. She slowed to a jog.

The wolf howled again. Closer.

It was answered by another howl on the other side of the road.

Shit, shit, shit. On her right, a clump of beech trunks that would be easy to climb offered themselves in the near darkness. Mila left the road and headed for the trees. The branches were higher than she'd thought. She removed the bolt from the crossbow, sprang its release, and slid it back over her shoulder. When she had climbed to the natural platform of the lowest branches, she reloaded the crossbow and sat down.

Ouch. Tree bark on her bare ass reminded her she was still only wearing the wraparound traveling dress. She pulled as much cloth under herself as she could.

One of the wolves howled. It seemed even closer, but this time it was answered by something new.

"I hear you, my beauty," whispered a man's voice.

A dark shadow crept past the base of her tree. She could hardly make out the thin lines of the longbow he held ready in his hands. Her legs chose that moment to cramp up again. *Seriously?* As Mila suffered silently above him, her pain-addled mind decided this stranger in the dark forest in the middle of the night might be her salvation. Through gritted teeth she asked, "Do you have any water?"

As the shadow spun toward her, the sound of the bowstring straining under the pressure of a full draw told her she might have made a mistake.

"Who are you?" The man crept back toward her tree. "You sound foreign. Are you French?"

"No," said Mila. "I'm thirsty."

"And a woman." The man chuckled. "Come down here."

"Why? Do you have anything to drink?"

"I do," he said. "But do you have anything to trade for it?"

Mila took a mental inventory of what she had on her and realized she had very little. She should have taken some of the silver. They all should be carrying some silver. But it was a bit late now, wasn't it? As she stared down at the stranger in the dark, she realized she was aiming her loaded crossbow at the center of his shadow. She was actually already in a standoff, and this guy had no idea. Could she shoot him? Did she have the balls, if he called her bluff? Was she willing to kill a man for his water? Her thighs shouted, *yes, do it*.

The shadow grew to twice its size in a flash, and something brushed the hair off her ear in the same instant. His screams and the deep growling of a wolf provided the explanation. It must have been the man's arrow that had flown past her face when the wolf took him. Correction: wolves. In a daze, Mila counted two, no, three individual shadows pulling in opposite directions. The screaming stopped and was replaced by the tearing of sinew and slapping of flesh on hungry lips.

She tried not to vomit down on the wolves. She didn't know how well they climbed or how high they could jump, and she really couldn't see a need to find out.

Mila couldn't tell how long she sat there listening to the wolves eat, but suddenly they stopped eating and went quiet. The silence chilled her. Had they finally detected her presence? She couldn't have been more than fifteen feet above them. A rustle of undergrowth accompanied the shadows as they moved away and disappeared into the forest.

Mila didn't hear anything, but something must have spooked the wolves. She sat, listening. She even took a deep sniff of the slight breeze. She couldn't smell anything either. A long way back along the road, a yellow light bobbed slowly into view. It was a torch. The clop of hooves came next and then the squeak of wooden axles and the rumble of wheels on the stones of the road. She welcomed the sound and the light—whoever came with them could be no worse than the dead wolf hunter. As they drew near, Mila decided she must take a chance or she would be stuck in the tree until dawn.

She unloaded the crossbow, shouldered it, and climbed to the ground. The light grew closer and began to throw slithery shadows across the remains of the wolf hunter. Mila crawled to the grisly... torso, really: its limbs were all missing.

Mila choked back the bile in her throat. She needed to search the corpse, because while she was safe from the wolves for the moment, she was still in desperate need of water and food, if he had any. She felt along his stomach, looking for pockets, but there wasn't even any clothing left, just the slick remains of his intestines held in place by two leather straps. Still warm. Mila dry-heaved. When she recovered, she rolled the torso onto its back. Surely these straps would be attached to a bag of some kind. One strap led to a quiver of arrows of no use to her, as they were far too long for the crossbow. The other strap was attached to a leather pouch. Inside the pouch she found an apple. The most delicious apple that existed on the entire planet. She devoured it, slurping at the juice that ran down her chin, not wanting to waste a single drop.

The torch moved past her on the road. It was mounted on a post at the front of a large two-wheeled cart. The driver hadn't seen her, and she knew he could not have heard her slurping over the noise of his passage. The island of light thrown by his torch began to move away as the cart moved on through the forest. Mila had to act. If she stayed put, there was nothing to stop the wolves from returning. The mounded load in the cart eclipsed the torchlight, creating a long shadow behind the vehicle. She loaded the crossbow and crept back to the road. She ran up behind the cart and then slowed to a walk, matching its pace. She could walk there in its shadow, and the driver would never see her.

CHAPTER TWENTY-THREE

April 28, 1341

When the road finally left the forest behind, it crossed a long series of fields as it approached the town. Mila unloaded her crossbow and slung it across her back. She guessed the wolves were no longer a threat. They hadn't appeared again in the forest, and now with the town in sight they weren't likely to. After all, they had just fed. Besides, her arms were killing her. She'd been holding it loaded and at the ready for over an hour.

The darkness of the forest had morphed into a gray light from the moon. And here in the open, Mila would become a silhouette to watchful eyes. She wasn't worried about the driver so much as a town watch. Would the town have a wall? What if they had a gate and a guard posted? She stepped to one side and walked where she could see past the cart along the road. A long line of silvery thatched roofs reflected the moonlight, but still she couldn't make out if there was a wall. At ground level, there was only black except for one small flame.

Mila stepped back behind the cart and continued to

follow in its shadow. If she couldn't see the gaps between the buildings, there was probably a wall. And if there was a wall there would be a gate. The flame must have been a torchlight at the gate.

Behind Mila, a whinny broke over the noise of the cart. Mila spun around. Two riders approached at a trot, and another cart followed them. *Shit.* They couldn't help but see her when they caught up. The fields on either side beckoned, but if she ran off the road, she would be clearly visible, both to the approaching riders and the town wall. She stepped up and gently touched the back of the cart with one hand while she felt the load with the other. Short lengths of rough wood filled the cart. Firewood, she guessed. She could easily climb onto the back of the cart and lay still but couldn't risk the horse or the driver sensing the change in the load or balance of the two-wheeled cart. And there was no guarantee that the wood itself wouldn't shift when she added her weight to it.

Mila felt along the underside of the cart. There was nothing but planking making up the floor.

The approaching riders were near enough that she could hear them talking. She resisted the temptation to turn and see exactly how close. Instead she crouched down and walked in under the back of the cart, keeping one hand in contact with the underside to gauge its speed. The floor of the cart was about three feet off the road. She had to lean over so far that her knees bumped into her chest. There was no way she could keep this pace up without falling on her face.

Her quads began to cramp. Mila involuntarily straightened them and drove her back into the underside of the cart. Her crossbow knocked the wood flooring, but no louder than the solid wooden wheels trundling over the stones on either side of her. With her legs almost straight, it was easier to move, and the cramp faded. Keeping her back in contact with the cart, she was able to match its speed.

The voices of the approaching riders grew loud enough to discern as a man's and a woman's. The man passed on her left, and the woman on her right. Their voices faded as they moved on ahead. The only threat of discovery now belonged to the driver of the cart behind her.

She could not risk turning to look, because her crossbow might make a noise on the underside of the cart, or worse, she might fall. It was already awkward enough. She just had to hope it was dark enough to mask her.

The light under the cart increased. They must be approaching the gate. Mila felt the cart slow to a stop and matched it, ceasing all movement when the cart came to rest. She relaxed, slowly bending her knees to let them rest on the ground.

"What business have you in Sussbury at this hour?" asked the gate guard.

"Firewood," said the driver, "for the tournament on the morrow."

More light began to spill in under the cart as the cart behind her approached. It had a torch mounted similarly to the cart she hid under and it felt like a follow spot dialing into her face. Surely the second cart driver must see her. She had to risk a move.

She slowly shuffled farther under the cart. She could only move forward a little before she reached the axle. She relaxed again and lowered her knees to the ground. They never made it. Instead her crossbow strap bit into her ribs and held her up. *Shit.* The crossbow itself was caught on something attached to the underside of the cart. Of course, that was when the cart started to roll again.

It dragged her forwards, but she was able to get her weight back onto her legs before she lost her balance. She crept forward with the cart. Once they were clear of the gatehouse and moving through the sleeping town, she reached up behind to figure out what she was caught on. *Ouch.* Something poked her forearm. Mila twisted her neck.

Something bit into her ear and she stifled most of the "Shit!" that erupted from her mouth, but the damage was done.

The cart stopped. Her crossbow came free, and she fell on her knees. She saw the cart driver's feet hit the ground as he jumped down on the right side. Mila glanced up at the underside of the cart as she crawled out the opposite side. Nails.

She gained her feet and ran into the shadows between the two closest houses. Once in the darkness, she crouched, froze, and cupped her bleeding ear. The driver circled the cart once and looked under it before he climbed back onto his bench and continued along the street.

Mila felt her own blood warming the skin under her ear. She pulled the neckline of her dress up and held it on her ear. It wasn't the most absorbent cloth, but it helped a bit. Once the pain was under control, she gingerly felt the ear. The cut was on the back and shallow, not through the cartilage. John had once told her that head and facial wounds always looked worse than they were because they bled more. Small comfort, but she decided not to worry. She had to keep moving. Jess needed her.

Mila stepped back into the street. The cart was still

visible about a hundred yards ahead. She caught up to it and resumed her place in its shadow. If this load of wood was for the tournament, then it had to be bound for the castle. It had worked once—maybe this was her ticket into the castle too.

The cart rumbled along and took a right turn at an intersection. She was surprised that the houses did not show more light from within. She expected to see candlelight, or firelight, but only occasionally did she see a glow in a window. For the most part the streets were dark except for the light cast by the cart's torch. The cart took a left turn, and Mila got a sense that the town was laid out on a grid, much like a modern town.

The street they were on opened out onto a large square. The town's cathedral took up one entire side. The other three sides were bordered by two-story houses that had tables or shelving in front of them: shops closed for the night, most likely.

Mila bumped into the cart. It had stopped while she was looking around the square. The driver jumped down and started walking back toward her. The cathedral was closest, and its front door was open. She ducked and ran, as quietly as she could.

When she reached the entrance, she risked a glance behind her. The driver had no interest in her. He had walked straight past the end of his cart and across the square to one of the shops. He banged on the door. It opened to his knock, and a warm light and the sound of people talking spilled out into the square. The door closed quickly, and Mila was alone.

So much for her ticket into the castle. She crossed to the dais in the middle of the square. A short flight of steps brought her up onto a stone platform with a well in its center. She turned in a slow circle. The castle should have been visible, but she couldn't see it. She climbed up the side of the well and balanced on the stones. The extra meter of elevation was just enough to reveal a single stone tower.

Mila jumped down carefully. It would be just her luck to fall into the well after having made it this far. She left the square and walked toward the tower she'd glimpsed. The streets were mainly deserted, but she hid in the shadows whenever she heard horses approaching. The ground began to slope up, and she knew she must be going in the right direction. When she'd seen it from the treetop on the first day, the castle had appeared to be on a hill. In addition, all the horse traffic she'd seen so far had been either coming toward her or passing her from behind. Where else would people be coming and going from at this time of night? It had to be the castle, because the cathedral and the town square were behind her.

Mila was avoiding the real problem. Her stealth, luck, and detective work had gotten her to the castle. But even if she could get inside, she still had no idea how to free Jess. Who goes on a rescue mission with no plan? *Dammit.* She was so out of her league.

The road bent to the left, and there was the castle's barbican gate. And almost immediately in front of her was a horse-drawn cart at the end of a long line of horse-drawn carts. Mila walked back around the bend into the shadows. She found an intersection and followed the cross street until it was intersected by a street parallel to the one with the line of carts. She followed the parallel street back toward the castle until it ended at the wall. A space between a house and its stable allowed her to work her way through until she could see the line of carts. She stayed in the shadows to watch and listen.

———

Mila had been standing in the shadows across the road from the barbican gate for far too long. The line of horse-drawn carts stretched along the road as the porter checked his list and admitted them one at a time, but people on horseback continued to bypass the cart line and ride straight up to the gate. These people reminded her of the wealthy couple that had passed her in the forest, with bits of fur and lace peeking out from under their riding cloaks. Each time one of these wealthy couples rode up to the porter, he had to stop what he was doing and see to them, so the carts waited. The privilege of wealth was clearly an age-old concept.

Mila took a deep breath and stepped out of the shadows. She had to move. Even though she had no plan, she figured if she just found Jess, then Jess could come up with their exit strategy.

She strolled down the line of carts away from the castle. She kept her eyes on the drivers. Near the end of the line, she found one who was snoozing in his seat. She stepped in front of his horse and faced the cart in front of it. It was larger than most and reminded her of a prairie schooner with its four wheels and large canvas cover. A loose flap revealed a space inside the cart. With one final glance to confirm the driver behind her was asleep, she climbed inside and pulled the flap closed.

When her eyes adjusted to the relative darkness, she could just make out stacked chests on both sides of a tiny aisle. She removed her crossbow and quiver and crawled forward to a spot where the aisle was wide enough for her to lay down. She shut her eyes and listened. She wasn't really worried about being caught. The porter hadn't been searching the carts, he'd just been identifying their owners and sending them in.

"Next!"

A man's voice. Close. Mila's eyes flew open. How long had she been asleep? Crap. The cart moved forward and stopped.

"This is the property of Sir Raymond," said a second voice, even closer. It had to have come from the driver of the cart she was riding in.

"So, he is coming." The first voice laughed at his own joke. "I thought Wessex might have scared him off."

"Not bloody likely," said the driver. "Sir Raymond don't scare easily."

"Wessex has never been unhorsed. He is unstoppable."

"He has never met Sir Raymond, has he?" The driver snickered.

"You are a cocky one."

"Look, friend. I have been driving all day. Is this leading to a wager?"

"Come see me later." The first voice paused. "Straight in, turn right. Go all the way to the north wall. Sir Raymond has the spot just to the right of the circular tower. Got it?"

The cart started to roll. It lurched left and rocked right as the wheels climbed off the stone road onto the open field. Mila's head bounced on the wooden floor, and she stifled a curse.

The torchlight of the outer bailey surrounded the cart and lit the interior, revealing the chests and crates she rode with. A corner of white linen peeked from under one of the lids. The well-oiled hinges opened easily to reveal neatly folded white robes. Mila picked them up. They reminded her of a nun's habit but beneath them lay folds of blue silk. She set the robes aside and pulled out a magnificent dress trimmed with delicate white fur.

Mila held the dress up to the light. She absolutely had to try it on. She shrugged off her woolen traveling dress and stepped into the folds of silk, delicately pulling them up her legs. This would be perfect for sneaking into the castle. It must be the kind of dress that the wealthy ladies wore under their cloaks. She slid it up around her waist. She slipped her arms into the sleeves and pulled it up over her chest then reached behind her. Crap! The bodice ribbon hung loose at one side. It would have to be laced through both sides and tightened... at the back... by somebody else. So that's why fancy ladies needed help dressing. She had to see herself in the dress before she took it off. A breast plate with a polished surface hung on a stand in the corner near the front of the cart. She took a step toward it and kicked a sack of loose metal.

"Whoa." The clatter must have caught the attention of the driver.

Mila lost her balance as the cart braked and toppled forward. She put her hands out to break her fall and landed in a push-up position on the rough wood floor of the cart. "Shit!" She was about to look at her palms to assess the damage when the driver stuck his head in through the front flap.

"Oy! Who are you, then?"

Mila glanced up at the driver. He wasn't looking at her face. He was staring at her chest. The dress was bunched around her wrists on the floor. The fat little man was ogling her breasts. A creepy smile overtook his face as he began to climb in through the opening.

Her crossbow was well out of reach behind her and unloaded. If any of the chests around her contained weapons, she had no idea. She would have to bullshit her way out of this, but what could she say? *Dammit.* She just wanted to be clean. Was it too much to ask to put on a nice dress and feel like a princess?

That was it. Royalty.

"*Arretez-vous!*"

That stopped him cold.

French was the language of the ruling class in England. She was probably the tallest woman he had ever seen. Her acting teacher would have said *live the moment.* Own it. She drew herself up to her full height, shoulders back, chest out, and chin up. The dress still hung off her wrists and around her waist, and this cretin was getting a front row seat to her naked chest. She fought the urge to cover herself with the dress. Any sign of weakness would spoil the effect. She towered over him and, in her haughtiest French, she shouted, "Have you forgotten your place? Return to your horse at once." He might not understand French, but he would certainly get the gist of her tone. "Or would you like me to tell the king?"

He seemed to recognize the word for *king* because he said, "Please forgive me, my lady. I beg you." He averted his eyes and backed out of the wagon as fast as he could.

The cart started to move. She shuddered as she reached for her JumpGear dress but then she dropped it back to the floor. A quick look in each of the chests revealed one filled with men's clothes. She found chain mail, leggings and a simple tunic. It all fit rather loosely. She found an ornate sword and its studded belt. That went around her waist, to cinch the chain mail and hold up the leggings as much as anything. She had no idea how to use a sword. A chain mail coif helped to disguise her hair. She lowered it over her head and adjusted the hole to the front. Leather boots finished the look. She made her way to the back of the cart, grabbed her crossbow and quiver and lowered herself out.

She hit the ground walking and headed behind the nearest tent.

CHAPTER TWENTY-FOUR

April 28, 1341

Reginald sat alone by the fireplace with his wolfhounds at his feet. His tournament guests continued to arrive, but he was content to let them address one another. The great hall was filled with knights and ladies, and their chatter and revelry was broken only by the gasping and clapping that occurred each time the servants paraded a new dish into the room. The din washed over Reginald but did not penetrate his demeanor. He scanned the room for Henri. The man had yet to report.

And then there was Evelyn. She had been away for so long he wondered if he would even recognize her. He still did not know why he had agreed to invite her to the tournament. Well, he could not very well invite her husband without inviting her. He needed Raymond's reputation to attract the other knights to his tournament. And so he had offered his sister an olive branch. She had of course gracefully accepted the opportunity to return, but he could not help feeling suspicious. She had always made him feel this way and now, even before she arrived, his knotted stomach reminded him of her powers. *Damn that woman.*

He scanned the room again. She was supposed to have arrived by none, but vespers was almost upon them.

Henri approached the fireplace. The dogs lifted their heads. Henri stopped and bowed. "My lord."

"What news?"

"One of the heretics is now secure in the dungeon."

"And the treasure?"

"We did not find it, my lord."

"Henri! I must have that silver."

"Yes, my lord. I will send a search party at first light."

"See to it personally."

Henri bowed and backed away.

Bishop Edward drew Reginald's attention as he made his way around the room, chatting with each guest. The man made a show of welcoming and blessing them, but his real interest lay in the gossip they always brought from court. The bishop approached as Henri left the hall. The dogs growled and stood up. They sniffed his robes and poked their snouts into his genitals.

"I wish you would teach these dogs some manners." He pulled one persistent snout from between his legs.

Reginald smiled. "I've always found them to be excellent judges of character. Sit, boys!" The dogs sat but stayed between him and the bishop.

"Did the captain bring good news?"

"The guards have captured a heretic."

"Only one?" Edward frowned. "When can I schedule the execution?"

"Do you not think it would be wise to talk to her first? See what she has to say? My God, man." There would be no execution until Reginald had questioned the heretic about the lost treasure chest.

The bishop bowed his head. "Of course, my lord. I only meant I need time to prepare for the execution. The interrogation can proceed whilst we prepare."

"The execution is a foregone conclusion?"

"A lesson must be taught." The bishop's eyes blazed in the firelight. "It is God's will."

The bishop was always a little frightening when he said *God's will*. Reginald waited to see if he would start ranting on about *God's will*, but he seemed to have finished. "The execution will be on Saint Philip and Saint James day. I do not want it interfering with my tournament."

"Next week, my lord? I am not sure it would be wise to wait that long. The dungeon is a dangerous place. If something were to happen—"

"Let that be the end of it."

"Yes, my lord. Saint Philip and Saint James day, an excellent choice."

"I am so glad you approve." Reginald returned to his fire and waited for the bishop to leave.

———

Bishop Edward stood outside the keep door at the top of the steps while he waited for the forester to climb up to him. One heretic burnt at the stake would be a good start. More would be better. The villagers would gape in awe at the sight of the cleansing flames eating away the evil that had possessed this unfortunate soul. Edward's cheeks flushed as he imagined the smell of the cooking flesh and crackle of the fat dripping off the body onto the flames beneath it.

The forester arrived at the top of the stairs. "Your Grace. How may I be of service?"

Edward upended his purse and dropped three coins into the forester's hand. "Prepare a pyre in the square."

"When would you like it ready, Your Grace?"

Edward closed his eyes. He drew in a long breath, then smiled as he opened his eyes. "Perhaps tonight. One never knows."

"Yes, Your Grace." The forester bowed and hurried down the steps.

CHAPTER TWENTY-FIVE

A*pril 28, 1341*
     Lady Evelyn paused at the entrance to the great hall. She had not set foot in the castle since the day Reginald had come of age. She had been his guardian for five years, but when he'd taken possession of their father's lands he had banished her. Henri had escorted her to the edge of the barony and deposited her in the Abbey of St. Mary. There she had remained until Sir Raymond crossed her path. Raymond had been good to her, but his lands were small and far away across the channel in Falaise. Today she would begin expanding his holdings.

     She straightened her back and lifted her chin as she stepped into the room. Two guards stood just inside the door. She recognized Eric and nodded to him, lowering her eyes. Eric snapped to attention, slamming his armored heel on the flag stones. *Perfect.* All eyes followed her as she strolled toward Reginald. The din died away as her green silk and ermine-trimmed gown drew stares, but of course that was why she had chosen it. The ladies envied her beauty, and the men lusted after it. She could not have hoped to make a better impression with her entrance.

Reginald had not yet seen her but the dogs leapt to their feet and rushed to greet her as she approached the fireplace. She leaned over to pet and nuzzle them. "Good doggies. Good."

"Hello... Evelyn," said Reginald without turning to look at her.

She smiled. Her father's dogs had always liked her better than Reginald, and while these were surely not the same dogs, they seemed to have inherited that same good sense. She drew out the moment to remind Raymond of that fact. "Have you been starving my babies? They look so thin."

"They are not your..." He stood, took her hand, and held it for the briefest moment. "Thank you for coming."

She controlled the urge to slap him. *Patience. You've waited this long. Just play it out.* She glanced at the fire, expecting to feel more warmth. This used to be her home. One day soon, it would be again. "Did you think I wouldn't?" *You ungrateful swine.*

"No, no. I just thought it should be said." He sat down. "I have prepared your old chamber."

"Thank you." Reginald always had babbled at these functions, and his conversational ability had not improved in her absence. She glanced around the hall to be certain all eyes were still upon her, then took a seat next to his.

"Where is Mary? I had thought I would meet her at the feast."

Reginald's eyes opened wide. "You know of Mary?"

"How could I not? News travels, Reginald. Little passes that I do not hear." And her well-paid network of spies helped enormously.

"I see."

"And Mary is...?"

"In her chamber."

"Whatever for? Is she ill? Has something happened?"

"Calm yourself, Evelyn. She is quite well."

"I do not understand. Should she not be at your side at such an event? How do you expect her to become a lady of manners if you do not give her these experiences?"

"Evelyn." Reginald raised his voice.

"Why are you so stubborn when it comes to Mary? You should have sent her to live with *me* when her mother died."

"Do not speak of the Lady Catherine." Reginald's face flushed red.

Lady? She was barely a woman. It was little wonder she died in childbirth. "But still, you should have sent her."

"I do not need nor seek your counsel. Let that be the end of it," said Reginald.

"Very well. I only pray Mary has not suffered because of your foolishness."

Reginald whipped his glare toward her. "Why do you test me?"

"Do forgive me, Reginald. Father charged me with your care from his deathbed."

"I am quite certain he meant only until I came of age."

"Have you come of age?" She raised one eyebrow.

"Evelyn! How dare you speak to me in this manner?" Reginald stood up, knocking his chair over. "Do you think you are untouchable?"

The crowd uttered a collective gasp and stared at Reginald. Evelyn stifled a smile. If he was trying to look intimidating, he needed practice. With his hands on his hips, it only served to accentuate his little paunch.

"You have met Raymond, have you not?" She paused to let him think about that for a moment then raised her voice just enough that those closest would hear her clearly. "Oh yes, you chose not to attend *my* wedding. But surely you must have heard of his prowess in the tournaments, otherwise you would not have featured him so prominently in your announcements."

The hatred in Reginald's eyes did not bother her in the least. She had disturbed him, and that was sufficient for now. "I think I will retire to my chamber."

She smiled sweetly, stood, and gathered her dress. "I shall return shortly. I do hope Mary is in attendance."

As she moved through the staring, open-mouthed crowd, she cringed at the crooked tapestries and cracked floorboards. She had hoped Reginald would have taken better care of her castle. There was work to be done.

———

Evelyn left her chamber and climbed the stairs in search of Mary. She was not about to rely on Reginald to introduce them. He might yet find a reason to keep them apart.

From the third-floor landing she entered the hall of tapestries. Reginald's chambers took up the entire third floor, but there were some small rooms built into the walls. Evelyn left the north tower stairs and made her way along the narrow hall. She had walked three sides of the square before she found a lone guard. He stood in front of the door to one of the wall rooms, with his hands behind his back. This had to be the place. "I wish to see my niece."

"I am sorry, Madam." The man bowed his head but did not meet her eyes. "Baron's strict orders. No one goes in."

"You are new here, are you not?"

"No, Madam. The baron has been my lord these past three years."

"What is your name?"

"Nigel."

"Do you know who I am?"

"No, Madam."

"I am the baron's sister." She raised an eyebrow. Nigel was handsome enough. A bit timid, but he definitely followed orders well. "Do you doubt my word?"

"No, Madam. I am sorry if I have offended you."

"Shall I drag the baron away from his guests to prove who I am?"

"No, Madam." The keys on his belt jingled as he dropped his hands to his sides and stood up straight. "That will not be necessary."

"Will you open the door for me?"

"I cannot, Madam. Baron's orders."

"I see." She put her hands on her hips as she turned away. Holding down the bodice of her dress, she stretched her head and shoulders backwards. When she released the dress, its bodice cupped under her breasts and brought them higher as it eased back into place. She stepped in front of Nigel as if to pass in the narrow hallway but paused directly in front of him and leaned forward.

He struggled not to glance at her décolletage as he stepped backward, bumping his back on the door. "What are you doing?" His hands came up, but he hesitated. He had no idea where to put his hands to ward her off.

Evelyn struggled not to smile as she moved toward him until her breasts touched his chest. When she was sure he could feel her body heat through his thin tunic, she flexed her chest muscles as she placed her hands on his waist. Her breasts shuddered from the movement, as she knew they would. She almost laughed when the shudder seemed to continue from her body directly through his, but she maintained her composure and held Nigel's eyes. "Would it be all right if I just stood here and spoke with Mary through the door?"

"Yes, Madam." He blushed and stood there, shaking.

Evelyn took as deep a breath as she could without popping her breasts out of the dress. She watched the sweat break out on his brow, and she let out the breath against his neck and said, "Thank you. Would you be so kind as to get me some wine?"

"Yes, Madam, of course." He stepped sideways to get clear of her.

She glanced down at his privates and was not surprised to see a bulge in his breeches. Men were so simple. She put Nigel's key in the lock and opened the door with one hand while she pulled the neckline of her dress higher with the other.

Mary lay on a bed in the corner with her back to the door, but she rolled over at the sound of Evelyn's entry. Evelyn's heart stopped when she saw the girl's face. It was like looking through a window to the past, and for a moment, she couldn't breathe. Mary was her, twenty years earlier, right down to the bloodshot eyes, red nose, and soaked sleeves.

"Hello, Mary."

"How do you know my name?"

"I am your father's sister."

"Auntie Evelyn?" Mary's smile was both hopeful and sad.

Evelyn nodded.

Mary stood and rushed into her arms.

Evelyn hugged her for a long time. "Let us have a look at you." She squatted and held Mary at arm's length. "You are a beautiful young lady."

"Thank you." Mary smiled bravely.

"What is the matter, child?"

"Nothing." The girl clenched her jaw and dropped her eyes to the floor.

"Mary, you do not have to be brave with me. You can tell me anything. I will not think any less of you for it."

"Father says I must be brave always. I must learn to hide my feelings."

"Has he been training you to be a knight?"

"No. If only he would." Her face brightened. "That would be so exciting."

"Your father means well, child, but he has no idea what a noble lady is, let alone how to raise one on his own." She took Mary's hands. "Do you think I know more about being a lady than your father?"

Mary giggled and nodded.

"Good. When a woman asks you what is the matter, jump at the chance to tell her. Even if she cannot help you solve your problem, just the act of sharing it will make you feel better. Do you understand?"

"I think so." Mary nodded.

"Good. Now let us hear your story."

Mary glanced at the door before returning her eyes to the floor.

"Your guard is not at his post," said Evelyn. "Just keep your voice low, and no one will hear you." Mary raised her chin and searched Evelyn's face. Evelyn smiled encouragingly and nodded. "It will be all right."

"Father says I am to wed the Lord Wessex."

The words took Evelyn's breath away. How could she not have heard of this? Her spies were everywhere. This must be new, or it surely would have leaked. Evelyn stood and almost stormed to the door, but Mary's upturned face stopped her. The child was on the verge of tears. Evelyn took Mary in her arms. "But surely you are not yet twelve years old. Is he mad? I will speak with him. Perhaps I can make him see reason."

Mary wrapped her arms around Evelyn's waist and held on.

Evelyn stroked the back of Mary's head. "When is this wedding to occur?"

Mary's tiny voice was muffled in Evelyn's dress. "Sunday."

My Lord. Not only was this new, it was soon. Evelyn had only a day and half to try and stop this madness.

Nigel's boots echoed from the stairwell.

"I must go." Evelyn pulled free of Mary's grip. "When I return I shall bring glad news."

Mary's eyes were glued to Evelyn's. Evelyn broke the contact as she stepped from the room and locked the door.

Nigel arrived with a goblet of wine and handed it to her without meeting her eyes. She tipped her head back and guzzled the wine, making sure plenty poured down her chin and snaked between her breasts. When she had drained the wine, she let out her breath. The bulge in his breeches had returned, and she upended the goblet and tried to place it over his member. He instinctively pulled his hips to the side. She had shocked him enough to finally look her in the eyes. She smiled at him and held out the goblet. He took it mutely as she walked toward the stairs.

Nigel's gasp told her he had just discovered his keys within the goblet. She hoped all of this groundwork would make it a little easier the next time she came to see Mary.

CHAPTER TWENTY-SIX

April 28, 1341

John opened his eyes to wooden rafters supporting a thatched roof. They weren't drinking ale in the forest anymore. A foot scraped the floor and he lifted his head. Sandra walked toward the bed he was lying on.

"So, you're awake?" She stopped next to him.

He put his head back down and took a breath. With three little words, she'd told him that she was pissed, scared, and that it was his fault. "What did I miss?"

"The girls are gone."

"Where?"

Sandra burst into tears. He sat up and reached for her. She stepped back and crossed her arms. "Jess has been captured by the guards, and Mila has decided to go off and play the hero."

"Are you serious? What can she do?"

"I tried to stop her, but she just ignored me."

He lowered his legs off the side of the bed. The room dimmed. He squeezed his eyes shut and shook his head.

When he opened them, the room was light again, but it tilted to the right.

"Okay, give me a chance to get my balance." He gripped the edge of the bed to brace himself against the tilt of the room. He was only sitting, but his pulse thumped in his throat. He took a deep breath. "Where are my pants?"

Sandra stepped in front of him and bent over to look in his eyes. "You're not going anywhere." She touched his shoulders. "Your pupils are spinning like pinwheels."

"I can't just lie here." His girls were out there. Alone. He leaned forward and started to push himself into a standing position.

"John! Don't do it." She held him down.

"Dammit, Sandra." He wiped her hands off his shoulders and struggled to his feet, using her as a human crutch.

"Fine." She stepped back. "If that's the way you want to be, fall on your ass. Maybe you'll learn something."

The room added a spin to the tilt. *Crap.* His head twitched to the side like a sprinkler. "Will you please tell me where my pants are?"

"On the bed."

His head followed one of the room's rotations around to the bed behind him. His pants came up to meet his face. He closed his eyes and lay there.

Sandra's hand rubbed the back of his head. "Just rest, tough guy. Margaret's bringing supper."

———

MILA WALKED AMONG THE PAVILIONS. BRILLIANTLY painted lances and shields leaned against each tent, proclaiming their owner's identities and reputations. It was like a theme park, except this was real. She kept her eyes moving, alert for danger, but taking in all the bright banners. Campfires burned between each pavilion, surrounded by men focused on eating. No one paid any attention to a solitary armored *man* walking among them. She'd developed her man walk on the fly, settling on a half swagger, half stomp with her legs well apart, as though she carried something important between her thighs.

She went behind the last pavilion and stood in the shadows by the curtain wall to study the gatehouse and its two flanking towers. She kept her back to the wall and moved toward the nearest tower. She edged around it, stopping before she reached the spill of light from the entrance. Voices drifted out of the passage, one feminine, one masculine, both speaking French.

"*Bonsoir, Claude!*" said the woman.

"*Bonsoir, Madame Evelyn.*"

"Have you seen my husband?"

"*Oui, Madame.* Sir Raymond was here not long ago."

"*Merci, Claude.*"

Footsteps echoed from the stone tunnel, then the woman emerged and moved toward the pavilions. Mila stared at Lady Evelyn's green silk gown shimmering in the torchlight. With its ermine trim and matching gloves, it was much like the blue dress Mila had seen in the cart. So, this was what that dress would have looked like. The cloth hung perfectly and flowed like water over the curves of Lady Evelyn's body. It was exquisite.

"You there!" Lady Evelyn called to Mila and stopped.

Too late to run, Mila lowered her chin to hide her face. "Yes, Madame," she answered in a low masculine voice.

"Why are you wearing my husband's sword?" Lady Evelyn said.

"You are mistaken."

"I assure you I am not mistaken." She poked the ornate sword belt around Mila's waist. "This is the very belt I gave my husband last season."

What were the chances of running into somebody who would recognize the stuff she'd stolen? She had to talk her way out of this, or her search for Jess would end right here.

"Well, have you nothing to say?" The woman crossed her arms over her chest.

Mila breathed in through her nose and let herself react to the moment. Damn this pushy bitch. What had Claude said her husband's name was? "Raymond gave it to me," Mila said without disguising her voice.

Lady Evelyn grabbed Mila's chin and lifted her face to the light. "And why would he give it to you?"

"Why do you think?" Mila batted the woman's hand off her chin.

Lady Evelyn appeared shocked, but it was more than that. Her anger seemed to lose some of its intensity and she almost smiled. "So, my husband is an adulterer?"

Lady Evelyn left the question hanging and hurried away.

Mila massaged her chin as she watched Lady Evelyn's receding back. *Okay, so maybe don't rile the locals.*

She needed to move. The woman might be back soon if she found Raymond quickly. Two men approached the gatehouse. One carried a basket of swords over his shoulder. The other carried a yoke with empty buckets hanging from each end. Mila came out of the shadows and entered the passage ahead of them.

"Halt. What business have you in the castle?" said the porter in poor English.

"*Bonsoir, Claude!*" said Mila in gruff French.

"How do you know my name?" asked Claude, switching back to French.

"Lady Evelyn told me. She lost one of her gloves and asked me to come and fetch it."

Claude took his time considering her request. The two men behind Mila shuffled from one leg to another. The man with the swords puffed out a sigh, the weight of his load growing on fatigued muscles.

"Come on, Claude. Do us a favor?" said the man with the buckets.

Claude glanced at the impatient men behind Mila. "*Vite.*"

Mila stepped past him into the inner bailey. She made a show of walking slowly and looking down at the ground. She spotted the stairs that led to the keep and drifted in that direction. She reached the foot of the stairs and snuck a glance over her shoulder. The man with the swords moved toward the smithy. The man with the buckets had reached the well. Claude watched her from the gatehouse doorway.

Mila started up the stairs. She took one step at a time, stopping to search it from one end to the other. At any moment, she expected Claude to come running toward her, but she reached the landing, crossed it slowly, and stepped through the giant door into the keep. Now what?

The entranceway led to a large room. The din of a crowd told her which direction would bring immediate trouble. On her right was a hallway. She peeked around the corner. A boy approached, carrying a platter heaped with small cooked birds. The aroma called to her stomach, and she swore she could hear it reply. She rubbed her tummy and forced herself to focus. On her left, an archway led to a circular stairway. She started down the stairs. Voices, growing louder, came from below. *Crap.* She rushed back up the stairs, two at a time. She passed the archway and kept going up. The next landing opened onto a long, narrow hallway.

Mila snuck into the hall and stopped at the first door. The door opened easily, and she glanced inside. Empty. She slipped through the opening and closed the door behind her. It was somebody's bedroom. What if they came back? What the hell was she doing? She was alone and cowering in a castle she knew nothing about. If only she hadn't yelled at her mother and stormed off. If John was at a hundred percent, he would probably have Jess rescued by now.

Mila forced herself to breathe slowly and leaned her back against the door. *Jess.* That's why she was here. John was out of it and Sandra was useless, so Jess needed her. She was going about this all wrong. Improvising would get her killed. This was real. If she was ever going to rescue her sister, she needed a plan. Popular belief held that prisoners were kept in dungeons and that dungeons were under castles. *Great.* Then what?

Stop it. Just find her.

CHAPTER TWENTY-SEVEN

April 28, 1341

"She said you gave it to her!" Lady Evelyn stood in the entrance to their pavilion with her hands on her hips.

"I assure you, darling, I have no idea what you are talking about." Raymond drifted to the other side of the pavilion and bent to lift the lid of a chest. He removed the white robes, and she watched the muscles in his back ripple as he rummaged deeper into the chest. He was magnificent, and she briefly wondered how she might feel if he ever did betray her. She smiled. That would never happen.

"Why do you continue to search for it? I have told you she has it. All I want to know is why."

Raymond stood and came toward her. His soft voice rumbled in his chest. "I do not know why she has it, Evelyn." He took her hands. "Perhaps she stole it. I will speak with the carter and see if he saw anybody loitering."

"I trusted you." She pouted.

"And I have done nothing to betray that trust. Just give me a little time to find proof of my innocence."

"How could you?" She turned her back to him. The ache in his voice made her smile. She almost felt sorry for deceiving him. She wanted to tell him she believed him, but she needed to keep him out of the castle for a while longer. Her brother knew not what Raymond looked like, and that fact might prove useful before the night was over.

Lady Evelyn made a show of storming from the pavilion in a huff. Raymond called to her, but she ignored him and continued toward the castle. She had to find the foreign woman who had Raymond's sword. What was the real reason for her disguise? And did she have access to Chad's ceremonial orb? She quickened her pace.

———

Evelyn hurried into the great hall where she was deafened by the noise of the banquet. Two long trestle tables ran the length of the room. All of the lesser knights and ladies sat along these tables, lost in boisterous conversation. The men's wine-fueled shouting was occasionally overshadowed by the high-pitched giggling of the ladies. Evelyn scanned the crowd for any sign of the foreign woman in Raymond's armor. Not finding her, she stepped onto the dais where Reginald sat with his most honored guests.

"Evelyn, you are late." Reginald sounded pouty.

Evelyn walked behind the table and stood behind Reginald. "There is a most urgent matter I must discuss with you."

He ignored her. "May I introduce Lord Wessex?"

The giant man sitting on his right stood and bowed

formally while his eyes roamed her décolletage. She resisted the urge to show her contempt. Wessex was an unknown, and she did not yet know if she would have use for him. She would take his measure before deciding if she would allow him to wed Mary and thus ally with the family.

"Lord Wessex." She curtsied and paused with her head down, so Wessex could take in the view.

"This is my sister. Do sit down, Evelyn," said Reginald, pointing at the empty chairs on Wessex's right. "Where is Raymond?"

Evelyn straightened. "He has been detained. I must speak to you."

"Not now. The bishop is about to bless the feast."

The bishop sat on Reginald's left, chatting with Captain Henri. He did not look at all like he was in a hurry to start the blessing.

"Edward!" Reginald poked the bishop's shoulder.

The bishop glanced at Reginald in shock, but he stood and raised his arms, waiting for the crowd to grow quiet.

Evelyn climbed onto the dais and sat down. She searched the crowd sitting at the two long trestle tables. The foreign woman was not among the guests.

The bishop started into the Latin, and everyone bowed their heads. Claude appeared at the door. He had his eye on Reginald. The bishop lowered his voice and slowed his delivery, took a long breath, and continued even more emphatically.

Reginald seemed to grow bored and opened his eyes to look around. Evelyn smiled inwardly. Reginald had no idea what the bishop was saying, because he could not speak a word of Latin. He spotted Claude and waved him over.

Claude walked around behind the dais and whispered, "My lord."

"Why are you not at the gate?" asked Reginald without whispering. Several guests opened their eyes and raised their heads. The bishop continued with his blessing. Apparently, interruptions from Reginald were not new or unusual.

"I must report that a young squire has snuck into the castle." Claude lowered his eyes. "I have no idea what his true intentions are, but he gained entry with a falsehood."

"Henri!"

This time the bishop did stop. He opened his eyes and glared at Reginald.

Henri stood up and stepped around the bishop. "Yes, my lord?"

"Go with Claude. He will explain."

Claude and Henri strode from the hall.

"I lost track. Are you done yet?" Reginald yelled at the bishop, who stood glaring at him.

The bishop took a deep breath, raised his eyes to the ceiling, and crossed himself. "*In nomine Patris et Filii et Spiritus Sancti. Amen.*"

"Let us feast!" Reginald slapped the table with his palm.

The music started up in the gallery, and the din of renewed conversation filled the hall. Evelyn stood and walked over behind Reginald. "Excuse me, Reginald. I shall return shortly."

Reginald grunted.

Evelyn hurried after Henri and Claude.

CHAPTER TWENTY-EIGHT

A*pril 28, 1341*
"What is the matter?" Henri stood in the passage that led to the keep door.

"A young French squire has entered the castle with a falsehood." Claude refused to look him in the eye.

"*Mon Dieu.* When?" Henri's hand slipped to the hilt of his sword, and he glanced around the passage.

"Just a few moments ago. He wears a hauberk with coif and carries an ornate sword and a crossbow."

"Return to the gate. We will discuss your failure at a more convenient time."

"Yes, Captain." Claude nodded and stepped out of the keep.

Henri returned to the entrance of the great hall, where Eric and Paul stood guard. He signaled, and they followed him toward the circular stairs. It was probably just a squire from the retinue of one of the invited knights. He would find the lad and teach him a lesson in manners.

"Henri."

He stopped. That soft voice. It could only be Lady Evelyn. He had not yet had the chance to speak with her since her return. "My lady. It is good to have you back in the castle. We have missed your company."

"Thank you, Henri. You are most kind." She stepped toward him and rested a hand on his arm. "There is something else you should know about the person you seek."

"You have information about this boy?"

"She is not a boy. She has stolen my husband's armor to disguise herself."

"Thank you, Lady Evelyn." This was more serious. Women did not dress in armor.

"Henri?"

"Yes, my lady." She had stepped even closer, and his upper arm brushed her chest as he turned.

"I should like to ask you a favor, if I may." Lady Evelyn's voice was low and melodic. The heat from her breasts still lingered on his arm as he stared into her captivating eyes. She was as beautiful as the day he had escorted her from the barony. When she had been Reginald's guardian, Henri had taken his orders directly from her. They had spent many long hours together, supervising the young baron's lands. It had always been a pleasure to be in her company. She placed a hand on his shoulder, and her fingers slipped up his neck and around to the back of his head. The hair on the back of his neck stood up as she drew his head down to whisper in his ear.

"I would like to speak to the girl before you give her to Reginald. Can you arrange that?"

He continued to lean toward her as he considered her request. Her perfume engulfed him, and for a moment he would have done anything she asked.

Paul shuffled his feet, and the spell was broken.

"Of course, my lady." Henri lifted his head. "Please follow at a distance while we search the castle."

"Thank you, Captain." She stepped back and Henri led his men up the stairs.

———

MILA HAD HER EAR PRESSED TO THE DOOR. SHE hadn't heard anything for a while, so she opened the door and peeked into the hall. Deserted. She snuck toward the stairs. Footsteps tumbled up toward her. She spun around and rushed back to the room, closed the door, and slid down between the bed and the wall. Her weapons scraped along the stones and she froze.

The footsteps stopped outside her room and the door swung open.

She held her breath.

"No one here, Captain," said a gruff voice.

"Next room," said another.

The door closed, and the footsteps moved away. Mila lay there, spent, her heart racing. She closed her eyes. She couldn't give up. Even if she didn't find Jess, she still had to get out of the castle. She opened her eyes. A spider crept along the wood of the bed, next to her face. *Okay, time to go.* There may have been armed men in the hallway, but there was no way she was staying under the bed with a spider. She pressed her back against the wall and dragged herself out from behind the bed, keeping both eyes on the spider until she could stand up and get clear. Only then did she let out her breath for what seemed like forever.

She returned to the door, and after a thorough search of its surface, pressed her ear to the wood.

———

HENRI FINISHED CHECKING THE SECOND FLOOR AND led his men up the stairs to the third floor, nearly colliding with Nigel as he rushed down toward them. "Have you seen any strangers?"

"Yes, sir. Surely you passed them on the stairs." Nigel pointed past Henri.

"Them? Describe them."

"A woman in blood-soaked clothes, and a man in filthy rags."

"Enough! Turn around!" It had to be the heretics from the dungeon.

"But sir. I assure you." Nigel stood, blocking his advance.

Henri drew his sword. "Nigel! Turn. Around."

Nigel finally obeyed and started up the stairs.

"Is Mary's chamber secure?"

"Yes, sir."

"Good. Check the baron's chamber then return to Mary's door."

Henri addressed the others. Eric and Paul stood below, but Lady Evelyn was not behind them. He had no time to wait for her. "Come, we will check the passage." He rushed up the stairs.

CHAPTER TWENTY-NINE

April 28, 1341

Hearing nothing, Mila slipped out of her room and started to sneak down the stairs. As she approached the main-floor archway, the crowd noise swarmed into the stairway. *Own it.* Mila stopped sneaking and resumed her man-walk. She made it past the opening and continued toward the lowest level of the castle.

At the bottom of the stairs, she came to an open gate of iron bars. That was a good sign. Bars meant cells, right? She crept through the gate. A narrow, torch-lit, stone hallway lined with heavy wooden doors stretched into the gloom. Each door had an opening the size of a face.

At the first door, she stopped and peered in. Darkness filled the cell. She checked behind her then whispered, "Jess?"

No answer. She tried the latch. Locked. She moved to the next door. This room was even darker. "Jess?"

Nothing and locked. A torch hung from a wall sconce back near the iron gate. The next torch hung at the end of the hallway at what appeared to be a right-angle corner at least thirty feet away. The three cells between her and the next torch would be even darker. If she had a torch with her, it would maximize her light and minimize her need to whisper into the dark rooms. Who knew what might lunge out of the darkness toward her face? She walked back to the gate.

A muted shuffle came from the bottom of the stairs. Mila's heart leapt into her throat. Scenes from too many horror movies leapt to her mind, but no one appeared at the gate. She took a deep breath and reached for the torch. It refused to come loose. No matter how hard she pulled, she could not free it. Her luck wouldn't last forever, so she gave up and returned to her search.

At the third door she didn't even bother to look into the gloom. "Jess?"

No answer, but when she tried the door, it moved. She pushed it open to maximize the light. The door swung until it knocked into the stone wall. She stood in the entrance, letting her eyes adjust to the darkness. The cell was empty. She moved to the next cell.

This door was open, and her foot hit something soft as she stepped in. A fat little man lay in a dark puddle. There wasn't enough light to make out the color, but it had to be blood.

"Shit!" Her hand flew up to her mouth as the curse echoed off the stone walls. She stepped back out of the room.

"Who are you?" asked a quiet voice behind her.

"Shit!" Mila spun around, drawing her sword. The heel of her sword hand drove into the wall long before the sword came clear of its scabbard. *Crap.* She'd forgotten how narrow the hallway was.

"That won't be necessary," said Lady Evelyn as she

stepped in close and held up a dagger. "I only have a few questions."

Mila jerked her face away from the dagger and bumped the back of her head into the door frame. "Dammit!" Mila let her sword slide back into its sheath.

Lady Evelyn smiled and lowered the dagger. "How is your head, my dear? Have you hurt yourself?"

Mila massaged her head with the heel of her hand.

"Who are you and who is this Jess you seek?" Lady Evelyn asked.

Mila had to decide how to play it. Honesty or fiction. Jess was already missing, and who knew what had happened to her since she'd disappeared? Lady Evelyn was clearly a member of the ruling class. Maybe she could help. "My name's Mila and Jess is my sister."

Lady Evelyn nodded slightly, but her dagger hand hung at her side, twitching. "She is why you snuck into the castle?"

"Yes."

"Why did you steal my husband's sword?"

"Um, the belt made the chain mail look more flattering?"

A smile ghosted across the Lady's eyes. "I find the truth to be of value in a case like this." Twitch.

"I needed a disguise."

"Ah. Honesty. Is that so hard?"

"No, I just..."

"Why would your sister be in my brother's dungeon?" Twitch.

This was getting old fast. "The bishop had her captured."

"Why?"

"He thinks we're witches." Mila smiled and rolled her eyes.

Lady Evelyn raised an eyebrow. "And are you?"

"Seriously?" Mila waited for Lady Evelyn to crack a smile, but she just stood there. Mila stopped smiling. "No."

"Why does the bishop believe that you are?" Twitch, twitch.

"I have no idea." Mila glanced at the dagger.

"Why do you not look me in the eye, child?"

She forced herself to lift her eyes to Lady Evelyn's face. "Your dagger keeps twitching."

"Shall I put it away?" Lady Evelyn lifted the dagger.

Mila spun away and ran to the corner before Lady Evelyn's words registered. She stopped and glanced back. Lady Evelyn still stood by the open cell. She hadn't chased her. She hadn't even moved.

"Here, I'm putting it away." Lady Evelyn slipped the dagger into a fold in her dress and her hand came away empty. "Is that better?"

"I guess so."

"Do come here. Look me in the eyes and tell me why the bishop thinks you are a witch."

"But I—"

"Your best guess, then."

Mila wandered back toward Lady Evelyn. Any mention of time travel would probably convince her that Mila was a witch. But she didn't have any choice. Jess wasn't in the dungeon. If not here, then where? Mila had no plan beyond the dungeon. "I believe the bishop has found out where we are from. He may even have seen us arrive."

"Is this a riddle?" Lady Evelyn cocked her head to the side.

"I'm sorry." Mila couldn't think of a way to describe their arrival that didn't sound like magic.

A scream from the stairwell echoed down the stairs.

"It seems my attention is needed elsewhere." Lady Evelyn walked to the stairs.

Mila followed her.

When Lady Evelyn stepped through the iron gate, she closed it. "Please wait here." She smiled and hurried up the stairs.

Mila tried the door, but she already knew it would be locked. *Dammit.* Now she was trapped. Worse than that, the more she replayed the scream in her head, the more she was convinced it was Jess.

CHAPTER THIRTY

A*pril 28, 1341*
     Edward sat listening to Reginald fawn over Wessex. Reginald asked him about horses, hunting, weapons, even women, hanging on every word. Yet Reginald had no interest in any of those subjects, and Wessex's responses to all of Reginald's inquiries were guarded. He was civil but not open. He wasn't drinking his wine, and he seemed uncomfortable with Reginald's attention. What was he hiding?

Edward sipped his wine. These two lords had struck an alliance over the marriage of Reginald's daughter, but they could not have been more different. Reginald was a merchant to his core. His only real interest was money, and he certainly had no religious convictions. Wessex was a pious man with a reputation for violence bought with the blood of his enemies, both in the lists and on the battlefield.

Wessex accepted a serving of capon from the carver, but before he picked up his knife, he closed his eyes and crossed himself.

Edward smiled. It had been a long time since he had shared a meal with someone as devout as Wessex. This was good news indeed and presented Edward with an irresistible opportunity. "My lord?"

"What?" Reginald dragged his gaze off Wessex.

"I think we should discuss the execution of the heretic." Edward kept his smile fixed in place.

"Heretic?" Wessex spoke with his mouth full. "Why have you not told me of this?"

Reginald glared at Edward but smiled at Wessex. "It is nothing, Wessex. A civil matter that shall be dealt with presently."

"I should like to see this heretic." Wessex put his knife down on the tablecloth. "I have never seen one."

"Why do we not execute the heretic tonight, my lord?" said Edward. "I am sure Lord Wessex would enjoy the spectacle of a witch burning."

"Yes, Reginald, that would be most satisfactory." Wessex pushed his chair away from the table as though he expected Reginald to comply immediately.

Edward held his tongue. He had but to wait as Reginald came slowly to the inevitable conclusion that he must satisfy Wessex.

A scream pierced the din of the crowd. Everyone fell silent and twisted their heads toward the passageway.

Edward stood and followed Reginald and Wessex, already headed for the hallway.

"Henri! Take your foot off that woman." Evelyn's voice came from the stairway. "At once!"

Edward felt the rest of the guests crowding in behind him as he stood behind Reginald and Wessex outside the archway that led to the stairs. Evelyn's eyes were glued to something up around the bend. Edward followed her gaze to where Henri stood with one foot on a woman's back. She lay awkwardly with a sword handle visible beneath her. Blood dripped onto the stair below. Henri dragged her to her feet, and Edward was impressed by how the blade skewered her breast like a side of meat. Henri pulled the sword up and out of her, handing it to the guard behind him. The woman whimpered and then collapsed. If Henri had not already been holding her, she would surely have fallen.

"Henri! What have you done?" Evelyn glared at him.

Henri addressed Reginald. "My lord. We recaptured the witch trying to escape with the man who drove the carriage. She has tried to escape twice since then and failed both times. This grievous injury was by her own hand."

That was hard to believe. Why would she have driven a sword through her own appendage? How? Edward wrestled with the mechanics of it for a moment then set that aside. The woman was clearly dying. Perhaps this was an opportunity.

"She is quite beautiful." Wessex ran a finger down the cleft of his chin.

"The hand of almighty God is at work, my lord," Edward said as he raised both palms toward the spectacle. "See how he has begun to spread his righteous justice even before we had intended."

"Surely you must burn her immediately. You cannot allow these wounds to rob you of the opportunity to serve the Lord," said Wessex.

The woman hung limp in Henri's grip. Edward longed to see the flames lick their way up her body but he forced his eyes to Reginald. "Indeed, my lord. We must make haste."

Reginald stood pondering and said finally, "Henri. Take this witch to the village square. She will be burned at the stake before the night is over."

"Yes, my lord." Henri dragged her toward the keep door.

"Reginald!"

"Not now, Evelyn." To his guests, he said, "Let us prepare to move to the square for this evening's unexpected entertainment."

The crowd let out a cheer.

Edward scurried past him and followed Henri out the door.

CHAPTER THIRTY-ONE

April 28, 1341

Mila was certain the screams had come from Jess. She heard Lady Evelyn yell at Henri to take his foot off, but then they lowered their voices. She strained to hear what they said, but she caught only the occasional word. Then there was a cheer. *Not good.*

She had to get out. Pulling a bolt from her quiver, she loaded the crossbow. She backed down the hallway into the shadows, where she had a clear view of the barred gate.

Lady Evelyn appeared almost immediately. She unlocked the gate, peering into the darkness. "Mila? There is no time for games. Something horrible has happened to your sister."

And whose fault is that? Mila stepped forward. She held the crossbow angled toward the floor but made sure Lady Evelyn knew it was loaded.

"That will not be necessary. I have come to help you get out of the castle."

"I'm not leaving without Jess."

"I know, but do come along, there is no time." Lady Evelyn hurried to the stairs.

Did she really think Mila would just follow her? Mila raised the crossbow. "Lady Evelyn!"

"What is it, child?" She turned at the stairs. "We really have no time."

"I just have a few questions." Mila held the crossbow aimed at her head.

"I will explain on the way." The woman folded her arms across her chest. "You will never get past the guards with a loaded crossbow."

Was she fearless? Or did she know Mila wouldn't shoot her? Mila got the feeling she was testing Lady Evelyn's patience. This was a waste of time. She couldn't trust Lady Evelyn, but she had to find out what had happened to Jess. She had no choice. "Fine!"

Mila unloaded and shouldered her weapon. At the top of the stairs, the crowd exiting the castle slowly shuffled past. Lady Evelyn reached for Mila's coif, and Mila forced herself not to bat the hands away. Lady Evelyn pushed Mila's coif back and let it fall down around her neck.

"There." Lady Evelyn combed her fingers through Mila's hair. "Claude will hardly recognize you." She took Mila's hand and stepped into the crowd.

They moved with the other guests until they were out of the keep and down past the well. Two lines were forming. Lady Evelyn led her around the one headed for the stable and joined the one leading out through the gatehouse passage.

It was time for some answers. Mila took a breath.

"Not here, dear." Lady Evelyn did not even turn to

look at her. "Keep your head up and look Claude straight in the eyes as we pass."

It was good advice, but how had she known Mila was about to speak? They reached the gatehouse, where the line became single file as Claude let the guests into the passage. When their turn came, Lady Evelyn released her hand. "Will you be joining us at the execution, Claude?"

"No, Madame, my place is here." Claude gave a slight nod.

Lady Evelyn was past him but she continued to speak, drawing his attention toward her. "That is unfortunate, Claude. Please have a horse saddled for me. I shall return presently."

"*Oui, Madame.*" Claude faced Mila. She nodded at him as she stepped through the door. A grimace flickered over his face, but Lady Evelyn took her hand and pulled her out of the passage. She half expected Claude to call out, but he was engaged by the next guest.

When they emerged into the outer bailey, Mila stopped Lady Evelyn. "Execution?"

"Keep your voice down," Lady Evelyn said, squeezing her hand.

Mila snatched it away and whispered, "What execution? And don't you dare say you'll tell me later." Mila drilled her with what she hoped was her most withering stare.

"Do come along." Lady Evelyn stepped around Mila and walked away.

Mila's jaw dropped open.

The line had thinned as it drifted toward the barbican gate. Small groups of people, some mounted, some walking, made their way out of the castle. Mila rushed after Lady Evelyn then slowed to walk beside her.

Lady Evelyn did not look at her. "My brother has seen fit to let the bishop execute your sister."

"When?"

"As soon as the fire is prepared in the town square."

"And all these people are going to watch?" The people around her chatted amongst themselves as they walked. They smiled and nodded, their faces bright with expectant grins. "You people are sick."

"Not all of us." Lady Evelyn stopped as they neared the main gate.

A large man separated himself from a group chatting around the porter and walked toward them. As he approached, his eyes were fixed on Lady Evelyn. A smile grew across his face.

"I have good news." He grabbed Lady Evelyn and lifted her into a bear hug.

"Put me down, Raymond. There is work to be done."

He lowered her gently until her feet touched the dirt. She straightened her dress. "Let me introduce Lady Mila."

Raymond glanced at her and his smile disappeared. He bowed. "My lady." To Evelyn he said, "I thought I had made progress toward the thief, but as usual you have bettered me by simply finding her."

Lady Evelyn patted his shoulder. "Do not feel badly, Raymond. The Lady Mila presented herself to me at the castle."

Well, that was an exaggeration, but Mila needed this little reunion to be over so she could see what kind of help Lady Evelyn would offer. She removed the sword and belt and presented them to Sir Raymond. "My apologies."

Raymond raised an eyebrow but accepted the sword and strapped it on.

Mila plucked at the chain mail she wore. "May I have the use of the armor a little longer, sir?"

"Of course," he said.

"Raymond, darling," said Evelyn, "Surely you have heard about the execution."

"Indeed. I saw the witch as they took her out. She is a real beauty, that one. Even covered in blood."

"Raymond!" He stopped talking. "She is Lady Mila's sister."

Raymond bowed his head. "That is most unfortunate."

Lady Evelyn pulled Raymond's ear down to her mouth. She whispered something Mila could not hear, released him, and said, "Mila is trying to rescue her sister. You will accompany her and keep her safe."

"Yes, my lady."

Lady Evelyn pulled Mila's coif back up over her hair. "It is a crime to dress as a man. Did you know that?"

Mila rolled her eyes. "You're telling me this now?"

Lady Evelyn smiled and held Mila's hands. "Godspeed. Now go!"

"Wait. Why are you helping me?" The cliché about the gift horse crossed Mila's mind. This was all just a little too convenient.

"I have my reasons, and you have no time." Lady Evelyn nodded toward the village.

Mila huffed. Did Lady Evelyn ever give a straight answer? But she was right about the time, so Mila ran out the barbican gate with Raymond close behind her.

CHAPTER THIRTY-TWO

April 28, 1341

A   Reginald and Wessex rode slowly past the alley, followed by a squad of four guards on foot. Evelyn urged her horse forward, and it stepped into the street behind the guards and matched their speed. She had questions for Reginald. He was behaving oddly, letting Bishop Edward and Wessex convince him the foreigners were heretics or even witches. Father had taught him the truth about heresy and witchcraft, so why now was he falling back on the ignorant opinions of his guests? There had to be something else at work here. She nudged her horse forward and came alongside Reginald.

"Evelyn. I wondered where you had disappeared to."

"Lady Evelyn." Wessex nodded to her.

"I had to speak to Raymond."

"Ah," bawled Wessex, "And how is your husband? Ready for a good thrashing, I hope."

She raised a single eyebrow. "I'm quite sure if thrashings are to be had, they will be delivered *by* him, not *to* him."

"Bah!" Wessex looked away, shaking his head.

Evelyn studied Wessex. She had not yet decided if he was worthy of Mary, but everything she had seen so far was a disappointment. "I did not come to argue jousting, sir. I would much rather discuss the witch. You said she was very pretty, did you not?"

"Indeed," said Wessex.

Evelyn had to engage Reginald if she was to learn his interest in the foreigners. "Did Reginald tell you he does not believe in witches?"

"He did not." Wessex glanced at Reginald.

Reginald kept his peace.

"Oh, yes. Our father was quite adamant. Witches are simply women who are too smart for their own good." She waited to see if Reginald would take the bait.

Reginald pursed his lips and glanced sideways at her before he addressed Wessex. "It is true. Father always favored the practical explanation."

"So, you do not believe this witch is possessed by evil?" Wessex crossed himself.

"Of course not." Evelyn shook her head.

"Evelyn. I can answer for myself."

"Please do." She waited, but he grew silent as he maneuvered his horse around a family moving slowly down the middle of the road.

"Well?" asked Wessex.

That was a blessing. If she waited long enough, Wessex would pry the information from him. She just needed to be present to hear it.

Finally, Reginald addressed Wessex. "It is true. I do not believe the woman is possessed. But the bishop does. Edward says the people are drifting away from the church, and he blames these witches."

"Witches?" Wessex stared at Reginald. "How many are there?"

"We counted four yesterday."

"Four! It is nothing short of an infestation, sir." Wessex shook his head.

"I must disagree, Wessex." Reginald paused as though working it out for the first time himself. "I am sure there is a perfectly rational explanation for their behavior. I had hoped to discuss it with the woman before she was so grievously injured."

"So that is why you agreed to the execution?" Evelyn said. "She was no longer of any use to you? Reginald, I am appalled." Evelyn's horse drifted back, and she squeezed it gently with her thighs.

"I agreed to this execution for a number of reasons, all of which are my own." Reginald threw a glare at her.

Evelyn ignored his warning and pressed on. "So. I have guessed the first one. Would you like me to continue, or should I give Wessex a turn?"

Wessex seemed uncomfortable. Perhaps he was unaccustomed to a woman badgering a man in Reginald's position. Evelyn smiled while she waited, but Wessex remained silent. "No? Then I shall guess again."

"Evelyn. That is quite enough." Reginald stopped his horse.

They had reached the village square, and Evelyn and Wessex stopped their horses next to Reginald's and looked out across the gathered masses. They had a clear view of the bishop, standing on the platform with his arms up and waiting for the crowd to acknowledge him. Reginald would not be very receptive to her pestering until after the show, so she let him be. She did hope Mila had some success rescuing her sister. That would rattle Reginald immensely, making it far easier to pry loose the information she required.

CHAPTER THIRTY-THREE

April 28, 1341
Mila spotted a knot of guards ahead in the crowd. She slowed to a walk as she came up behind them. Ten guards formed a loose *V* across the front and sides of a cage mounted on a wagon. Their task was to clear a path and they weren't particularly interested in protecting their prisoner.

Mila was able to walk casually up to the back of the wagon. She bit back a scream. Jess lay on her back in a pool of her own blood. Jess's left eye was nearly swollen shut. The bastards had beaten her. Mila didn't know if she was alive or dead until Jess slowly raised one hand and gingerly explored the holes in her chest. Blood flowed from a gash in the top of her left breast, a hole in the bottom, and a slice down the outside of her ribs. Jess rolled onto her side and managed to push herself into a sitting position with her right arm only.

Jess began to remove her tunic and was immediately rewarded with jeers and curses from the guards. Ignoring them, she bunched the shirt next to the wounds and tried to wrap the sleeves behind her back like a strapless halter.

Good job, Jess. But Mila saw the problem before Jess, who was obviously thinking slowly through her fog of pain. Mila wanted to shout to her but knew it would draw the guards' attention. *Use your pants.* Mila willed her to think of it.

Jess laid down.

Don't give up. Some blood must have reached Jess's brain, because she started dragging her pants off.

Yes. Good girl.

The cheers and curses intensified. "Witch!" The guards grabbed the bars of the cage and shook it. "Heretic!" They spat on her and pawed at her like apes.

If Mila had a machine gun, she would have just mowed these assholes to the ground.

Jess struggled to the center of the cage where they couldn't reach her. She knotted one sleeve to one pant leg, then wrapped the long cloth around and around her torso. She pulled it as tight as she could, then folded herself in a ball and lay on her side.

The cage wagon bumped along the village road. Jess bounced on the wooden floorboards. She lay there with her eyes closed for so long Mila thought she might have passed out.

All Mila could do was walk behind the cage... and watch her sister die. If only she knew how to use a sword, she could fight off the guards... She glanced at Raymond, who followed behind her. Lady Evelyn had told him to keep her safe. Would he fight off the guards long enough for her to get Jess out? Could she even get her out? She had no idea if the cage door was locked or, if so, what kind of lock it was.

First things first, then. Mila stepped up to the back of the cage and walked close enough to study the lock. It was a sliding bolt secured with a padlock. *Shit.* That meant somebody had a key. One of the guards? Maybe, but how likely was it that she could convince Raymond to kill all the guards so she could search them for the key? Not very. And was this horror-hungry mob going to stand by and watch that happen? No. But what else could she do? It was her only move, and it was suicide.

As she was pondering, Mila drifted close enough to the back of the cage to reach out and touch the bars, and nobody said boo. A quick glance at the closest guards told her they hadn't noticed. Jess hadn't moved for a few minutes, and Mila had to know if she was still alive. If Jess were already dead... *Stop it. She can't be dead.* Mila put her face to the bars and whispered, "Jess?"

Jess didn't move. Maybe she hadn't heard.

"Jess." This time Mila spoke it. Jess just lay there. Mila thought she could detect the slight rise and fall of Jess's ribs, but she couldn't be sure with the bouncing cage floor.

"Jess." This time Mila was certain she'd said it loud enough for Jess to hear.

Jess opened her eyes.

Mila's throat constricted, and she swallowed hard. She had to keep it light, had to give Jess hope, a reason to hang on. "Suck it up, buttercup."

Mila hated herself for quoting John. He used to say that to them when they were little and they had fallen down. But she couldn't think of anything else to say.

Jess stirred.

"So you did hear me," said Mila.

Jess's eyes finally focused. A smile slipped onto her

lips, but it was immediately crushed by a scowl. "Mila!" she whispered. "Get out of here." Jess tried to drag herself closer to the back of the cage.

"Shut up, bitch." Mila smiled. "I'm getting you out."

"Don't be stupid. Run!"

"Oy! You there." The nearest guard stepped toward Mila. "Not that close."

Raymond placed himself between Mila and the guard, bumping him aside.

"Run!" Jess yelled. She grabbed her chest.

Raymond put his arm around Mila's shoulders.

"You know this guy?" Jess said.

"We must go, Lady Mila." Raymond began to pull Mila back from the wagon.

Mila locked eyes with Jess. "You hang on," she ordered, but her voice cracked. "Okay?"

Jess was still staring at Raymond, still more concerned with Mila's safety than her own. Mila's face reddened. She wanted to scream and lash out. At anybody, but really at herself. Her sister was about to die and she was powerless to do anything about it. Every move she could think of would also end in her own death. Why was she so frightened? Why couldn't she just...

The crowd bunched up in front of them as they reached the town square. The guards forced their way through and disappeared with the cage wagon.

Mila spun free of Raymond and glared at him. "Will you fight the guards for me?"

Raymond placed one meaty fist on his chest. "No harm will come to you."

"What does that even mean?" Mila rolled her eyes and shoved her way through the crowd. Villagers, merchants, off-duty guards—it seemed like everybody had come out to see her sister's execution. Even the nobles sat on their horses at the edge of the mob. They were all focused on a raised platform in the center. Mila didn't dare glance toward it. She didn't know how she would react to seeing Jess tied there. Instead she kept her head down and her anger focused.

She had to find John. He would know what to do, he had to. Even if he couldn't fight, he would give her a plan. She checked each storefront she came to, then plunged into the next person who stood gawking at Jess. She shouldered as many of the bloodthirsty villagers as she could while she made her way around the outside of the square, searching for the inn with the hanging cock.

She had no idea if she could trust Raymond, but he did seem to be solving disputes behind her. From time to time she heard the villagers she'd bumped begin to shout and then suddenly grow quiet. She never looked back. Whether Raymond was calming them or killing them made no difference to her.

There it was, two doors away, a dead chicken hanging above a door. She put on a burst of speed and shouldered her way between two men. They shouted, but Raymond drew their attention.

As she arrived, John rushed out the door.

CHAPTER THIRTY-FOUR

April 28, 1341

A Sandra had first watch. She sat with her back against the door. Margaret slept stretched out on the floor, and John snored in the bed. She could only hope her babies were okay. Her eyes drifted to the gouges on Margaret's chest, and she shuddered.

The noise of the crowd woke Sandra. She cursed herself for falling asleep. Why was there a crowd gathered outside the inn? Had the innkeeper turned them in while she slept? She stood and crossed to the window. There she saw a sea of people, but they were not looking up at her window. They faced the center of the square.

A squad of guards formed a perimeter and held the crowd away from a raised platform, where a muscular woman tied to a pole held everyone's attention. The woman's head lolled to one side, and her hair hung across her face. Her clothes had been removed and wrapped around her torso to stem the bleeding of a wound. Her hair was caked with blood. A pile of stacked wood surrounded the base of the pole. A guard stood nearby with a torch, watching a man dressed in golden robes. The man in gold held his palms to the crowd, gesturing for silence.

The figure tied to the stake stirred and raised her head.

Jess. The word jammed in her throat.

Jess's left eye was swollen shut. Blood flowed from under her makeshift bandage. It ran down her thighs and dripped off her feet onto the wood beneath her. She was half-naked. Sandra spun away from the window, trying desperately to shut out the images of torture and rape that flooded her. She needed to think. Act. But she stood there, shaking.

"Juh," she rasped. She swallowed hard. "Je..." Her throat constricted like a vice. "John!" The scream tore its way out. Sandra fell toward the bed. She grabbed him by the shoulders and shook him awake.

"What?" He opened his eyes and struggled into a sitting position.

He was in rough shape, but he was the only chance Jess had. Sandra pointed out the window. "Do something! They're going to..." Her voice strangled to nothing. She sucked in a breath and clutched at her throat. "... burn her!"

John staggered to the window. His back seemed to swell as he took in the view. He straightened and picked up his chain mail. All signs of his dizziness had vanished by the time he'd donned the armor. His eyes focused and his nostrils flared as he grabbed his sword and headed for the door.

Sandra grabbed his arm and squeezed. "Don't let that son of a bitch hurt my baby."

John put his hand over Sandra's. His eyes locked with

hers as he pried her fingers loose. "I won't." He opened the door and was gone.

Sandra stared at the door. Had she just sentenced him to death? Despite his adrenaline-fueled recovery, he wasn't ready to fight. He would trade his life for Jess's in an instant, but knowing that didn't ease her guilt. If she had to choose between him and Jess, she would choose Jess every time, but not because she loved John any less. He had to know that, didn't he?

CHAPTER THIRTY-FIVE

April 28, 1341

"John!" Mila's smile felt so wrong, but just seeing him on his feet made her giddy. Maybe Jess did have a chance.

"Mila." He hugged her. "Are you okay?"

"Yeah." She pulled away. "Do you have a plan? What should I do?"

"Go up to our room." He pointed above his head at an open window overlooking the square. "Shoot anybody who tries to light that fire."

"What about the *don't kill anybody in the past* rule?"

"Fuck it. All bets are off."

Raymond came up behind Mila. She had to get upstairs, but she couldn't just leave Raymond with John without some kind of explanation. "John, this is Sir Raymond. His wife helped me escape from the castle and told him he had to protect me. I don't know whether to trust him or not. Maybe he can help you?"

"I'm going to get my daughter off that platform," said

John. "I'll kill anybody who gets in my way. Is that what your wife had in mind?"

"I am afraid Lady Mila is mistaken. I have been tasked with keeping *her* safe. Alas, I cannot accompany you on such a noble emprise." Raymond bowed his head, looking slightly embarrassed.

"That's what I figured." John took his hand back.

The crowd grew quiet.

"If you're going to keep Mila safe, you need to guard the stairs." He nodded to the inn. "Once she starts shooting, it won't take them long to figure out where she is."

"That, I can do. No one shall pass." Raymond placed a hand on John's shoulder and bowed his head. "Bless you, John. Your quest is righteous. Fight gloriously or die in the attempt. May God be with you."

John nodded and waded into the crowd.

"You should be helping *him*," Mila yelled at Raymond as she rushed into the inn.

———

Mila climbed the stairs, opened the door, and raced to the window where Sandra stood watching. "Hello, Mother."

"Mila." Sandra's double-take morphed into a smile, accentuating the tear streaks on her dusty face, but the greeting was short as Sandra's attention returned to the view out the window.

Mila pulled the crossbow and quiver off her back. She laid the quiver on the floor, pulled a bolt, and loaded the crossbow. She tried to nudge her mother to the right. "Mom."

Nothing.

"Mom?"

Nothing.

Mila put a hand on her shoulder and pulled it backwards, forcing her mother to turn and look at her. "I need the window."

"Of course. Sorry." Sandra took a breath, swallowed, and nodded. "What can I do?"

"I don't know." Mila pointed at the door. Sandra picked up her sword and wandered toward the door. She seemed to be in a daze and probably wouldn't be able to do much if somebody was determined to get in, but at least she was out of the way. Mila lifted the crossbow to her shoulder and took aim out the window.

The squad of guards that had escorted the wagon now formed a perimeter and held the crowd away from the raised platform, where Jess was tied to a pole. The bishop that Jean-Pierre had told them about stood with his palms to the crowd, gesturing for silence.

Not knowing if Jess was alive or dead, Mila had an overwhelming urge to shoot the bishop as he addressed the crowd. She swung her sights toward him, but somebody in the audience threw a rock toward the stage. It bounced off Jess's chest, and she stirred. Jess was still alive. Mila's chest shuddered. She gritted her teeth and sniffed back her tears. Then she puckered her lips and slowly let out her breath, tracing her aim back to the torchbearer's heart.

CHAPTER THIRTY-SIX

April 28, 1341

A	Bishop Edward held up his hands and waited for the crowded square to quiet. The villagers pressed against the detail of guards surrounding the platform. At the back of the throng, the baron, Wessex, and the other guests sat on their horses watching him. Beyond the crowd, every shop window and doorway was filled with faces. Everyone was here. He could not have prayed for a better turnout. Here at last was his chance to demonstrate God's will.

Finally, the crowd grew silent. Edward lowered his hands and folded them in front of his robes as humbly as he could. "Welcome. This is a joyous occasion. Tonight, we will together witness the salvation of a lost soul. Over the past season, many of you have spoken with the travelers that visit in the carriage. No doubt, they have shared stories with you about the way things are in *their* land. And quite naturally, you have wondered why things cannot be like that *here*."

The crowd murmured as they stared at the witch.

"My children, I am here to tell you that you have been deceived. There is no such place." Edward paused and pointed at the pathetic, bleeding woman. "These people are no different than you or I. *They* have been led astray, and now they lead *you* astray with that same evil."

He paused to let them hang on the very word. *Evil.* Let them feel its danger. Someone coughed in the back, and a few people cleared their throats. That was enough of a pause.

"But no more! Tonight, we will rejoice while the purifying flames cleanse this girl and return her to the path of righteousness from which she has surely strayed."

Somebody threw a stone. It bounced off the witch's chest. Edward smiled inwardly as the witch winced from the impact. It seemed she could still feel some pain.

"Let us pray." He raised his hands palms down toward the masses. "Each of you must reflect upon what is happening to this heretic. Here, you must see the work of our lord Jesus Christ." He gestured to the witch with one hand as ominously as he could. "If you fail to learn from *her* suffering, then *you too* will be doomed to endure the same lesson." The crowd gasped. *Good, let them worry.*

Edward knelt and assumed the silent prayer position with his eyes closed and his head down. He listened carefully to the crowd and prayed. *Lord, help me choose the perfect moment to open my eyes and complete your service.* As usual, he felt nothing, but when he opened his eyes, every face was fixed on the witch. *Thank you, Lord.* This was the moment. This would bring them back to him. It had to. He stood and nodded to the torchbearer.

———

JOHN REACHED THE FRONT OF THE CROWD AS THE torchbearer stepped toward the edge of the woodpile. A crossbow bolt ripped into the man's arm, pinning it to his ribcage. He cried out, dropping the torch and staggering off the platform onto the dirt behind the perimeter guards. The closest guard glanced behind him to see who had screamed. John stepped around him. When the man returned his attention to the crowd, John took his head. The crowd gasped and backed away. The next guard along the perimeter drew his sword and came at John. He took his arm. The man fell to his knees, clutching the gushing stump. The element of surprise was spent. All he had left were his reach and his rage. John ran for the stairs.

The remaining guards abandoned the perimeter and converged on John. The man unfortunate enough to be closest swung his sword. John blocked the attack and stabbed the man in the face. A scream erupted behind him. John swung around in time to see a guard let go of his sword to clutch at a bolt in his neck. The blade glanced harmlessly off John's shoulder as it clattered to the ground. John pushed the dying man aside as another soldier rushed to engage him.

———

AFTER MILA SHOT THE TORCHBEARER, SHE WATCHED John decapitate the nearest guard. But there was no sign of Raymond. He had ignored her and must be cowering in the inn below her. Mila reloaded. She had to help John.

Mila couldn't possibly miss. She just had to make sure she missed John. She aimed at the guards closing in behind him and released her bolt. It hit a guard clean in the neck as he swung at John.

Mila reloaded as fast as she could.

She watched John work his way toward the stairs, taking out each guard he encountered. She shot as often and as safely as she could. He was like a machine—Jess's own personal angel of death. It wouldn't be long now.

Movement on the platform. The bishop inched toward the fallen torch.

"Dad!" It was Jess. She collapsed after the costly scream. The bishop reached for the torch.

Mila loaded her last bolt.

The bishop picked up the torch and walked toward Jess.

Mila fired over John's head and her bolt disappeared low into the bishop's flowing robes. The bishop spun around and glanced toward her window. Mila waited for him to topple over, but he did not. He threw the torch into the wood under Jess. *Dammit.* She'd missed.

The torch landed near the bottom of the pile and the flames appeared instantly, eating their way up the dry pyre. The bishop retreated to safety behind Jess's pole.

"Dad," pleaded Jess.

"I'm coming!" John rushed the stairs.

Five guards stood between him and Jess. If he didn't get through them quickly, he would be too late. The man at the bottom of the stairs sliced down at him. He deflected the blow to the side and skewered him. The rest of the guards had taken up defensive positions on the stairs. John shook his head and glanced toward Mila.

She was out. How could she tell him? She held the quiver upside down.

Jess let out a shriek as the flames licked up against her feet. She writhed against her bindings, trying desperately to pull her feet up the pole.

"Hang on!" John picked up a second sword from the nearest corpse and ran toward the stairs.

CHAPTER THIRTY-SEVEN

April 28, 1341

A Reginald wished he were a fighting man. Father would have spurred his horse and driven through the crowd toward the fight. All Reginald could do was watch helplessly as the heretic with the sword cut down his men. Wessex stared at him.

"Shall we ride to their aid?" Wessex drew his sword. He obviously assumed Reginald would rush into battle at his side.

Reginald glanced behind them. Evelyn sat there watching him. She had always believed him a coward.

The crossbowman's window was just across the square. That had to be where the rest of the heretics were hiding. Perhaps he could reverse this disaster.

"No, Wessex. I need this man captured. We cannot fight him directly without risk of killing him. But perhaps there is a way he would give up willingly." Reginald gestured to his guards. "Get inside that inn. Bring me whoever is shooting out of that window. Now go!" Reginald smiled as his guards pushed through the crowd.

"Put away your sword, Wessex. We will have him shortly."

————

Mila gaped helplessly as the flames licked at Jess's feet. She'd missed the bishop. The only shot she'd missed was the only one that mattered. Why was it taking John so long to get up the stairs?

The crowd parted below her as four guards made their way toward the inn. She tore herself away from the window.

"Mom, they're coming for us. We need to get out. Now." She ran toward the door. Margaret took Sandra by the hand and followed. Mila rushed down the inner stairs and almost collided with Sir Raymond.

"What are you doing in here? Why aren't you helping my father?"

"I am sorry, Lady Mila." Raymond spoke quietly. "That is not my fight."

"Bullshit." Mila glared at him. "You're a coward!"

The four guards rushed into the inn. Raymond came *en garde*. The men skidded to a stop. The nearest one was within reach and paid with his life. The other three fell over each other trying to stay out of his way. They seemed to have forgotten about the three women huddled at the foot of the stairs. They slowly circled Raymond until one of them had his back to Mila. Big mistake. Mila took Sandra's sword and drove it into his exposed neck. The guard gurgled and fell, clutching his throat. The other two men glanced at their dying comrade.

It was all Raymond needed. His sword came up, and

the nearest guard fell where he stood. He spun toward the last guard, his sword blurred, then stopped.

Mila stared as the dead man's skull pulled Raymond's sword to the ground. Fear was obviously something Raymond would never know. He was a master swordsman.

Raymond put his foot on the head and pulled his sword free of the eye socket in which it was lodged. "Are you harmed, Lady Mila?" He bowed his head slightly.

"No."

Raymond's eyes glanced at the floor as he slammed his sword back in its scabbard. It was clear he had more to say, but he kept it to himself.

"I'm sorry, Sir Raymond. You are not a coward." Three men lay dead or dying at his hand, and it had taken less than a minute. So why wasn't he helping her father? Shit, if he were out there, they'd have Jess rescued by now. Mila's eyes widened as she studied Raymond's face. He was taking Lady Evelyn's instructions verbatim. He was protecting... her.

"Margaret. Take Sandra back up to the room." Mila ran out of the inn, plunging through the crowd. She glanced behind her just once, to be sure.

Raymond rushed after her.

———

THE CLOSEST GUARD TOOK A STEP DOWN THE STAIRS and slashed at John. He deflected the blow and punched him in the groin. The man doubled over, and he stabbed him in the neck.

Flames caught a corner of Jess's bandage and quickly licked up toward her body. She screamed uncontrollably.

"No! Jess, I'm coming." The tears welled in his eyes. He forced himself to focus on the fight, one man at a time. He was nearly there.

The armored man at the top of the stairs ordered the last two guards toward him.

Jess screamed, the sound impossibly loud.

They came at him together. The one on his left slashed down at him. He blocked it. The one on his right thrust straight while John was engaged. His chain mail took the brunt of the blow, but he felt the tip of the sword penetrate his ribs. He dodged away and felt the warmth of his own blood under his tunic.

Jess's scream tore at his ears, swamping him with adrenaline.

The guards advanced again, driving him farther away. He stumbled over a body and landed hard on another corpse.

Jess writhed on the pole, straining against her bindings. Flames devoured her hair. Her face blistered and bubbled.

He shook his head to keep the thought out, but it grew and demanded more and more of his attention. He wasn't going to make it. He had to focus. But Jess was... dying.

John's hand found a dagger on the corpse as he pushed himself to his feet to fend off another attack. Jess's weakening screams owned his mind. He surprised the last two guards by charging them. The first man fell headless at his feet. The last guard choked, clutching the dagger in his throat as he sank to his knees.

But John was too late. Jess's screams had died away, replaced by a faint gurgle. She twitched in the flames, the fire roasting her like meat.

All he could do was end her pain. Through his tears,

he pulled the dagger free of the guard's neck, flipped the blade into his palm, and threw it. The dagger buried itself in her forehead. He had failed.

SANDRA WENT UP THE STAIRS WITH MARGARET. SHE stepped to the window, and her world ended.

Jess wasn't tied to the pole anymore. Her baby was gone and, in her place, hung a strange creature. Its blackened face lolled to one side with a dagger handle protruding from its brow. The thing on the pole steamed and sizzled as the sick bastard of a crowd just stood there watching. How could they? Every single last one of them deserved to die.

Sandra turned away from the window. The bed invited her to just lie down and shut out this horrible place. But she couldn't. She wandered back toward the door. Her whole body weighed her down, pulling her toward the floor with every step. Margaret tried to take her hand, but she brushed her aside and started down the stairs. John and Mila needed her.

JESS'S SHRIEKING HAD STOPPED. MILA TRIED NOT TO think of what that might mean. She raced to the front of the thinning crowd and pushed her way into the open where the ground was littered with dead and dying guards.

There was only one armored man between John and Jess. But Jess was completely engulfed in flames. She had stopped moving, stopped screaming. John backed away.

No. John. Mila dropped to her knees, staring up at Jess's charred body. Jess was dead.

And it was her fault. She'd left Jess alone in the forest. She'd wasted precious moments cowering in the castle. And now she'd taken far too long getting Raymond into the fight.

It was all her fault.

"Lady Mila?" Raymond glanced around the town square, then lifted her into his arms.

Mila hadn't the strength to resist. He carried her back to the inn.

"Mila?" Sandra stepped to Raymond's side when they were inside the inn.

"She is unharmed, Madame."

"What happened to her?" Sandra wiped Mila's hair out of her face.

Mila brushed the hands away. "Sandra." She climbed out of Raymond's arms and stood. Sandra tried to feel her forehead. "Mom!"

"What?" Sandra stopped scanning Mila's clothes.

"Jess is..." Mila stopped, refusing to say the word.

"Shh." Sandra pulled her close and hugged her. Mila lifted her arms to return the hug, but Sandra let go. "Where's your father?"

Sandra stood there looking very concerned, like she did when he was late for dinner. Why wasn't she crying? Her whole life, Mila had seen her cry easily and often. She was the most emotional person Mila knew. She was in shock. That had to be it. She reached out to her. "Jess is... dead."

Sandra took a step back. "Yes. I heard you." She spoke

quietly but firmly. To Raymond she said, "Do you know where my husband is?"

"Madame, he was walking away from the square when I returned with Lady Mila."

"We should go and find him. Will you please escort us to where you saw him last?"

"Yes, Madame, it would be an honor." Raymond bowed.

Mila stared at Sandra. She'd expected her to be a useless mass of blubbering, but here she was, composed and lucid. Somehow, she'd boxed up her grief and put it away. Mila couldn't believe it.

"Mila." Sandra stood waiting at the door with Raymond. "Stop staring. Let's go. We need to find your father and get him off the streets."

Mila's chest still ached from her tears. All she wanted to do was curl up in a ball and hide, but Sandra was right. They needed to find John. Mila swallowed hard and followed her out the back door.

CHAPTER THIRTY-EIGHT

April 28, 1341

Edward peeked out from behind the stake. The crossbow danger seemed to be over. The heretic swordsman limped away, and the crowd parted to let him pass. Henri just stood there at the top of the stairs.

"Will you not pursue him?"

Henri pointed to the ground in front of the platform. "Can you not see, Your Grace?"

The bodies of the dead and dying guards were everywhere. Henri walked down off the platform and knelt next to the nearest man, who yet breathed. The crowd closed behind the heretic and Edward lost sight of him.

"He is escaping!"

Henri acted as if he had not heard him. Edward hated being ignored more than anything.

Much of the crowd had run away when the fighting began, but those who remained now looked to him. Did they want him to say something? He had nothing else prepared. Who knew the heretic would jump out of the crowd and ruin the execution?

Edward walked down the stairs and knelt by the corpse of the torchbearer. He closed his eyes and crossed himself. He peeked out at the crowd while he prayed. They seemed satisfied with his actions and began to drift away. He finished praying and moved to the next corpse to repeat the performance.

Why was Henri so afraid to engage in the Lord's work? Did he not know that God would protect the righteous? Edward seemed to be the only one who understood the urgency of suppressing this evil. His entire existence depended on the unwavering belief of the villagers. Without them, he had nothing... *was nothing*. The heresy must be stamped out at all costs. The lives of a few guards seemed a small price to pay. If the baron and his captain had tired of the task, then Edward must find another way.

———

REGINALD CONTINUED TO WATCH THE HERETIC AS HE walked, unmolested, from the square. The man was tall and easily visible above the crowd. Reginald glanced at the door to the Hanging Cock. The crowd had cleared away, and he had an unobstructed view of the building. At any moment he expected to see his men come out, dragging the crossbow-wielding heretic behind them. Yet no one came. How could this be?

"The heretic has sought refuge in an alley," said Wessex. He stood in his stirrups, keeping an eye on the heretic. He lowered himself back into his saddle and lifted his reins. "Shall we take him?"

"Hold," said Reginald. The massacre that had been wrought by this one man lay before him, and he had never seen such carnage. Henri was kneeling next to the dead and dying men.

And why had his men yet to emerge from the inn? He glanced behind him, and there sat Evelyn, with what looked like a smile on her face.

Damn her. He hated to look the coward in front of her but, including those he had sent to the inn, fifteen men had died this night, attempting to subdue one man. With only Henri and Wessex, Reginald could not possibly risk another attempt at confronting so dangerous a foe. He would rather lose face in front of his sister than lose his life at the hands of this heretic. He would have to regroup at the castle and send out a stronger party.

———

EVELYN SAT QUIETLY BEHIND REGINALD AND Wessex. She was sad to see the girl die, but the failure of the bishop's display was quite pleasing. Reginald kept glancing over at the inn. Perhaps he still hoped to see his men emerge with another hostage. Evelyn had no such illusions. She had seen Raymond charging out after Mila. He had carried her back into the inn as the crowd dispersed. She knew there were no living guards inside.

"Captain!" said Reginald. Henri knelt next to one of his men and did not respond. "Captain!"

Henri released the hand of the dying man and crossed the square toward them.

Reginald did not wait. "Report to me immediately upon your return to the castle." He wheeled his horse. "We have much to discuss."

"My lord." Henri said it without bowing or even lowering his eyes. He glared at Reginald galloping back toward the castle with Wessex close behind. Henri was the most loyal knight Evelyn had ever met. She had never seen him show Reginald such bold disrespect. The loss of so many of his men had taken a toll, indeed.

"My lady." Henri nodded to her then turned to follow the horses.

"Captain, wait." She dismounted and approached him. "I am sorry about your men."

"Thank you, my lady."

She placed her hand on his arm. "The entire spectacle was a foolish waste of life."

"So it was." Henri bowed and walked away.

Evelyn led her horse toward the inn. Up ahead, she saw Raymond lead Lady Mila and two other women from behind the inn. When they had left the square and disappeared into one of the darkened streets, she mounted her horse and rode back to the castle.

CHAPTER THIRTY-NINE

April 28, 1341

A John stumbled into the dark alley. His balance abandoned him, and he fell against the wall and slid down to the dirt. His tears came again, though he squeezed his eyes shut. Jess, charred and screaming, came at him from the dark. He whipped his eyes open and yelled. As long as he yelled, he couldn't hear her screams.

When Jess said *Dad,* it had always embodied hope and respect. She had used it with pride, and as a rebuke, but never harshly and always with love. Her last word to him had been *Dad.* With that one word she had pleaded for him to save her. Now that word could only ever mean one thing. Failure.

"Dad?"

"Jess?" He spun desperately toward the voice, but it was Mila who ran into the alley. He'd forgotten how similar they sounded. He must have sagged visibly when he recognized her, because Mila froze where she stood. Some part of him knew he should reach out and comfort her, but he could not. He leaned his head back against the wall.

Mila put a hand on his shoulder. John studied it. He wished Mila's shot at the bishop had been as accurate as the rest of her shots. If she hadn't divided her focus and shot the men attacking *him*, she might have made a better shot at the bishop. This was why the military model broke down when you thrust it on a family. The mission was to save Jess. They each had a role to play. Hers was to keep the torch away from Jess. His was to fight his way to her side. They had both failed. But it was a conversation he could never have with her. Mila was not one of his men, she was his daughter. He should never have expected her to blindly follow his orders. She never had back home— why had he thought this would be any different?

He reached up and put his hand on hers. "Are you okay?"

Mila shook her head. She squeezed her eyes shut and turned her head to the side. She swallowed. "I'm sorry."

"Mila, don't." He squeezed her hand.

"It's all my fault." The tears ran freely down her cheeks.

John shook his head. "How can that possibly be true?"

"I dragged the whole family on this stupid vacation." She sniffed hard. "I left Jess in the forest. I took too long in the castle." Her voice dropped to a whisper. "I missed the fucking bishop."

"There you are." Sandra walked into the alley, followed by Margaret and Raymond. "What's going on?"

"Mila, you did your best," said John, ignoring Sandra.

"No, I didn't." Mila choked back her tears. She stood there shaking.

John tried to get to his feet, but his limbs were leaden.

He had to use his sword like a cane to pull himself up. When he was standing, he reached out to her.

———

"No." MILA PULLED BACK. SHE SPUN AWAY AND raced into the road. She didn't want a hug, and she didn't want to be consoled. She needed to be alone.

Raymond came to the mouth of the alley and watched her. Mila rolled her eyes. She didn't need Lady Evelyn's watchdog, either. Couldn't he figure out that the mission was over? A failure? Mila sprinted into the shadows.

"Wait, Mila!" Sandra yelled as she emerged from the alley.

But Mila kept running. She had to get away: from Sandra's needy pleas, from John's forgiveness, even from Raymond the watchdog. But mostly she had to get away from the square where Jess had been murdered.

CHAPTER FORTY

A*pril 28, 1341*
As Evelyn entered the keep, Reginald's voice echoed from the great hall. "Seventeen men dead?"

"Yes, my lord," said Henri.

Evelyn stopped in the entry passage and stood in the shadows.

"That's almost half the watch." Reginald paused. "Can we still hold the castle?"

"I believe so, but we will be stretched to the limit."

"Well, there it is, then. We will have to use Wessex's plan."

"My lord?"

"Wessex is in the outer bailey gathering the tournament knights, even now. They are the best in the land. He has promised to have the heretic captured by daybreak."

"Captured?" said Henri.

"Of course. I cannot speak with him if he is dead."

Evelyn had heard enough. She walked toward the great hall. If Wessex was gathering knights inside the castle walls, he had just sealed his fate. He would not have this castle, or Mary.

"My lord, do you think it wise to give these foreigners that kind of power?" said Henri.

"What do you mean?"

"He means," said Evelyn as she stepped into the great hall, "if you hand over control of the barony to Wessex and his knights, you may not get it back."

"Evelyn! How long have you been listening?"

"Long enough to know you are behaving like an ass." Evelyn crossed the great hall to the hearth, where Reginald stood with Henri.

"Captain, escort Lady Evelyn to her chamber. Then see if Wessex needs any assistance."

Henri did not move.

"Henri also thinks you are being foolish, but he is too loyal to say so." Evelyn stopped next to Henri and faced Reginald.

"Henri! Did you not hear me?" Reginald's face reddened as he stood with his hands on his hips.

"Reginald." Evelyn kept her voice light. "I have a plan that will let you keep your barony and your pride. Would you like to hear it?"

"No!" Reginald turned his back and sat by the fire.

"Please, my lord, do listen to Lady Evelyn."

"Evelyn's plan, whatever it may be, will come with a price." Reginald sniffed. "It always does."

"Reginald, you wound me. I simply want to ensure Father's lands remain in the family." She watched the back of his head for any reaction.

Reginald sneered at her. "And you want *nothing* in return?"

"Why do you not hear my plan?" She sat down next

to him and began to peel off her gloves. Reginald glared at her.

"Please, my lord, for the good of the barony," offered Henri.

She was thankful for Henri's support. His loyalty, after all these years, had not diminished.

"Fine," said Reginald. "I will hear it, but I make no promises."

Evelyn smiled inwardly. "Would it surprise you to learn that Raymond is already in the company of the heretics?" Evelyn waited for that to sink in before continuing. "Henri and I can seek out Raymond and return with the heretics before daybreak. You need not spill another drop of blood, nor pay a single penny to foreign knights."

"And exactly how do you propose to accomplish this miracle?" Reginald crossed his arms over his chest, but he was listening.

"I will simply invite them here to talk with you as your guests." She folded her gloves and placed them in her lap.

"And they will come?"

"They believe I am their friend and confidante." She held her tongue as Reginald studied her. He was teetering. She almost had him.

Reginald raised an eyebrow. "Am I to believe you are now *my* friend and confidante?"

"Of course not. But these people pose a real threat to peace in the barony. That I cannot abide." Her devotion to the barony was unquestionable. Even Reginald knew that in his heart.

"Indeed." Reginald nodded.

She had him.

"Henri." Reginald sprang to his feet as though he had just had an original idea. "Accompany the Lady Evelyn and help her enact this plan. I will tell Wessex his assistance is no longer required." He tugged at his tunic.

"Yes, my lord." Henri bowed his head and left the hall.

Evelyn lingered. "Reginald, there is one more thing."

"Of course there is, Evelyn." Reginald sighed. "There always is."

"I ask for nothing tangible. I simply wish to ask a question." He did not interrupt, so she stood and stepped toward him. When he answered, she had to be able to hear the truth in his breath and see it in his eyes. "It is the same thing I asked you on the road. I know you do not believe in this rubbish about witches, so why are you continuing the charade?"

Reginald looked away. "I cannot say."

"Is it Edward? Does he have some leverage over you that I am unaware of?"

"Hardly." Reginald snickered. "It is nothing like that."

"Then why?"

"Enough." Reginald strode to the door.

Evelyn watched him go. Had Reginald learned of the magical orb while he'd held Chad prisoner? She could not think of any other reason worth changing one's beliefs.

———

Edward left the cathedral door open as he entered the alley. He carried a candle, and its light revealed his eight well-armed guests. He walked from one killer to the next, blessing them and handing each a small pouch of silver. He stepped back to address the group.

"Thank you for answering my call. If any of you were at the execution, you have already seen the heretic, and you know what he is capable of. The man who brings me his head will receive a second pouch."

Several of them snickered. Peter, the largest of them, spat on the ground. "I will be back for it on the morrow."

"Hold on." Geoffrey, the weasel, pouted up at Peter.

"Shut it!" said Peter. To Edward, he said, "Keep it handy."

Edward nodded. Confidence was very refreshing. "There are also two women much like the one who burned this night. I do not care what you do with them. Just make sure they never enter my bishopric again. Do we have an understanding?"

The killers grunted and nodded. There was a chorus of, "Yes, Your Grace," as they bowed and slipped away into the night.

Edward returned to the cathedral and closed the door. He would soon be rid of these witches, and his village could return to its God-fearing ways.

CHAPTER FORTY-ONE

April 29, 1341

At dawn, a lone villager untied Jess's burnt corpse and lowered it from the platform into a wheelbarrow. He started to push it down the road when John stepped from the shadows, blocking his way.

"Oy, move it," the man said. He lifted his eyes up to John's bloody face and dropped the wheelbarrow handles. The man scurried away, and John gently picked up the handles of the wheelbarrow and rolled it into the shadows of the alley, where Margaret waited.

He knelt and touched the blackened remains of Jess's cheek. From the moment she was born, she had shone with optimism and beauty, forever smiling at what life had to show her. He searched her charred face for some hint of that little girl, but there was only death. Burnt hair and smoke stung his nose. His throat constricted, and he squeezed out a growl through gritted teeth. He closed his eyes and tried to find the words to say goodbye. The only thing that came to him was *I'm sorry*.

He stood and drew a long breath. He opened his

mouth to speak and closed it again. Any sound he might make would be unintelligible: too high, too strained, too quiet, too violent.

"Go, John. Your family needs you," Margaret said as she picked up the handles of the wheelbarrow.

John nodded but stood rooted to the ground. He'd always told himself he would never let anything happen to his family. Everyone in his unit quietly prided themselves on the unholy wrath that would befall anybody foolish enough to mess with their families. Last night he'd brought it. His full rage had fallen on this tiny village, but Jess had still died. He'd failed at the only thing that really mattered. He played it back in his head over and over, but each time he couldn't see a choice, couldn't see the error, couldn't find a faster way up the stairs.

"I will keep her safe," said Margaret. She nodded toward the end of the alley.

He forced himself to put one foot in front of the other. Margaret was right. For a young peasant woman, she had an unshakable grasp on priorities. He'd failed to keep Jess alive and now Mila and Sandra were in danger. He lifted his head. There was work to do. When his family was safe, they would have a funeral for Jess, and then... there would be payback.

WHEN THE SUN CAME UP, THE TOWN CAME BACK TO life. Sandra walked among the villagers, searching every face. They filled the roads. Their pathetic lives continued in spite of what they had witnessed the previous evening. And while she still thought they all deserved to die for watching Jess's execution, her focus was on finding Mila.

It had been hours since she'd last glimpsed her only living daughter. She could only hope Raymond was still following her and keeping her safe. Sandra had spent the night wandering the streets and hiding. She wanted to stand in the road and shout Mila's name, but that would bring unwanted attention. Instead, she kept moving and tried not to think of Jess.

Sandra returned to the village square, where the market had opened. She hoped Mila might get hungry and try to find some food. The central platform loomed in her peripheral vision, and she turned to keep it behind her. She stood there, shaking, not daring to look at the stake. Whatever might hang there could quite possibly undo her resolve.

If she circled the platform, being careful to keep her head aimed away, she would be able to see all of the shops that faced into the square. But she would miss the stalls set up with their backs to the platform. *This is stupid.* Her irrational fear of what she might see hanging there impeded her search for her living daughter. She took a breath and turned around to face whatever might be waiting.

The stake was empty. She let out a sigh and refused to think about what might have happened to Jess's body. *Find Mila.*

She walked from stall to stall, checking every face. She turned around frequently and searched in all directions. People probably thought she was crazy, but she didn't care.

A well-armed man grinned at her with no teeth. She moved around to the front of the nearest vendor and glanced back to see if he followed. The man strolled past and kept going. He looked familiar, but she had seen so many faces that morning, it wasn't surprising. She walked around the next stall and came to a cart selling shoes. The grinning man slouched nearby, looking back at her. *Shit.* She spun around and bumped into the chest of another well-armed man.

"Sorry." She backed up.

She tried to walk around him, but he grabbed her in a bear hug, pinning her arms and hoisting her off the ground. His garbage breath stung her nose as he laughed in her face. She stifled her gag reflex and kneed him in the groin. His eyes widened and he stopped laughing but he did not let go.

Plan B. She raised her head and bit his chin. He tried to pull his face back, but she held on. She tasted blood and continued to bite down. Finally, his arms released her.

As soon as her feet hit the ground, she bolted. She didn't glance behind her until she was past the vegetable cart. The bear-hugging man was lying on the ground, staring at the sky. She hadn't bitten him that hard.

She swerved to avoid the grasp of yet another ugly man. She ran as fast as she could. The ugly grasper ran after her, and the toothless grinner was with him.

She dodged villagers, children, and small dogs in the thick market crowd as she ran. But the shouts, curses, and smashing pottery behind her indicated that her pursuers weren't as polite. When she heard shocked gasps and screaming, she stole another glance. The ugly grasper was on his knees, holding his intestines in his hands. The toothless grinner lay beside his own head. *They must have bumped into the wrong villager.* She left the square and plunged down a side road.

"Sandra." It was all she heard: just one word, spoken

softly. She forgot everything but that familiar voice, face, and the arms she knew would be there. They always were.

John took her hand and guided her to safety in the alley behind him.

"Was that you?" She nodded back toward the square.

The muscles around his jaw tightened, and his voice came out raspy. "I'm just getting started."

"Well, it's about time." She pulled him into a hug.

"I'm sorry." He gently pulled away and led her out of the alley.

"Are you okay?"

He exhaled heavily. "Barely keeping it together."

The knot in her throat poked her, but she swallowed it down. "I know."

He glanced behind them. "Have you seen Mila?"

"Not for a while."

———

EVELYN STOOD FUMING OUTSIDE THE DOVER DOVE. Raymond had arrived alone. He had been forced to leave the parents behind when the daughter went off on her own. At least he had followed her orders and stayed with Mila. But now her plan was in ruins.

Henri and his two knights pushed themselves off a nearby wall and wandered toward her. She raised a palm, gesturing for them to stay back.

"I cannot believe you have let me down." She glared at Raymond.

"I am sorry, my love." He reached for her, and she took his hand in hers.

She had to salvage her plan. "Where is she now?"

"She rests in the next street." Raymond pointed into the nearby alley.

"Why did she leave them?"

"I know not." Raymond shook his head. "She was crying, and then she rushed away."

Evelyn took a long breath and reminded herself that nothing was ever easy. Now she would have to reconcile the estranged family before she could convince them to come to the castle. But she was running out of time. She had promised Reginald she would return with them by daybreak, but it had already come and gone.

Henri again walked toward her. "Lady Evelyn, is there a problem?"

"No, Henri, just a slight change in plans. Raymond, you will go and bring the parents back to the Dover Dove. Once you have done that, come and find me. I will be with the Lady Mila. Henri, you and your men will stay out of sight until you see me go up to the room. Any questions?"

The men shook their heads. Evelyn disappeared into the alley.

———

JOHN LED SANDRA DOWN THE ROAD. HE HELD HER hand so he could keep his eyes up and moving, or so he told himself. In truth, he needed to feel her hand. Her touch kept him grounded. "Okay, let's work a grid pattern. We'll go to one end of town and work our way up and down the roads. We don't really have the manpower to do it properly, but at least it's organized."

"You're the boss." She squeezed his hand. But John

pulled her to the side of the road and into the mouth of an alley. "What is it?"

He pointed across the road and down two houses. A man stood watching the traffic. He had a sword on his hip, a dagger in his belt, and a longbow on his back. He was waiting for somebody—and odds were, it was them.

"Let's try the other side." They walked to the other end of the alley and checked the next road. There, three houses away, stood a big son of a bitch with a pair of broadswords crossed on his back. "It looks like somebody else has already started a search. When he looks away, we'll turn right and walk casually away. Ready?"

"Ready."

John stepped from the alley and led her up the road. At the intersection, he led them left and scanned ahead. A hundred meters up, a heavily armed, barrel-chested man stood on the side of the road. His head swiveled, searching the crowd, then stopped.

John gently guided Sandra in a slow arc that took them to the right, across the road and back toward the intersection. "I think we've just been made." He felt her start to look over her shoulder and squeezed her hand. "Don't look."

She stopped herself in time, and they continued to the corner.

"We're turning left. As we do, look at me. You'll get a clear view over my shoulder. See if he's coming. Big guy, ugly, brown tunic, too many weapons."

As they turned the corner, Sandra said, "Got him, and he's coming fast."

"Let me know when he can't see us anymore."

Sandra kept an eye over his shoulder. "Now."

"Let's go." John moved as fast as his leg would allow

and hung a left at the next intersection. They crossed the road and took a right at the first alley. As they entered, he checked their six. The man ran into the road behind them. "This guy's not giving up."

They exited the alley and made another left. They crossed the road and continued until they reached the intersection. He checked their six as they made a right. The man appeared in the mouth of the alley, but this time he was walking.

"He's tiring," John said. "If we can keep up the pace to the next corner, we'll lose him."

Sandra put on a burst of speed. They rounded the bend and slowed to a walk.

"Nice going." He gave her a squeeze as they caught their breath.

"Our search pattern is blown," Sandra said. "That's for sure."

"We're going to need to keep our eyes peeled for these thugs. Who knows how many there are? Why don't you focus your attention behind us? I'll watch the front."

"If you say so." Sandra glanced behind them then tapped John on the shoulder. A familiar face walked up behind them.

"The Lady Mila sent me to find you," said Raymond.

CHAPTER FORTY-TWO

April 29, 1341

As the sun came up, Mila sat at the side of a road, oblivious to the villagers moving past her and starting their day. A wall rose up at the end of the street, but it was the village wall, not the castle wall.

The castle. Jess. Burning.

Dammit. She forced herself to take a long breath and worked at replacing the thought with a memory of her sister alive and vibrant. Jess had an easy smile for everyone she met, and when she laughed, it was infectious. The lump in Mila's throat started to swell and squeeze out tears from her puffy eyes. Even thinking of happy times couldn't keep Mila from crying. Each memory came laced with the thought, *But that will never happen again.*

Mila tried to recall Jess's face in a desperate attempt to suppress the emptiness. Jess in the cage... *too beat up*, Mila thought. Jess leading the fight at the guide's cottage... *too bossy*. Jess arguing with her at Annie's inn... *too bitchy*. Jess having her back as always, on the hilltop... *a bit nicer*.

Jess had looked amazing in the warm glow of the holographic numbers right before their time jump. But the more she tried to picture Jess's face, the more her mind drifted to the numbers floating above it.

Was it really that simple? She told herself to get serious. It was her grief-stricken psyche grasping at anything. Jess was gone, and nothing would bring her back. But still... wasn't it worth exploring? She couldn't just give up on it. If she could hold out hope for Jess, she could pretend last night was just a bad dream. It wasn't healthy, but it was one way to cope. Her mother had found a way. This could be hers.

First, she needed to recover the MCV. Then she had to figure out how to use it. Even then it was a long shot. She had no idea how time travel worked. Was it like a train, and you just hopped on and off? Or was it more like parallel universes? She'd seen the advertisements on TV and thought, *Hey, wouldn't that be cool?* She never figured she'd need to understand how it worked. If only she'd paid more attention to the parade of geeks that had tried to date her in high school. They would have known all about this shit. Suddenly, she had a new respect for the pocket protector brigade. *Stop it. Work the problem.*

How would she find the MCV? The last time she'd seen it, it was in the chest in the carriage. That meant it was at the castle. But how would she get back into the castle? She glanced behind her to check if Raymond was still shadowing her. He was not. Maybe he'd gotten bored and gone home. *Home.* Her own bed, with its sun-warmed micro-fleece throw, beckoned her. She would sleep for a week if she survived long enough to see home again.

The villagers making their way to the fields and

market were beginning to glance in her direction and whisper as they passed. Mila stood and started walking back toward the square. Lady Evelyn had told her it was a crime to dress as a man, so she'd tried to keep her coif covering her hair and a swagger in her walk. But as she tired, the swagger diminished to the point where she was pretty sure she wasn't even doing it. The weight of the crossbow on her shoulder cramped her back. Every few minutes, she shifted the weapon from one shoulder to the other, but it didn't help. The chain mail probably weighed about ten kilos, but right now it felt like a hundred.

A shopkeeper across the road propped open his wooden shutter, revealing a long table about chest height. He put a tray of horn cups next to a wooden jug and began pouring an amber liquid into them.

Mila stopped walking and watched a line of people form next to the shop. The shopkeeper declared he was open, accepting coins with one hand while he passed out his cups with the other. Mila's mouth watered even though she knew it was that stinky ale.

Lady Evelyn's voice came from the shadows. "I would not recommend patronizing that particular establishment."

"Why not?"

Lady Evelyn lowered her hood. She was maybe the one person who could help her get back into the castle, and suddenly here she was.

"Have you been following me?"

"You have managed to find the worst tavern in the town." Lady Evelyn continued to search the traffic. "We should keep moving. The roads are unusually dangerous this morning."

Mila noted that Lady Evelyn had ignored her

question but let it slide and tried to follow her glances and see the danger for herself.

"Surely, you should not be wasting your time on food and drink?" Lady Evelyn raised an eyebrow.

"But I'm starving."

"Nonsense. Look at you. You are nowhere near starving."

Mila sneered. "I didn't mean it literally."

Lady Evelyn touched the back of her elbow and slid her hand down into Mila's. She started walking. "Whatever are you doing wandering the streets by yourself?"

"Why do you care?"

"Why have you abandoned your family?" asked Lady Evelyn.

Mila thought of her father standing in the alley, bleeding, and of her mother rushing blindly into the night, trying to find her. But how could she face them? She knew her parents would say they loved her, but deep inside she knew they blamed her for Jess's death. If she could save Jess, she would never have to deal with their lying. "I haven't abandoned anybody. I just needed time to think."

"You cannot walk the streets alone. Everyone in the village knows you are a stranger, and most will have figured out by now that you are not a man." Lady Evelyn reached up and tucked a strand of Mila's hair back into her coif. "It is not safe."

Mila batted her hand away. She didn't need another mother. Something was off. Lady Evelyn ignored Mila's questions and peppered her with her own. "Why are you helping me?"

"Because of what happened to your sister. It does not sit well with me."

That smelled like bullshit. Mila said, "In the dungeon, you told me to tell the truth. Why don't you take your own advice?"

"I do not know what to say." Shock registered on Lady Evelyn's face, but only for a fraction of a second. The silence stretched into the uncomfortable zone, but Mila refused to let her off the hook.

"You are a wise woman," Lady Evelyn said finally. "But we really should get off the street."

"Nice try," Mila said as she folded her arms.

Lady Evelyn smoothed the cloth on her sleeve and stared at the ground. When she raised her head she said, "Because you have been accused of being a witch. I know how that feels... I have also been accused of this, from time to time."

Mila smiled. "And are you?" She echoed Lady Evelyn's words from the dungeon.

"I have certain skills." Lady Evelyn glanced up and down the street.

"What?" Mila laughed. But Lady Evelyn did not. She showed no false modesty, as though she was simply stating a fact. And it sounded like an honest answer, not that Mila believed in magic or anything. Lady Evelyn was intelligent, and her natural beauty would be intimidating to anyone, especially the men in power. It made a kind of sense that they would brand her a witch out of fear.

"So you're helping me out of empathy and you want nothing in return?" Mila so wanted to believe her—she really needed Lady Evelyn's help right now—but her inner alarm bells were deafening.

"Perhaps a small compensation." Lady Evelyn

resumed walking.

Mila walked beside her. This felt like progress. If Lady Evelyn needed something from Mila, they could start to build a relationship based on trust and mutual benefit. She hoped Lady Evelyn would ask for something she could actually provide. Mila stepped in front of Lady Evelyn and faced her. "Now we're getting somewhere. I hope I can provide whatever it is that you need of me, but right now I need you to get me back into the castle."

Lady Evelyn just nodded with a hint of a smile.

That was way too easy. Mila said, "Don't you want to know why?"

Lady Evelyn cupped Mila's hands in her own. "I'm sure you will tell me when the time is right."

Mila thought the time was right now, but she saw movement from the shadows of a nearby alley. An ugly little man walked toward them. He carried more weapons than he could possibly wield: a sword at his side, a dagger in his belt, and a crossbow slung across his back. "There is a well-armed man approaching behind you. Is he the danger?"

"Perhaps. I was wondering when the weasel might show himself." Lady Evelyn raised her voice. "Good morning, Geoffrey."

"Good morning, Mother Abbess." Geoffrey bowed his head. "I did not recognize you. Have you abandoned the—?"

"Do not trouble yourself about my appearance, Geoffrey." Lady Evelyn held out a hand, and Geoffrey reached out to take it.

Mila assumed Lady Evelyn expected him to kiss the hand, but the man held it briefly, then released it and opened his own. She'd given him something.

"Who has hired you to stalk my friend?" Lady Evelyn nodded toward Mila.

"The bishop," said Geoffrey. "Why are you with her?"

Lady Evelyn cocked her head as she studied him. "Is that a question, Geoffrey? I am afraid you do not quite understand how this arrangement works. If you want information, you will have to return that coin."

Geoffrey leered at Mila. Lady Evelyn held out her hand. He tore his eyes off Mila and took it. When he released the hand, he again studied the contents of his own.

"How many men did the bishop hire?" Lady Evelyn asked.

Geoffrey started counting on his fingers then gave up. "I would say six."

"I see. He is a wealthy man." She repeated the payment ritual. "What were the terms?"

"Kill the man." Geoffrey let his eyes stray to Mila. "Make the women... disappear."

"Excuse us, won't you?" said Mila, motioning Lady Evelyn to follow her into the alley Geoffrey had emerged from. Mila nodded at Geoffrey, who stood watching them from the road. "Can I pay him to give up his contract on my family and hunt the other assassins?"

Lady Evelyn smiled. "I like the way you think, but you could not afford it. The bishop's wealth is infinite. He would simply outbid you."

"So, what do I do?"

"Trust me." Lady Evelyn's beautiful eyes crinkled at the corners. "Have I not made good on my promises?"

Trusting her was the last thing Mila could do. Lady Evelyn had proven, in the short time since they'd met, that she never said what she meant. Although she had helped Mila out of the castle and sent Raymond to keep her safe, the reason for this woman's generosity remained a mystery. But Mila could only nod. "You have."

"Well then, let me take care of Geoffrey. And then we should rejoin your parents."

"What?" Mila stopped whispering. "You know where they are?"

"Of course."

Mila stared at the Lady Evelyn. She didn't look smug. She simply returned her gaze, as though she did this kind of thing every day. Damn, she was good. This woman thought nine moves ahead, like a chess master. "How do we ditch Geoffrey?"

"Ditch?"

"Lose, get rid of—we don't want Geoffrey knowing where we are, right?"

"Ah yes, do not worry about Geoffrey." The Lady Evelyn beckoned the assassin to join them in the alley. Geoffrey wandered into the shadows and stood facing them, silhouetted against the light of the road.

Lady Evelyn reached out her hand as if to repeat the payment ritual, but she only fluttered her fingers and said, "Goodbye, Geoffrey."

His silhouette grew as a larger man loomed behind him. A hand snaked around his mouth and his eyes bulged wide as he was thrust deeper into the alley. Mila recognized Sir Raymond as the man pushing Geoffrey. Geoffrey seemed to collapse at Raymond's feet for no apparent reason, but Raymond wiped blood off his dagger with a white lace hanky. *That could be the reason.*

Mila's mouth fell open. Raymond and Lady Evelyn seemed unconcerned as Geoffrey died at their feet.

"He was scum." Lady Evelyn touched her arm. "Do not trouble yourself. It was a fate he earned a long time ago. With his current assignment, I am sure you will agree his death is of benefit to you and your family."

Mila stared. She was only now beginning to realize what this woman was capable of. Perhaps she wasn't quite the ally Mila had been hoping for, but she had no choice.

Mila shrugged and stepped toward Geoffrey's corpse. She bent and took Geoffrey's supply of crossbow bolts. She stood and placed them in her quiver. Raymond took a step toward her, reaching for his sword, but Lady Evelyn put her hand on his arm and led him away.

"Do come along," she said over her shoulder. "We should not keep your parents waiting."

What was that about? It was okay for Raymond to kill the assassin, but she had somehow crossed a line by stealing from his corpse? Men were so weird.

CHAPTER FORTY-THREE

April 29, 1341

John sat with his back against the inside of the door, studying the beams and rafters that supported the thatching. The second-floor room at the Dover Dove inn was larger than the one they'd had at the Hanging Cock. Unfortunately, that gave Sandra more room to pace. She stopped at the window and searched the road for the twentieth time. Raymond had left them there and gone to get Mila and Lady Evelyn, saying he would return shortly. As soon as he got back with Mila, John planned to take his family and get them out of town. Margaret had said she would meet them at the Hanging Cock and take them to the next village, where her father lived. Anywhere would be better than here.

Sandra spun from the window. "What if something happened to her?"

"Don't go there."

"I can't help it." She blew a hair off her face.

"She'll be fine," he said, but he didn't really believe it. He was as worried as Sandra, but sitting around waiting was something he had a lot of experience with. He knew how to stay in a constant state of readiness and stand down at a moment's notice. *Hurry up and wait* was his normal.

"You don't know that," she said bitterly. "Why aren't you out looking for her?"

"You heard what Raymond said." He watched Sandra walk back toward him from the window.

"That's true. I did hear that." Sandra put her fists on her hips and stopped in front of him. "What I didn't hear was what you said to Mila in that alley."

What was she talking about? He replayed the alley conversation in his head. He'd had some pretty dark thoughts, but he hadn't shared any of them with Mila. Sandra was probably digging for a fight. The stress of waiting was eating away at her, pushing her to lash out. "Babe, take a breath—"

"Don't manage me! God damn you, you arrogant fuck."

"I'm sorry." He stood up and stepped toward her to pull her into a hug.

She spun away and lifted one hand to ward him off.

———

MILA FOLLOWED RAYMOND AND LADY EVELYN UP the stairs at the Dover Dove. Raymond stopped at a door and stood to the side, while Lady Evelyn knocked.

Sandra pulled the door open.

"Mila!" She pushed past Lady Evelyn and wrapped Mila in a hug. "Are you all right?"

"I'm fine." Mila tried to extricate herself from the hug. "Can you let us in?"

By the time she got Sandra turned around, Lady Evelyn had already gone inside.

"You must be Raymond's wife," said John.

"I am Lady Evelyn." She touched his arm. "I am so sorry about Lady Jess."

John watched her without saying anything.

Raymond was the last one in and he shut the door behind them.

"Sandra, this is—"

"Lady Evelyn." She held a hand out to Sandra. "I have been trying to help your daughters."

"That's kind of you. Why?" John asked.

"John, leave her alone," Mila snapped, but then she regretted it. Maybe John could get answers from Lady Evelyn.

"You hardly know her," John continued. "I just want to know why she's helping us."

Lady Evelyn seemed undisturbed by his concern. She just stood there smiling pleasantly. Mila didn't say anything, letting John have the floor. How far would he get?

"John, stop it! I apologize for my husband."

"No apology is necessary. You have all been through a tragic ordeal." Lady Evelyn lowered her eyes, bowing slightly.

Since Sandra had put an end to John's questions, Mila said, "I have asked Lady Evelyn to help me get back into the castle—"

A knock at the door.

"That will be Captain Henri," said Lady Evelyn, "here to escort us to the castle."

John pulled Sandra behind him and went for his

sword, but Raymond's blade was at John's throat before he found the hilt.

"Sir Raymond!" Mila glared at him.

Lady Evelyn put her hand on Raymond's sword arm and pulled him away from John. "There is no need for violence."

"But you asked me to trust you," Mila said.

"And so you should." Lady Evelyn smiled. "You said you wanted to return to the castle, and this I have arranged."

Mila hadn't seen Lady Evelyn speak to anybody but Raymond since they had left Geoffrey in the alley. And Raymond had not left her side. So this meeting with Henri had to have been arranged before Mila had told Lady Evelyn what she wanted. Trust was dead. At least until she could figure out what Lady Evelyn was up to.

"Why do you want to go to the castle?" John asked Mila, keeping his eyes glued on Raymond.

"This is not the time." There was no way she was discussing her plans in front of Lady Evelyn.

"Fair enough," said John. "You can tell me later." He focused on Lady Evelyn. "Why do *you* want us to come to the castle?"

Lady Evelyn opened her mouth to speak, but there was another knock at the door. She touched Raymond's hand. "Would you ask the captain to wait at the bottom of the stairs?"

Raymond bowed, sheathed his weapon, and left the room.

Lady Evelyn returned her attention to John. "My brother, Baron Reginald, wishes to speak with you. I know not why. He had been raising an even larger company of armed men to seek you out. I suggested to him that there would be far less bloodshed if I simply asked you to meet with him, as his guests."

It all sounded logical to Mila, but this was Lady Evelyn. There had to be more to it.

"That sounds a bit too simple," said John. "What else?"

"You would like to go to the castle, yes?" Lady Evelyn ignored his question.

"Yes," John said. "You said guests, right?"

"I did."

"So we can keep our weapons?"

"Of course."

"Can you give us a minute?" John said. Lady Evelyn looked confused.

Mila pointed to the door. "Can you leave us alone so we can discuss it?"

"Certainly." Lady Evelyn stepped from the room.

It was clear that she had wanted them in the castle long before Mila had asked for her help. But why did she want them armed in the presence of the baron when she could have easily forced them to give up their weapons?

John stood staring at the back of the closed door.

"John." Sandra poked his arm. "Are we going to discuss it, or are you back to your one-man show?"

"Sorry. There's something off about this little visit to the castle."

"Ya think?" Mila rolled her eyes. John smelled it too, and she was glad he was on her side.

"But still, the best way to get information about the guide might be to talk directly to the man in charge."

"I can't believe you're even considering this." Sandra said. "He's the man who executed Jess."

"I know, but the only other option is to fight our way

out of this room. That means getting past Lady Evelyn and her swordsman, and then the captain and his posse. If we can manage to do all that—and I'm not saying we can—we're back at square one: on the run, and no closer to going home."

"So we don't have a choice?"

"Not really," said John. "What do you think?"

"I had a different idea." Mila glared at him. "I wanted to go to the castle, but not as a prisoner. I thought Lady Evelyn would sneak me in."

"Well, we can't expect to get an audience with the baron if we sneak in first."

"I never wanted an audience with the baron." Mila stopped talking. Lady Evelyn had said she might ask for a 'small compensation' in return for her help. Did she want John armed in front of the baron? So he could—what? Assassinate him? It felt more and more like she'd been played. This was just Lady Evelyn capturing all three of them without spilling a drop of blood. Mila's deal was probably off the table, long since forgotten.

The door opened, and there she was, Lady Evelyn, flanked by Captain Henri and Sir Raymond. "Shall we?"

———

MILA FOLLOWED HER PARENTS DOWN THE STAIRS AND out to the road. Lady Evelyn introduced them to Captain Henri. Sandra glared at him, and John refused to offer his hand. That was understandable. Henri had stood on the platform barring John's advance toward Jess, sending wave after wave of guards to stop him.

Henri and his two knights led the way up the hill toward the castle, Henri occasionally glancing over his shoulder to check on his charges. John and Sandra stayed a couple of meters behind him, and he seemed satisfied with that.

Mila walked behind her parents, and Evelyn stayed close to Raymond, whispering as the two of them walked hand in hand behind Mila. Mila shook her head. If she wanted to get back to the twenty-first century, she needed to stay focused. She stepped up close to her parents and nudged her way between them.

"How are you?" Sandra put her arm around Mila's shoulders.

"Not now." Mila dropped her voice as low as she could. "Nod if you can still hear me."

They both nodded.

"I think I know how to save Jess."

"Jess's dead," said John. Sandra reached out and touched her forehead.

"I'm not sick." Mila swatted the hand away. "Hear me out."

Her parents exchanged concerned looks, and Sandra said, "Okay. Let's hear it."

"Don't treat me like I'm seven. Are you going to be open-minded or what?"

"Your sister is dead," John said. He sounded pissed. "We're all trying to come to grips with that. You're talking about saving her. Do you know how crazy that sounds?"

"I'm not talking about resurrection or magic. I'm talking about time travel. Remember? The reason we're in this shit?" Mila let that sink in.

Sandra frowned.

John stared straight ahead while they walked up the hill toward the castle. Finally, he said, "I'm listening."

"Bob sent us back six hundred seventy-seven years.

He punched in the exact date. We all saw him dial it in on the MCV, right? I say we punch in a date two days sooner. If I'm right, that will put us here before Chad gets captured." The words began to tumble out more quickly, like a clamp had been released from her heart. When she said it out loud it sounded good—possible, even. A smile snuck onto her face. "We find him and warn him before he gets nabbed. Then we meet ourselves as we arrive and get him to send us back immediately, before anything happens to Jess."

Sandra continued to look worried. Mila started to wonder if she'd even followed the logic. To John she said, "Well?"

"We don't have the MCV. We don't know where it is or how it works." John's concerned look told her he wasn't buying into it. His list of excuses was his attempt to convince her he'd listened but nothing more.

"Look, we have to try." Mila couldn't abandon her idea. For the first time since the night before, she could breathe. "The MCV was in a chest in the carriage when Jess was taken. That's why I wanted to get into the castle. To search for the MCV."

"Great." John shook his head. "Now the baron has it. He'll probably wreck it, trying to figure out what it is."

"John..." Sandra waited until he looked at her.

"What?"

"If there's even a chance, we're trying it." Sandra had her stern face on.

"Not you too." John said. "Am I the only one who thinks we should be focused on finding the guide? Jess is dead. I can't... *won't* let that happen to you."

"I'm not going home without my baby." Sandra held his gaze, and it was over.

Mila smiled. Sandra always had the last word. Now that her parents were on board, she just had to find the MCV, figure out how to work it, and get everyone back to the meadow. Mila rolled her eyes again. What could possibly go wrong?

CHAPTER FORTY-FOUR

April 29, 1341

As Mila followed her parents into the keep, Lady Evelyn and Raymond disappeared up the circular staircase—ostensibly so Raymond could prepare for the tournament, but Mila wasn't so sure. She and her family were led along the short passage into the great hall. A force of six archers stood along the back of the room. They each wore chain mail, and they held their bows with an arrow knocked, ready to draw. Clearly being armed in front of the baron was not going to be an advantage. Lady Evelyn had simply been putting John at ease and telling him what he wanted to hear. If shit went bad, it wouldn't be long before somebody got off a deadly shot. They were going to have to "trust" Lady Evelyn. Mila sighed. Basically, they were already dead.

A man dressed in fur and silk strode into the room. He glanced at the captain then pointed at the two knights and gestured toward the archers. The knights retreated to the back of the hall. He stopped and stood with his hands on his hips, looking up into John's face. "I am Baron Reginald Fitzdumay, constable of Sussbury Castle."

"John McLeod. Lady Evelyn said you wanted to speak with me."

The baron walked over to the fireplace and sat. "Join me." He pointed to a chair near him. "Please."

John nodded toward the fireplace. They all moved up together. John pointed to a spot near the fire for Sandra and Mila to stand then pulled his chair around and sat between them and the archers. Mila checked the sightlines. It wasn't going to make a hell of a lot of difference, but it was something.

"I was very curious to meet you. I believe you killed fifteen of my men trying to rescue the witch." The baron pulled on his chin. "What was she to you?"

"She was my daughter." John's voice trailed away.

"Oh. I see." The baron eyed him. "Where did you learn to fight?"

"A long way from here."

"Will I not know its name?"

"Have you heard of the Americas?"

The baron leaned in. "You speak of a place of which I have not heard, yet you speak passable English. How can that be?"

"The place I came from was colonized by people from here... a long time ago."

"Colonized... I know not this word."

"Explored?"

"Explored... I know not."

"Invaded? Conquered?" offered Mila. Sandra elbowed her.

"Conquered. 'Conquered' I understand." The baron raised an eyebrow at Mila.

"Chad, the man you captured," John said. "Is he still in your dungeon?"

"Ah yes, the man who claimed he had a chest of silver." The baron returned his gaze to John. "He was killed while trying to escape with the witch."

Shit. With the guide dead, John's plan to seek information was over. Now Mila's plan was all they had.

Lady Evelyn entered the great hall. Four wolfhounds followed in her wake. She sat next to her brother, and the dogs sat in a pile at her feet.

The baron waited until she was seated. "My sister tells me you are trying to return to your homeland."

"That's true," John said.

Mila kept her eyes glued to Lady Evelyn. What was she after? Lady Evelyn kept her focus on the dog whose chin she was scratching. She seemed content to let Reginald make small talk.

"There is the issue of the men who have died since your arrival in my lands. Henri tells me the count stands at seventeen," said Reginald. "How do you propose to settle that debt?"

John didn't answer right away, so Mila jumped in. "I think that debt has already been settled."

The baron turned to her. "What is your name?"

"This is my daughter, Mila." John stared at her, trying to catch her attention, but she ignored him, locking eyes with Reginald.

"I see," he said. "And what were you saying about the debt?"

"Chad's chest of silver." Mila crossed her arms over her chest. "You already have it."

"Indeed?" the baron said excitedly. "Henri, has it been recovered? Why have I not been told?"

"We did not find it, my lord," said Henri.

"The chest. About this big." Mila held her hands four feet apart, demonstrating for Henri. "It was in the carriage when you took my sister."

Henri looked shocked.

"Your daughter is very bold." Reginald smiled. "Well, Henri? Is there any truth to this?"

"My lord. There was no chest in the carriage." Henri bowed his head slightly and closed his eyes as though that would be the end of it.

Mila took a step toward him. "You're lying!"

Henri put his hand on the hilt of his sword.

John sprang to his feet and placed himself between Mila and Henri.

The six archers pulled their bows to full draw.

"Mila." Lady Evelyn spoke quietly, without looking up from the dogs. "Henri is a knight. He has sworn fealty to my brother and keeps that vow with a passion matched by no man. He is incapable of duplicity and knows not what a 'bluff' is. If he says there was no chest in the carriage, then there was no chest in the carriage." She raised her head finally. "Quite simply."

"If that is the case," Mila said, glaring at Henri, refusing to let him off so quickly, "then I am mistaken."

Reginald gestured to his men. They lowered their bows, but Henri continued to face John, his hand still on the hilt of his sheathed sword. John had killed a lot of Henri's men in the last two days.

"Henri, why do you hesitate to do the Lord's work?" said the bishop.

He stood leaning against one side of the arched doorway to the great hall. Mila hadn't seen him come in and wondered how long he'd been there. He pushed himself away from the wall and walked toward the fireplace.

Reginald swung his gaze toward the bishop. "Hold your tongue, Edward, or I'll have it handed to you."

"My lord baron, how can you put a price on the life of a man?" As the bishop neared the fireplace, the dogs started growling. He stopped. "We have lost seventeen good men. Their wives and children yet mourn. How will they survive without their men? How ever will they pay for the funerals? Our community has been destroyed by these heretics. I cannot believe you are bartering over a chest of coins. I think of the story of Judas, and I weep for us all."

"Spare me your hypocrisy. You will not even pray for a man that cannot pay."

"My lord baron, please. I am but the messenger. It is God's will that I impart with every word I speak."

"Is it really?" said Reginald. "Well, do not worry, you will get your cut."

"My lord, surely you know the church does not take a cut. The people give of their own free will to ensure their place in heaven." The bishop steepled his fingers and raised his eyes to the ceiling.

"Fine. I will give willingly to ensure my place in God's good graces," Reginald said, dismissing him with a wave, but apparently the bishop had more to say.

"I only wish it was that simple." The bishop let his gaze drift to Mila.

"What are you looking at?" Mila tore her glare away from Henri and aimed it at the bishop.

"My lord baron, I was unaware prisoners could address members of the court so freely." The bishop let his eyes travel down and back up Mila's body. "Least of all women."

"These are not Reginald's prisoners. They are his guests," said Lady Evelyn.

"Indeed? My lord baron, I must protest." The bishop took a step toward the baron but stopped when the dogs growled. "If these people are allowed to live, the heresy in our village will only continue to grow. It must be stamped out." The bishop faced Henri. "Captain, you hold in your power the ability to execute them here and now, and yet you hesitate. God's justice must be both swift and mighty. Why do you not strike, sir?"

"Edward!" Reginald got to his feet.

The bishop addressed the knights and archers at the end of the room. "If any man here has the courage to see God's justice done, he will be well rewarded in this life and the next."

Mila checked the archers for any kind of reaction. If any one of them responded to the bishop's desperate plea, she and her family were done.

"Captain, remove Edward." Reginald pointed at the door. "At once!"

"Yes, my lord." Henri bowed, and took the bishop by the arm.

"This is not over," the bishop yelled toward John as Henri forced him from the room. "You will not escape God's justice."

John smirked. "Neither will you."

Reginald waited until the bishop was out of the hall and said, "As to the debt... If you have nothing else to offer, I'm afraid Edward will have his way after all."

He signaled to his men, and the archers once again drew their bows and aimed.

Lady Evelyn was still petting the goddamned dogs. Mila could have screamed. She showed no further interest in her or her family.

"Hang on a minute there, Reginald," said John. "What about that chest of silver?"

Reginald raised a hand to the archers without taking his eyes off John. "Do you know where it is?"

"No, but—"

"Then we have nothing more to discuss."

"Wait." Mila uncrossed her arms. "I do."

"Continue." Reginald kept his palm toward his men.

"Since the *honest* captain *swears* the chest *was not* in the carriage," Mila said, drenching every word in sarcasm, "there is only one place it can be. Give us a day to collect it."

"Well, John, what say you?" Reginald kept his eyes on Mila while he spoke. "Am I wasting my time?"

John surprised even Mila when he said, "It is always foolish to underestimate my daughter. If she says we can bring you the chest, then we can bring you the chest."

"Very well, then, one day. But since we have just met, there is a small issue of faith. Your daughter will retrieve the chest, but you and your lady will remain as my guests, awaiting her return."

"That is unacceptable," said John.

"That is beyond negotiation." Reginald smiled.

"Do I have your word we will be released when she returns with the chest?"

Reginald said nothing. The silence grew uncomfortable.

"Of course," said Lady Evelyn. "A knight's word is his very honor. Do not question my brother's honor, John. If he were to break his word, his men and his God would lose faith in him."

Mila stared at Lady Evelyn. She had finally found her voice. What was that about? She appeared to be speaking for the baron, and she had smoothed over the awkward silence. Reginald didn't seem to have much of a relationship with his God. But judging by the way his men responded to command, his relationship with them seemed pretty strong.

"Fine," said John. To Mila he said softly, "Margaret will be waiting at the Hanging Cock inn. She can help you. Are you sure you're up for this?"

"Seriously?" Mila said. "You just backed me in front of the baron."

"You're right. I'm sorry." John put his hands on her shoulders. "Be careful."

Mila studied Reginald. She had something to ask, though she wasn't sure if she would be pushing her luck. "I need two horses: one for myself and one for the chest."

Reginald nodded to Henri. "Arrange it." To Mila he said, "Will that be all?"

"Yes, thank you."

Sandra grabbed Mila in a big hug and kissed her cheek. "We're so proud of you. We love you."

"I know." Mila extricated herself from Sandra's slobbery grasp. "This isn't the time."

CHAPTER FORTY-FIVE

April 29, 1341

Mila stood by the well in the inner bailey as one of the guards led two saddled horses out of the stable. He held out the reins. She took one set, letting him keep the other.

"Hello, beauty." She reached up and stroked its head like she'd seen people do in the movies and on TV. The horse was enormous. It studied her with one huge eye, stepped away, and snuffled. She was so totally out of her league.

How was she going to find the silver and get back to the castle if she couldn't even get on the horse? She could walk them into town and ask Margaret to show her how to ride. But she only had one day to find the chest. She needed a faster solution. She searched the inner bailey for inspiration, and her gaze fell on the guard holding the other horse.

He was a young man, about her age. He seemed to be watching her with an indifferent expression, no doubt wondering why she was taking so long to mount the horse.

Play the princess. She glanced down and regretted that she was decked out in chain mail, but she would have to make do with what she had. She stood up straight to accentuate her chest, but with no bra, the weight of the chain mail totally flattened her. *Crap.* She smiled at him instead. "What's your name, soldier?"

"Beg your pardon?" said the guard.

She was doing her best Mae West, and the guy probably couldn't understand a word she was saying. Channeling an English aristocratic vibe instead, she said, "Would you be so kind as to hold the horse for me?" She toyed with the idea of batting her eyelashes but decided that would be a bit over the top.

"Yes, madam." The guard stepped forward and took the reins. He maneuvered the horse next to her until the stirrup was lined up in front of her.

She placed her left foot into the stirrup and lifted her left hand. He immediately put his own hand under hers and guided her hand to the pommel. The horse stood like a statue.

She smiled and caught his eyes. "I'm sorry, it's been so long."

"Other hand on the cantle, madam."

What the hell is a cantle? Thankfully he pointed at the back of the saddle before she had to ask. She reached up and gripped it with her right hand. That felt good, almost natural. She pulled with both hands and stepped up, swinging her right leg over the back of the horse. Her leg smacked into the cantle. She had to lift it much higher than she had expected to clear the back of the saddle and sit down. She found the other stirrup and slid her foot in.

The guard slipped the reins over the horse's head and handed them to her. He reached up and tied the pack horse's reins to her saddle. "Will there be anything else, madam?"

"How do I turn him again?" She smiled.

"You just pull gently on one side or the other." The guard squinted up at her. "Are you sure you want to do this, madam? It is dangerous for a woman."

Mila had to get going before this little guard man decided to get all protective and macho. She pulled on the left rein. The horse moved its head to the left and the movement of the big animal gave her a bit of a start. She squeezed her knees to steady herself and suddenly the horse started walking. The packhorse started to follow as soon as its reins tightened. She was moving. *Awesome.* Now what?

She gently pulled on the left rein until the horse's head lined up with the gatehouse. It walked in that direction. So far, so good, but the gatehouse door was closed.

"Open the door!" she called to the porter.

The horse sped up a bit. *Shit.* The porter had made no move to open the door, and the horse was heading straight for the wall of wood.

She recognized the porter. *What was his name?*

"Claude! Ouvrez la porte!"

Claude moved, but he swung open the small door within the larger one. She'd expected the large door to be opened, but the horse didn't care. It continued straight toward the tiny opening. Its head would barely clear the archway. She bent forward and put her head next to the horse's neck. The horse's hooves clattered on the cobblestones of the narrow passage. The crossbow on her back dragged along the stone ceiling, but then they were clear.

The outer bailey was alive with the tournament. She pointed her horse in the direction of the barbican gate and let the animal pick its way through the crowd.

Captain Henri led his horse out of the gatehouse passage, followed by the other knights who had been in the great hall.

"And here comes my babysitter," Mila said to nobody in particular. "Or not," she added as Henri and his men rode toward the tournament.

CHAPTER FORTY-SIX

A*pril 29, 1341*
    Lady Evelyn climbed into the stands and sat on a cushioned seat under the canopy next to Reginald. As she studied the new construction of the stands, the tilts, the lists, and the multitude of people below her, it finally made sense. Reginald had overextended himself preparing for his tournament, and he saw Chad's chest of silver as his salvation. He did not believe in witches—he simply wanted to relieve these strangers of their wealth in the basest and most opportunistic way. Her brother had a silly grin pasted to his lips. And why wouldn't he, thinking he would soon possess this windfall?

The crowd cheered as the main event of Reginald's tournament began. They stood ten deep around the lists, everyone anxious to see the infamous Raymond de Falaise face the English legend, Sir Wessex. Raymond stopped his horse at the base of the stands, bowed toward Reginald, and smiled and waved toward the masses. The crowd went wild.

Wessex slowed his horse and stopped next to

Raymond. He bowed toward Reginald, straightened, and drove a triumphant fist skyward. The crowd grumbled and grew silent.

Lady Evelyn chuckled. Wessex was not a popular man. Apparently, her assessment of him was shared by the masses. Reginald's announcements had proclaimed that two champions who had never been unhorsed would meet for the first time. The word must have spread for miles, for it appeared that everyone in the barony had come to witness Wessex's first fall. Raymond bowed in Wessex's direction then wheeled his mount and walked to his end of the tilt.

Wessex ambled his destrier in the opposite direction.

Raymond closed his eyes and waited while his squire hurried over with a lance, and Lady Evelyn wondered what was going through Raymond's head in those preparatory moments. When his charger snuffled beneath him and sidestepped, Raymond opened his eyes and raised a hand to the squire. The boy slowed as he neared the animal. Raymond accepted the lance and held it vertically.

Lady Evelyn waited for Raymond to look in her direction. When he locked eyes with her, she bowed her head ever so slightly. Raymond nodded and swung down his visor. He had received her message and knew what she wanted of him.

The umpire dropped the flag, and Raymond spurred his horse. The charger exploded down the lists. The crowd hushed until the only sound was the thumping of hoofs on soft turf. Raymond lowered his lance. The two knights thundered toward each other. As their lance tips met, Raymond deflected Wessex's skyward, letting his own bounce down to its target. Evelyn caught her breath.

If Wessex's lance failed to rise high enough, Raymond would certainly be unhorsed or killed. But the tip of Wessex's lance flew past the outside of Raymond's helm.

Raymond's lance cracked and shattered on Wessex's helm. But the placement had been perfect. Wessex's head snapped back as he was lifted from the saddle. The splintering shards rained down around him as he fell off the back of his horse. Raymond had already galloped past before Wessex's armor clanged on the turf.

The crowd gasped as Wessex tumbled to a stop. Raymond slowly reined in his animal. He stopped at the end of the tilt to watch and wait. He lifted his visor. The fickle crowd was hushed. They always hoped the downed knight would rise. When one of Wessex's gauntlets twitched, Raymond walked his horse out of the lists.

As Wessex's retinue rushed to tend to their fallen master, Lady Evelyn shook her head. Wessex's feigned allegiance to Reginald and his potential threat to Mary were one thing. But his bid to usurp the barony had marked him for death. The neck-snapping impact and fall would have killed a weaker man. Wessex had been lucky, but Evelyn would not rest until he breathed no more.

———

AFTER BEING TREATED SO DISGRACEFULLY, EDWARD wandered through the crowds, unwilling to sit in the stands with Reginald. Who did this cretin of a baron think he was dealing with? Edward was not some begging friar to be turned away without a second thought. As he walked among the pavilions, he heard the crowd grow silent then gasp and scream. He wondered absently which knight had been unhorsed. It mattered not. There was always another knight waiting in the lists to ride out and take the place of whichever champion had fallen out of favor. He found himself outside Wessex's pavilion, and a smile crept onto his lips.

Edward stepped inside the pavilion to wait. When his eyes adjusted to the lack of light, he saw a single wooden chair, a small altar, and a bed that looked like the ground itself might be more comfortable. The man was a monk. *This is perfect.* The pavilion flaps rustled, and two squires helped Wessex enter.

"My Lord Wessex. Are you quite well, sir?"

Wessex stood straight, and his attendants began to unfasten his armor. When the squires had pulled off his gauntlets, he massaged his hands. "Good day, Your Grace. I am not kindly disposed at the moment. As you may have heard, Raymond unhorsed me."

"That is most unfortunate." Edward brought his palms together and bowed his head slightly.

"Tomorrow my fortunes will change, and my honor will be restored." Wessex lifted his arms to let the squires unbuckle his cuirass. "I assume you will get to the point of your visit in due time."

Edward wanted to ask how Wessex planned to restore his honor but said, "Let me get straight to the matter. You saw the execution turn to disaster last night, did you not?"

"I did," said Wessex.

Edward nodded, emphasizing their shared assessment of the event. "This morning I learned Reginald had the remaining witches in his custody."

"Excellent." Wessex sneered. "I did not think he was equal to the task."

"He is not."

"Explain."

"He wavers. He has lost interest in seeing God's justice done." Edward shook his head and raised his eyes to heaven, crossing himself.

"Will he not execute them?"

Wessex's shock pleased Edward greatly. "He negotiates their release. Apparently, they are quite wealthy."

"That is disquieting," Wessex said. "The more I learn of Reginald, the less I like him."

Wessex's sentiment matched Edward's. This was very promising. "I tried to reason with him. I pleaded with Captain Henri and his knights. I asked if there was anyone in the room who was willing to do God's righteous work, but my call went unanswered."

Wessex shook his head. "I am sorry to hear of it."

"At that point my thoughts turned to you, sir." Now came the dangerous part. Would Wessex agree to the treason Edward was contemplating? Or would he throw him out, or worse, run him through?

Wessex nodded to his squires. They stopped what they were doing and left the pavilion.

Finally, Wessex spoke. "I will not act on hints and assumptions, Your Grace. If it is treason you have come for, you will need to speak the words aloud for you and I and God to hear them. If you can do that," Wessex said, slapping him on both shoulders, "*that* will be our pact."

Edward nodded. "You have gladdened my heart, sir. I will await you at the cathedral, where we will have privacy. There we can devise a plan that even the king will find satisfactory."

CHAPTER FORTY-SEVEN

A *pril 29, 1341*
When Mila found Margaret at the Hanging Cock, she still had the horse they had taken from Annie's inn. Together, they rode through the town gate and out into the fields. Two well-armed men walked out the gate behind them. Mila expected the baron to send somebody to follow her, but these men didn't look like castle guards. They reminded her more of Geoffrey the assassin.

Mila squeezed her horse with her legs, and it trotted up beside Margaret's mount. "When we reach the forest, we need to go faster."

"Why?"

"I want to put some distance between us and those two." Mila nodded behind her.

Margaret studied the two men. "How did they come to want you?"

"I think the bishop may have hired them."

Mila followed Margaret for what seemed like hours along the Roman road. The sun was long gone, and the moon barely penetrated the forest canopy, but Margaret rode confidently through the night, the steady jingle of her horse's harness somehow reassuring in the dark. Remembering the wolves, Mila asked if they could have a torch, but Margaret said that wasn't a good idea. Not only would it attract every forest robber for miles, but also, they didn't have one. Margaret's matter-of-fact manner made Mila smile in the dark.

Finally, Margaret reined in and dismounted. "This is the place."

"Okay. Um, how do I get off?"

"Honestly, Mila, how did you get on the horse?"

Mila shrugged. "A nice little guard showed me."

"Unhook one of your feet, swing it over the back of the horse, and lower yourself down."

Mila dismounted, thankful it was too dark for Margaret to see the flush that came to her cheeks. Getting off the horse had really been quite easy. They led their horses off the trail into the woods and felt their way up the forested slope about a hundred meters before tying their reins to a tree. Mila pulled her crossbow off her back and loaded it. "I'll take first watch."

———

April 30, 1341

"Wake up."

Mila's eyes popped open.

"I heard something," Margaret whispered in Mila's ear. She stood and stepped to the edge of the old oak under which they sheltered. She hefted a short length of wood over her shoulder like a bat and peered out at the dawn mist.

Mila stood to load her crossbow. The gray sea of icy

air swirled around her. She could barely see three trees in any direction. Down the slope something moved through the undergrowth, disturbing the quiet. A repeated crunch grew closer, and louder. Someone's attempt at stealth had the exact opposite effect.

Mila shouldered her weapon and aimed out at the mist. A dark man-shape appeared through the gray. It walked straight toward their tree and gradually became recognizable as one of the assassins that had followed them out of town. The man wore chain mail with two swords sheathed on his back. He held a longbow with an arrow already knocked. How had he found them so easily —and where was his companion? She could shoot this one easily as he approached but wasn't sure she could reload in time if the other was nearby.

One of Mila's horses let out a short whinny. The assassin must have heard the horse because he turned toward the sound. If he kept moving in this new direction, he would miss their tree. Maybe he didn't know where they were? But she couldn't let him get near the horses: with him moving sideways across her field of view, it would be a harder shot. She'd missed the only moving shot she'd tried, and the bishop had... *Stop it. Lead the target.* But how far? If she could somehow get him to stand still...

"Hey!"

The assassin stopped and lifted his bow in her direction.

Mila fired and ducked behind the tree as his arrow whistled past her head. She was rewarded with a grunt, and she snuck a look around the tree. The man stared at the bolt in his chest as he toppled forward.

The other assassin came thundering through the

forest on Margaret's side of their tree. Mila caught a glimpse of him, wielding a giant sword, but she forced herself to reload instead of run. She dropped the foot loop to the ground. Placing one foot in the loop, she bent both knees, hooked the string, and straightened her legs. The string came up and latched in place.

The man was almost upon them. *Shit. Breathe.*

"I can't!" Margaret dropped her club and ran the other way.

Mila slipped a bolt into the slot.

The assassin bounded around the tree with his sword swinging down at her. With no time to raise the weapon to her shoulder, she fired from the hip, and the bolt penetrated his throat and continued up into his skull. She sidestepped as the giant sword fell past her shoulder, followed by its dead owner.

Margaret screamed.

Mila spun toward the sound. "Margaret?"

Nothing.

She reloaded, shouldered the weapon, and advanced into the mist. "Margaret?"

"She's fine, Lady Mila. Please lower your weapon." A man's voice.

"Why would I do that?" Mila searched the fog.

"Because I'm sure you don't want to hurt us." Sir Raymond walked out of the mist carrying Margaret, one arm behind her back, the other under her knees.

Mila lowered her weapon. "What happened?"

"I twisted my ankle." Margaret offered a shy smile as she gently held on to Raymond's muscular neck.

"I fear I may have startled her when I stepped from the fog." Raymond stopped and lowered Margaret, feet first, to the ground.

"What are you doing here?" The last time she'd seen Raymond, he'd held his sword to John's neck.

"Lady Evelyn sent me to look after you, on your quest. I followed the assassins, but I am embarrassed to say I lost track of them in the fog." Raymond bowed slightly. "But you seem to have handled yourself rather well. How did you become so skillful?"

"Never mind that. Help Margaret up on her horse."

He helped Margaret limp over to the horses.

"That one." Margaret pointed at her spotted mount and giggled. She swung her leg over as he lifted her onto its back, but her fingers lingered along his sleeve as he stepped back out of reach. "Thank you, Sir Raymond."

Was Margaret that enamored with him? Mila remembered Raymond preparing to be in the tournament. Was he a jousting star? Did they even have stars in 1341? Perhaps he was a local celebrity. He was certainly a master of the sword. Mila smiled at Margaret's medieval fangirl crush and rolled her eyes.

Raymond stepped back from Margaret's horse, his eyes coming to rest at the brand on its hindquarters. He reached up and gently patted the horse's flank. To Mila he said, "It is a fine animal. How did you come by it?"

"Why?" She took an involuntary step back. It was the horse they had stolen from Annie's inn. Surely it wasn't Raymond's too...

Raymond breathed out slowly. "It is no matter."

Mila decided to let it go. "Are you here to help, or are you here to look out for Lady Evelyn's interests?"

He smiled. "What can I do to help, Lady Mila?"

"Answer the question, for starters." Mila crossed her arms over her chest.

"At the moment, Lady Evelyn's interests are aligned

with your own. Next time we see her..." Sir Raymond shrugged. "Who can say?"

He seemed to have some insight into Lady Evelyn's ability to change her mind, but he was still her man. *Great.* Now she had a babysitter who would report her every movement back to Lady Evelyn at the first opportunity. At which point he might be informed that their goals were no longer "aligned."

Mila raised an inner eyebrow. In theory, all she had to do to keep Raymond on her side was keep him from reporting to Lady Evelyn. For the first time in days, she was glad that texting hadn't been invented yet. "Do you think the baron will keep his word if I bring him the treasure chest?"

"Lady Evelyn says he always chooses what is most advantageous to him." Raymond adjusted his tunic. "It depends on whether he sees a greater advantage in not keeping his word."

"He stands to gain a great deal of money. What could be more advantageous than that?"

"Your father has proven himself to be a formidable swordsman. If the baron fears your father, he may not release him."

"What can I do to make him keep his word?"

"Perhaps you should find the chest." Raymond smiled. "Then you will have a position of strength from which to bargain."

Raymond was right. She took the reins of her horses and led them down the slope toward the road. She only hoped she could figure out where Jess had hidden the chest. Margaret nudged her horse down the hill after Mila. Raymond excused himself to retrieve his own mount.

When Mila neared the road, she retied her animals. She found the deep grooves in the mud where the carriage had been parked. With that position in mind, she peered back up the slope at the forest.

"Margaret, you look that way." She pointed to her right. "Check behind every tree, and crisscross back and forth as you go up. I'll go this way." Raymond joined them, and she set him to work on a central quadrant that overlapped the sections she and Margaret searched.

Mila went from tree to tree, keeping her head down and looking for any sign of disturbed earth. The higher she went, the more doubt crept into her psyche. Was she completely wrong? If Henri was to be believed, as Lady Evelyn insisted, the chest had to be here. This was the only place Jess would have had time to hide it. But where? Half the morning gone and still no sign of it.

She stopped and looked down at the road. She sat and tried to will the location to reveal itself. Her gaze drifted across to the other side of the road, where the forest continued.

Of course.

Mila ran down the hill. The others heard her rustling through the undergrowth and came to investigate.

"What is it, Lady Mila?" Raymond asked.

"I think we'll try the other side of the road now." Mila crossed the flat stones and stepped into the mud on the far side. She spotted a lone set of footprints leading into the woods. The footprints were deep, like a person might leave if they carried a heavy load. The prints led into the forest, where they ended at a tree. Behind the tree, Mila found the chest. *Nice job, Jess. The very first tree you came to?*

Mila bent over and lifted the lid. The MCV lay in

one corner on the pile of coins. She picked it up, choking back tears and not sure which emotion to blame them on. She was happy she'd found the chest, sad that Jess was dead, and desperately hopeful that she might just see her again.

"Have you found something, Lady Mila?" Sir Raymond stood on the edge of the road, looking concerned.

She pocketed the MCV and closed the lid. She grabbed the handles and bent her knees to lift the chest. It did not budge. *That's why it's at the closest tree.* It must have taken all of Jess's strength to carry it this far.

She smiled and stood up without the chest. "Sir Raymond, thank goodness you're here."

CHAPTER FORTY-EIGHT

April 30, 1341

Evelyn forced herself not to smile.

"Not here?" Reginald's forehead broke out in a sweat. "What do you mean Sir Raymond is not here?"

"Reginald, calm yourself." She stepped aside and let him and Henri into her chamber. "I sent him to look after Lady Mila in the forest."

"But Wessex awaits him. He demands satisfaction."

The chant of the crowd drifted in through Evelyn's window. *Ray-mon, Ray-mon.*

"How can he *demand* anything?" Evelyn closed the door to keep what little warmth there was in the room. "The tournament was yesterday."

"He has set up a blockade at the barbican gate. He says no man shall pass until Raymond agrees to face him. He's calling it a *pas d'armes.*" Reginald's gaze fell on Henri. "You. You should be in the forest, looking after the witch. Not Raymond. Whatever were you thinking?"

Evelyn let Reginald stew. He was clearly out of sorts

and might well agree to anything. Perhaps this could be turned to her advantage. Since Raymond was not here to finish Wessex himself, she might be able to use this opportunity to regain the trust of..." Might I suggest something?"

"No." Reginald glared at her.

Evelyn smiled but continued anyway. "Henri is a fine swordsman. Why not have *him* wear Raymond's armor and fight in his stead? No one will ever know."

"*Mon Dieu!*" It was Henri's turn to gape at her.

"Yes! That's very good, Evelyn." Reginald spun around to Henri. "Get suited up."

"But, my lord—"

"Shut it. You should have been in the forest. Now you will have to take Raymond's place in this *pas d'armes*. I will go out to the gate and tell Wessex that 'Raymond' is on his way." Reginald grinned and rushed from the room. "Hurry now."

Henri's face was an ashen mask.

"Oh, come now, Henri. I would never put you in such danger. Besides, Raymond's armor would never fit you."

"But—"

She put a finger to his lips. "Raymond is a full head taller than you. The crowd would see the counterfeit at once."

———

"No!" SANDRA STARED AT JOHN. SHE COULDN'T believe he was even considering Lady Evelyn's ridiculous idea.

"Sandra, think about it." John crossed his arms and

glanced toward the open door. He lowered his voice. "If I help with this, she'll owe us. We don't have a lot of friends here."

Evelyn and Henri waited outside the door for John's answer. Sandra stepped toward John and lowered her own voice to match his. "What makes you think she'll keep her word? Mila doesn't trust her anymore."

There had to be another reason, but he wasn't telling her. He refused to meet her eye and kept glancing at the door. Sandra took his face in her hands and made him look at her. "What is it? Why won't you tell me?"

John looked into her eyes and said, "I don't know what you're talking about," then looked away.

Sandra's heart broke a little bit. They'd been together for thirty-five years, and she was still surprised when John thought he could lie to her. Maybe she should be thankful he was so easy to read, but it always hurt when he pulled this shit.

She took a deep breath and released it before she started the all-too-familiar dance. "Really? Because I think you know exactly what I'm talking about. Let's look at the facts." Sandra held up her index finger. "One. You don't trust this woman any more than I do. You said so yourself. Two." She added another finger. "There is no evidence to suggest she will honor any kind of arrangement. And three." She added another finger. "You are not a stupid man, just a stubborn one."

John grimaced but refused to meet her eye.

Sandra put down her hand. "Please, tell me *why* you are so willing to risk fighting this man."

John stepped in and grabbed her into a hug. His warm bulk around her felt good, but she wasn't about to let him off the hook. She pushed him back and looked up into his face. His eyes brimmed with tears. Sandra's mouth fell open, and her heart leapt into her throat.

"I have to," John growled. "Evelyn said Wessex helped the bishop convince Reginald to execute Jess. No way he gets a pass."

And there it was.

John walked out the door.

"Henri will take you to Raymond's pavilion and help you get into his armor." Lady Evelyn handed John a cloak with a hood. "Put this on. You cannot be seen until you are in full armor with the visor closed."

———

JOHN KNELT IN RAYMOND'S ARMOR IN THE OUTER bailey. Lady Evelyn made a show of leaning over and kissing his helmet.

"Henri is waiting in the pavilion to help you out of the armor," she whispered. "I shall await your return with Sandra in the tower."

John stood and walked toward the barbican gate. The crowd opened and let him pass. As soon as John was in range, Wessex came at him with the largest sword John had ever seen. The grip had room for two hands, but Wessex only needed one. He brandished it above his head before slashing it down as though it were a toy. The hardened steel clanged off John's shoulder piece, but the impact resonated deep in his joint.

The crowd let out a collective *oooh* that echoed through the barbican gate.

John growled out a breath and sidestepped, focusing

his anger. Henri had said his armor would stop any slashing or hacking, but John decided not to press his luck. Sooner or later Wessex would try thrusting, and John needed the fight to be over before that happened.

He backed away, lifting his own weapon to his shoulder. Its armored shaft fit his hands perfectly, and the weight of its head promised damage and pain wherever it made contact. The *war hammer* was aptly named. Not only did it have the hammer side, but it also had a perfectly tapered back end with a single tine that could concentrate the force of a strike right through an armor plate. The spike at the end of the shaft added thrusting to the weapon's already extensive capabilities.

Wessex came at him again, this time with a horizontal slash from the right. John blocked it with the hammer handle, stepped inside, and clanged the hammerhead off Wessex's helm. Wessex staggered back and lowered his sword arm.

John took the opportunity to swing the weapon in a full circle behind his head. The weight of the accelerating hammer pulled on his arms, and he gripped the shaft tighter with both hands. Wessex took a step back, and John let the weapon do another revolution. As the hammer head came around from behind, he lunged for Wessex and aimed the swing into his left elbow.

It impacted with a satisfying crash. Wessex's shaped elbow piece pancaked under the pressure. John smiled and took a deep breath as Wessex tried to raise his sword arm. Henri had tried to teach him the names of the armor pieces in the short time they'd had, but in the end, John had just focused on learning the weak points.

"Damn you!" Wessex's elbow armor was binding nicely on the surrounding pieces. He couldn't flex the arm, making it effectively useless. Wessex deftly tossed the sword to his other hand and caught it, swinging the giant blade up toward John's legs in a single movement.

John managed to bend his leg, and the blow glanced off one of the fins on the outside of his knee. That was *too* close. He swapped his grip and hammered at Wessex's other elbow.

Wessex anticipated and took the blow on his chest-plate. Wessex's sword came for John's neck.

John tilted his head in the direction of the blow to make sure there was no gap between his helmet and chest-plate. As the blow struck, Wessex's arm was extended, and John thrust his hammer up into the exposed armpit. Wessex's armor absorbed most of the attack, but the hammer spike came away bloody.

Wessex backed away with his left hand under his right arm.

"Do you yield, sir?" John asked quietly, hoping he would not.

"Never!" Wessex raised his sword, but it came up slowly and only halfway. He couldn't lift the shoulder.

John swung the hammer around behind his head. The hammer accelerated and came out on his right, aimed at Wessex's helmet. Just before impact, John spun the hammer backwards, and the tapered end penetrated Wessex's helmet like a can opener. The crowd gasped as Wessex collapsed to his knees and fell on his face.

John walked out of the barbican gate and across the field toward Raymond's pavilion, leaving the weapon in Wessex's skull. He told himself it had been for Jess, but deep down he knew it was really for him. This world had taken his baby, and anyone even remotely connected with her death would pay the ultimate price. He was still mad as hell.

———

SANDRA STOOD AT THE TOWER WINDOW, LISTENING desperately to the crowd below. She had no idea if John would even survive this ridiculous *pas d'armes*. Ever since Jess's... She couldn't say it, even to herself, but ever since then, John was different. She knew he was grieving, but it was more than that. His behavior was reckless and even a bit frightening. Didn't that stupid, macho, selfish bastard of a man know that she and Mila needed him alive? She loved him, and she hated him, and he had to do something soon to help her decide which impulse was stronger.

Lady Evelyn appeared at the door, and a guard let her in. Sandra watched her close the door behind her. Lady Evelyn smiled briefly and walked over to Sandra.

"There are some things I need to say," Sandra said before Evelyn could speak.

Lady Evelyn gestured for her to continue.

Sandra struggled to control the urge to tell the woman off. "I think you used to be in charge here. Henri obeys you as readily as he does Reginald."

An unreadable look flickered across Lady Evelyn's face, but it was enough to tell Sandra she was on the right track.

"Little brother hasn't been doing a very good job of running the barony, and you're here to set things right." Sandra paused, but Evelyn had her mask back in place and revealed nothing. Sandra held up her hands. "I'm not judging. I get that you live in a harsh world, where men rule and women follow. You have to fight for everything you want with every means at your disposal. Believe me, it's not much different where I come from. Women still have to fight for what they want. If we let our guard down, even for a second, the old prejudices resurface."

"Why are you telling me this?" Lady Evelyn spoke softly.

"I am trying to say that you don't have to pretend with me. I get it. If you want something from me, just ask for it. Hell, if I can think of a way to help, I'll *offer* it." Sandra touched Lady Evelyn's arm. "But please, stop manipulating my family." Sandra's throat tightened up. She took a long breath to calm herself. "I need them alive."

Sandra searched Lady Evelyn's face for any sign of concession.

After an uncomfortable silence, Evelyn cleared her throat. "Mila is safe. I sent Raymond to watch over her on her journey."

Sandra stifled the urge to hug her. She wasn't quite sure how it would be received, so she simply said, "Thank you."

Sandra waited for Evelyn to speak next, hoping she would fill the silence with her own thoughts. But Evelyn just stood there smiling back at her.

———

JOHN STARTED THE LONG CLIMB TO THE TOWER WITH his hood up and Henri by his side. When he reached the top of the stairs, Henri stood aside and let him enter first.

Sandra spun from the window where she stood with Lady Evelyn. "Are you all right?" Her eyes flitted down his body and back up to his face before they drained of concern. "Do you feel better now?"

"Yes, thank you." He braced for what was to come. Sandra had been against the idea from the start, and of course she was right to be. It wasn't going to bring Jess back, and it put him—and therefore her and Mila—at risk. But damn, it sure as hell felt good to see that shit-sack sink to the ground.

"Well, that makes one of us." She crossed her arms.

"I'm sorry, babe. I won't do it again," said John.

"Yes, you will."

She was right. She knew it and he knew it, and there was no point in denying it. As long as he breathed, anybody who harmed his family would pay.

"Thank you, John," said Lady Evelyn. "Raymond's honor is intact. I am indebted to you."

"Okay, then let's go."

"That would not be wise." Lady Evelyn shook her head.

"Why not?"

"Because Lady Mila will return here with or without the prize my brother seeks. If you are not here, she will face his anger alone."

"She's making sense," said Sandra.

John clenched his fists. "I know. Dammit." He huffed. "But... she's out there. I can't just sit around and do nothing. What's the plan?"

"The plan?" Lady Evelyn glanced at Sandra.

"Yeah. If your brother decides to keep the money and not let us out, what's our backup plan?"

"Back up?" Lady Evelyn smiled. "Why would we back up?"

"Seriously?" John took a calming breath. He was sure

she was playing at not understanding him. "Our second plan. You know, if our first plan doesn't work?"

"I am sure I do not know what you mean." She glanced at Henri, still standing by the door, and stopped talking.

He had to assume Henri was not part of the backup plan.

CHAPTER FORTY-NINE

April 30, 1341

Mila, Margaret, and Sir Raymond rode out of the forest at dusk and made their way across the fields. The castle loomed above the town, its tan and brown stonework a stark contrast to the surrounding green.

"Thank you for your help today, Sir Raymond."

"You are welcome, Lady Mila."

Mila had the MCV and the silver to buy her parents' freedom, but something felt off. She should have been happy, but imminent failure hung over her like a blanket. She had no idea what she would do if Sir Reginald did not keep his word.

She glanced at Raymond. "If it were up to you, how would you negotiate my parents' release?"

"I would not."

What? Surely Raymond wasn't about to flip-flop his allegiance already. He hadn't yet had a chance to communicate with Lady Evelyn. "Why not?"

"It would not be necessary. I would simply rescue them." Raymond stated it like it was a fact.

Of course, *he* would, but that was no help to Mila. She couldn't rescue her parents. The guards knew what she looked like—they'd seen her leave. They would be expecting her. Unless... She smiled. "Exactly how would you rescue my parents?"

"Lady Mila, you do not possess the skill or the knowledge."

"But you do, so share it with me," she said in a matter-of-fact tone.

Raymond shook his head. "It takes a lifetime to develop the skills of a swordsman."

"Yes, but it only takes a minute to share your knowledge of the castle."

Raymond said nothing, and Mila gave him a moment to think. No doubt he was deciding if this would in any way contradict Lady Evelyn's instructions to protect Mila.

"You can't let me wander into the castle unprepared." Mila gave him a mischievous smile and added, with as much innocence and light as she could muster, "Surely that would be the death of me."

Raymond smiled.

"Tell me what I need to know."

He nudged his horse closer to Mila's and lowered his voice. "Evelyn says there is a narrow path that leads around the curtain wall along the clifftops at the back of the castle. You will come to a postern gate guarded by a giant idiot."

"Why only one guy?" Mila interrupted. "That's not very secure."

"There is nothing but a cliff beyond that wall. No sizeable force could attack the gate. They would have to approach in single file." Raymond closed his eyes and shook his head. "May I continue?"

Mila nodded. "Sorry."

"Inside, there is a long passage and a set of stairs."

Mila smiled and interrupted again. "Are you sure all this is necessary?"

"You said you wanted to sneak into the castle."

"Yes, but why don't you just come with me and show me the way? It would be the best way to ensure my safety." Mila smiled. "*N'est-ce pas?*"

"Indeed." Raymond broke out laughing. "*C'est vrai.*"

"There is just one more thing." Mila pointed at the chest on the packhorse. "Where do we hide this while we're in the castle?"

"They are very discreet at the Dover Dove," Raymond nodded. "Lady Evelyn often makes use of their services."

Once again, it all came down to trust. Mila was confident that Raymond could rescue her parents. The silver was just her backup plan. She would keep the MCV with her. That was her lifeline. "That sounds fine," she said.

Raymond led them through the town gate and down a back alley to the stables behind the Dover Dove where he carried the silver up to Lady Evelyn's room.

Mila held the door as he walked in and placed it on the floor. She beckoned Margaret in so she could close the hall door. "How's your leg?"

"It is feeling much better." Margaret walked around the room with only a slight limp.

"Maybe you should stay here and rest it. You could watch the silver for us."

"No." Margaret shook her head emphatically, and a big grin spread across her face. "If you are rescuing John and Sandra, we can rescue my Chaddy at the same time."

Mila felt like shit. Chad was dead. She'd known it for twenty-four hours and still hadn't found a convenient time to tell Margaret. She reached for Margaret's hands. "There's something I should have told you." She paused for a breath. "Yesterday at the castle, I found out that Chad is dead."

Margaret closed her eyes and nodded.

Mila pulled her into a hug. "I'm so sorry. There is no excuse."

Margaret pulled out of the hug and smiled bravely. "Do not worry. I have been expecting this news."

"We should hurry, Lady Mila." Raymond stood at the door with his hand on the handle.

"Raymond." Mila gave him a *back off* look but doubted he had the ability to read it. "Would you like to stay here and rest?" she asked Margaret.

"Of course not." Margaret moved to the door. "You might need me."

———

Mila and Margaret followed Raymond around the outside of the curtain wall. Mila focused on finding quiet but sturdy foot placements in the gloom. Raymond hadn't been kidding about the cliff. She could put her left hand on the stone wall and look down over the edge to her right without even leaning. The path was definitely single file. In the dying light she couldn't make out any detail of the ground at the base of the cliff.

Raymond stopped.

"What is it?" Mila said.

He held a finger to his lips. Liquid splashed the stonework somewhere ahead.

"I will take care of it." He drew his sword.

"Wait." Mila touched Raymond's forearm. "We cannot add to Reginald's body count against my family. Can you take care of it in a way that doesn't involve killing?"

"I am not certain." Raymond shook his head. "A fight is unpredictable enough. To wound an opponent is to make him angry and even more dangerous. The safest course is to kill."

"Perhaps I can take care of it without fighting." She squeezed past Raymond.

"How? Lady Mila, I must insist." Raymond stepped toward her. "You put yourself at risk unnecessarily."

Mila put her hands on his chest. "Let me try." She lifted her hands away and slowly raised them, palms skyward, as she stepped back. "You see, I am no threat."

She crept forwards before Raymond could object again. He was exhibiting the same macho bullshit she resented so much in her father. *Men.* Why was fighting their answer for everything? As she came around the curve of the wall, the tallest man she had ever seen stood peeing against the wall. He had to be seven feet at least and could have modeled for a muscle magazine. He finished his business and rearranged his breeches then shouldered an enormous battle-ax and disappeared into a depression in the wall.

A metallic jingle accompanied his walk. Mila moved closer until she could peek around the edge of the depression. The giant stood in a semicircular alcove. The chain around his neck led through a small gate in the wall behind him.

Raymond and Margaret came up behind Mila.

"Well?" said Raymond. "Is it the idiot?"

"I have an idea." She motioned them back around the bend of the wall until they were invisible from the giant's latrine, which she assumed was located at the extreme end of his chain, because why would anybody pee on the ground where they knew they would have to walk in it? She hoped her logic was sound. "Wait here."

Mila walked back to the splash zone. Her plan was no plan. *Just talk to him, see what comes up, show some interest.* Channeling Oprah, she took a long breath in and slowly blew it out on the silent word... *care.* "Hello at the gate!"

"Who's there?" The giant rushed out of the alcove and stomped along the narrow trail toward her until his chain pulled on his throat.

"My name's Mila." She smiled up at him. "What's yours?"

"Richard." The man spoke very slowly and backed up until his collar no longer pulled on him. He gripped his battle-ax in his fists and stood with his legs apart and slightly bent.

"I'm not going to fight you." She held her empty hands high to put the thought out of his head. Keeping a friendly tone in her voice, she said, "Why are you chained up?"

Richard watched her for a long time. "They never told me."

"Who are 'they'?"

"Captain Henri and the baron," Richard said with great respect.

"Are you a slave?"

"No," Richard said. "I am a guard."

"No, you're not." Mila shook her head.

Richard stomped his feet. "Yes." He took a swing at Mila with the ax. She was out of reach but close enough to feel the wind.

"Easy, big guy. I'm saying you can't be a guard."

"I am a guard." Richard swung the ax with one hand and reached out as far as he could.

Mila had to step back to stay out of range. "No, you're not."

"Stop saying that." Richard dropped his ax and pulled on his chain with both hands.

"Do you want some help with that?"

Richard stopped straining. "Why would you help me? I'm trying to get this free so I can make you stop lying."

"I'm not lying, buddy."

Richard whipped back to his chain and started yanking on it again.

"Hey!" Mila had to yell to be heard above the clinking and scraping of metal on stone. "Give me a chance to explain, okay?"

Richard kept pulling, ignoring her.

While he had his back to her, she hefted his abandoned battle-ax up onto her shoulder and walked back out of range. She let Richard work on his chain for a while. "Are you getting tired yet?" No answer. She just hoped he didn't pull it free. She had to assume this wasn't the first time he'd tried.

Richard stopped to catch his breath, and Mila said, "Nice ax you got here."

Richard's head spun around. He came running the two steps his chain would allow before it pulled taut and he fell back on his ass in the puddle of pee. He reached out with open palms. "Give it back. Please."

"Why? You'll just swing it at me."

"No. I promise. Just give it back."

"Why?"

Richard dropped his eyes to the ground. "If I lose any more axes, Henri will not feed me."

"That doesn't surprise me. Henri's an asshole."

Richard smiled. "Yes. He is. Will you please give me my ax?"

"Yes." Mila lowered the ax to the ground where Richard could reach it easily then moved back casually, trying not to make it look too obvious.

Richard clutched the ax to his chest but made no move to get to his feet.

"Are you ready to listen to me?"

Richard nodded.

"Okay. I'm going to tell you why I don't think you're a guard."

Richard glared at her but remained silent.

"I've been all over this castle, and the other guards are not chained up. They come and go as they please. They ride horses. They eat and drink when they feel like it. Sure, Henri tells them what to do, but they do it because they agree with him. Not because he won't feed them." The irony of the invisible bonds that chained the other guards to Henri came to mind, but she let it rest.

Richard had stopped glaring at her. "Do they really get to ride horses?"

"Yes, and carts. And they can walk all over town and visit the cathedral, too."

A tear rolled down Richard's cheek. "I want to do that."

"Maybe you can."

"How?"

"Show me where this chain is attached." It was a long shot, but maybe she could see a way he hadn't.

Richard smiled and got to his feet. He walked back toward the depression in the wall.

Mila signaled to Raymond and Margaret to move up, then scurried to catch the giant. Richard's long, slow gait covered a lot of ground.

Inside the gate, Richard went through a door on his right and stood in a small room built into the wall. A cot was the only furnishing. A metal loop buried in the stone held Richard's chain to the wall. Richard's constant pulling had loosened the mortar. It wouldn't have been long before he would have freed himself.

Mila held out her hand. "May I borrow your ax?"

"No." Richard held the ax out of reach, looking horrified. "It will dull the blade."

"I'm not going to use the blade."

"What are you going to do?"

"I need a lever."

"A what?"

Mila reached out for the ax again. "May I?"

Richard slowly handed it over. Its handle was sheathed in metal. As long as the wood inside didn't crack, it would make a perfect lever. Mila slid the point of the handle inside the loop from above. She pulled it away from the wall. Nothing happened. She strained on the handle with all her strength. Nothing. She climbed up the wall, holding the handle of the ax, until her feet were on each side of the loop and still she couldn't budge it. "A little help?"

Mila let go of the ax and dropped back to the floor. Richard stepped over to the wall by the loop. He put his back to the wall above it and with one hand pushed outward on the ax handle like he was putting a giant transmission into first gear.

The loop ground its way out of the stonework and clanged on the floor.

"You've done it," Mila said.

Richard still held his ax in the hand he'd used to pry out the loop. He studied the end of the handle where the metal banding had been crimped by the force. Tentatively, he placed his hand around the injured metal but pulled it away almost immediately. There was a small cut in his palm. He tossed the ax to the ground. "It is ruined." He sat down on his cot. "Henri will not be happy."

"Richard." Mila waited until he looked up. "Why are you worried about Henri? Don't you remember why we pulled your chain off the wall?"

He shook his head.

"Now you can walk outside the castle, ride a horse, see the cathedral, all of it."

Richard stared at the ruined ax. "But what about Henri? When he sees the ax..."

"He won't." Mila bent and picked up the ax. "Because you're taking it with you on your adventure."

"I am?"

Mila walked out of the room and nodded through the gate. "Come on." Then she walked outside without waiting for him.

Raymond and Margaret stood outside. Mila shushed them and pointed to the side to keep them out of Richard's way, then she faced the entrance. The tinkling of metal on stone preceded Richard's appearance.

He stepped outside and spotted Raymond and Margaret in the alcove. "Who are you?"

"These are my friends Margaret and Sir Raymond. Say hello to Richard."

"Hello, Richard," they said, carefully keeping their distance from the giant man.

Mila handed Richard his ax. He took it one-handed and walked away, dragging his chain behind him. The end of the chain slid out of the gate and followed him around the corner, but it stopped before it was out of sight. Richard trudged back around the corner. A tear rolled down his cheek.

Mila walked over to meet him. "What's the matter, Richard?"

"I don't want to go on my adventure."

"Why?"

"I do not know where the cathedral is, or where the riding horses are, or where to get a drink." Richard walked back toward his gate where Raymond and Margaret were standing.

"Wait. Richard. I know how you can still have your adventure. You need a guide."

Richard stopped. "What is a guide?"

"A guide is somebody who knows about all the things you want to know about, and they love to show you those things."

Richard frowned. "I do not know a guide."

"Yes, you do."

"Stop saying that."

"It's Margaret." Mila pointed. "I just introduced you to her."

"Will you show me where the cathedral is?"

Margaret glanced at Mila. Mila nodded vigorously, then stopped when Richard looked toward her.

"I will." Margaret took her cue seamlessly and laced

her fingers around Richard's arm, leading him back down the trail. "The first place I am going to show you is the blacksmith's, where we can get rid of this chain."

Mila stood with Raymond, watching them walk away. "That took longer than I had hoped."

"Killing is faster, too," Raymond said.

CHAPTER FIFTY

A *pril 30, 1341*

Edward climbed the keep stairs in his finest armor. At his back were five of the tournament's knights dressed as he was. With Wessex's demise, it had fallen to him to see God's work done. He had called on the knights Wessex had originally recruited to hunt the heretics, before Reginald—under Lady Evelyn's influence—had told Wessex they would not be needed. They were surely needed now, more than ever. With these men at his back, he would hunt down the heretics and put an end to this menace once and for all.

Edward entered the keep with his men and heard shouting coming from the great hall. He held up a hand to hold his men back while he listened.

"Henri!" Reginald's voice echoed. Something wooden scraped across the floor, and one of the wolfhounds whimpered. Edward had to smile at that divine justice.

Henri said, "Yes, my lord?"

"Why did you kill him?" Reginald yelled. "Even I

could see that he couldn't raise his sword, and I was standing several yards away."

"Kill who... my lord?"

"Wessex, of course. Have you lost your mind?" Reginald paused. "Do you know what your foolish pride has cost me?"

"No..." said Henri.

"You will stand while I address you, sir." He paused. "Henri!"

"My lord," said Henri. "There is something I must tell you."

"Does it explain your behavior of late?"

"It does."

"It had better. If I find the story lacking in any way, you will no longer be my captain. Begin."

"It was not I in Raymond's armor."

"What? My god, man, who was it? I'll have his head!"

What news was this? Had Reginald conspired to kill Wessex? Edward crossed himself and thanked the lord for this bounteous revelation. He began to imagine how he might best put this information to use.

Reginald continued, "How did this man come to be in the—"

"Please, sir, there is more," said Henri. "After you agreed to Lady Evelyn's plan and left to tell Wessex, Lady Evelyn said I was not tall enough to fill Raymond's armor convincingly. She suggested that the heretic was the only man tall and capable enough to pull off the counterfeit."

"My God, Henri!"

"I agreed with her and the plan. But I assure you, I had no idea the heretic would kill Wessex."

"Where is the heretic who is finding my treasure?"

"I know not, my lord."

"Henri, you continue to disappoint me. I would have given her a full escort and a work party of laborers had she asked for it. She needs to be protected. If there is even the slightest chance of finding that money..." Reginald paused. "Bring me the hostages. And Evelyn!"

Henri rushed from the great hall and came face to face with Edward and his knights. Edward nodded solemnly as Henri rushed into the stairway and climbed out of sight.

"Let us speak with Reginald," Edward said to his knights, leading them into the great hall.

———

MILA FOLLOWED RAYMOND INTO A LONG, DARK passage and up the stairs. When they reached the top, they emerged into a hallway from behind a tapestry that hid the opening to the secret passage.

Raymond pointed her across the hall to another set of stairs leading up. "Your parents have a single guard." He smiled. "Might I assume you do not want me to kill him either?"

"Correct." Mila loaded her crossbow and went up the stairs ahead of Raymond. Behind her, she heard someone say, "Hello, Raymond." It was Lady Evelyn. Raymond stopped and returned to the base of the stairs to greet her. Mila rushed up the stairs, not knowing how long she had before Raymond was reprogrammed by Lady Evelyn.

Mila reached the top of the tower. A guard stood facing the stairs with his back to a door. She raised the crossbow to her shoulder and walked out of the shadows until she was certain he could see the weapon.

Mila spoke in as gruff a voice as she could muster. "Put your hands on your head."

He did what she asked. But his eyes strayed from the crossbow and drifted to her face. He started to smile and lowered his hands toward his sword.

"That would be a mistake, Colin." Lady Evelyn emerged from the stairs behind her.

He sneered. "But she is just a girl."

"Did you not hear tell of the crossbowman who shot the guards at the execution in the square?"

Colin stopped sneering and moved his hands back up to his head.

"Can I trust you?" Mila maintained her aim. "Or have you changed your mind again?"

Lady Evelyn whispered in Mila's ear. "Not in front of the guard, dear."

Mila rolled her eyes. She would have to improvise. Lady Evelyn would be on her side until it suited her not to be. She would just have to keep an eye on her and be ready when the switch came.

"Open it." Mila gestured Colin toward the door.

He unlocked it, and swung it open. John's huge arms encircled Colin's neck, pulling him into the cell.

Sandra stepped out and gave her a hug. "Are you all right? Did you find it?"

She had to point the crossbow at the ceiling to keep it out of Sandra's way. "This is not the time. It's a rescue."

There was a ruckus in the cell. Mila pried Sandra off and advanced into the cell with her weapon raised. "Colin!"

The man stopped struggling.

John took his chain-mail shirt and sword. "Ready."

Mila nodded at Colin.

"Right." John ripped off Colin's tunic as though it were tissue. Colin stood helpless under the threat of Mila's crossbow. John tore the shirt into strips, then bound and gagged him.

The two of them stepped into the hall, where Sandra and Lady Evelyn chatted quietly.

"You two seem rather chummy," Mila said.

Sandra gave her a scolding look, and Lady Evelyn produced her usual sphinxlike smile.

"We should go." Mila led the way down the stairs. She had reached the tapestry when raised voices drifted along the hall toward her.

"Raymond! I insist you let me pass."

"Do not raise your voice to me, Henri." Raymond slurred his words in a crappy impersonation of a drunk.

Lady Evelyn brushed past her. "I will see to Raymond. We will meet you at the Dover Dove."

Mila wanted to find out what was going on with Raymond, but Evelyn was right as usual, so she led her parents behind the tapestry. "There's a long staircase. Go slowly and feel your way."

When they came out of the passage by Richard's gate, Mila led them along the curtain wall. She pointed straight down the cliff with her left hand. "Don't fall."

She glanced behind periodically to make sure they stayed close. "We need to talk about our next move."

"Get the hell out of here?" John said.

"What about the baron?" Mila asked. "And the money?"

"Fuck him."

"John, if Reginald gets his money, he might not come after us. But if he doesn't..." Sandra left it hanging.

"But how do we give it to him without getting

captured?" Mila climbed over a rock that blocked the path and made sure her parents were aware of the obstacle.

"Mila's right." John helped Sandra over the rock. "We can't risk it. But it might be useful, so we'll take it with us. If Reginald finds us, it's our bargaining chip."

They reached the point where the cliff was replaced by a shallow slope leading down to the town. Mila took a long breath and picked up the pace.

————

LADY EVELYN DESCENDED THE STAIRWELL UNTIL she'd reached Raymond. He stood in the middle of the circular stair—there was indeed no way for two men to pass.

Henri seemed relieved to see her. "Lady Evelyn, please speak with your husband. I must get through."

"Raymond." Evelyn put her hand on his back. "Do come upstairs with me."

"Yes, my darling." Raymond followed her to the third floor.

Henri shook his head and climbed up the stairs after them. He stopped when he reached Evelyn. He sighed and refused to meet her eye.

Raymond's hand drifted to the hilt of his sword. Evelyn lifted her palm toward Raymond and waited for Henri to break his silence, but she could not wait forever. "What is it, Henri?"

Finally, he said, "Did you know the heretic would kill Wessex?"

"Of course not." So Henri had found out, and now he was consumed by the guilt of knight's honor.

"My lady, I would never have agreed, had I known."

"Henri, the fault does not lie with you. Wessex brought it on himself by demanding the confrontation of arms."

Henri seemed to consider that for a moment. "But he did not deserve to die."

Evelyn put a hand on Henri's shoulder. "I'm sure he would have preferred a warrior's death to the alternative."

Henri nodded slowly. "Reginald is not pleased that the heretic was in my place."

"You told him?"

"I had to."

Evelyn took her hand off Henri. "Of course."

"He has demanded your presence in the great hall. I am on my way to retrieve the hostages."

"We will meet you there." Evelyn watched Henri turn and walk along the hallway toward the tower stairs.

When he was gone, she reached up and kissed Raymond on the lips. "Thank you."

He returned her kiss and slipped his hand around the small of her back, pulling her toward him.

She bit his lip. "Not now. We need to be gone by the time Henri returns from the tower."

———

As EDWARD LED HIS MEN INTO THE GREAT HALL, Reginald sat staring into his fireplace, his back to the door. Edward decided to open with a civil tone, despite his eagerness to bring Reginald down from his undeserved barony. "My lord."

"What now?" Reginald said without turning from the fire.

"Might we have a word, Reginald?"

Reginald stood and faced him. "What is this?"

The shocked look on Reginald's face gladdened Edward's heart. Edward aimed his palms skyward. "Justice must be done. It is God's will. I had asked Wessex to do what you would not, but since he is dead, I must now insist that you hand over the heretics."

"Edward, have you lost your wits?" Reginald studied the knights. Each was one of his tournament guests.

"It is for the good of the kingdom. All of these noble men are of like mind." Edward nodded at the knights behind him. "They do not want the heresy to spread to their lands. It must end here. We are quite sure the king will agree."

"Damn the king." Reginald shook his head. "His bloody war tax brought us to these desperate times."

"Reginald!" Edward's mouth fell open. "I will not tell the king of your treasonous words if you hand the heretics over at once."

"Do not speak of treason while you threaten me in my own castle." He sniffed. "Do you think the king will stand by while I am usurped?"

Henri ran into the great hall. "My lord, the hostages have escaped, and Lady Evelyn is gone."

"Good god, Henri." Reginald's face reddened. "You seem quite incapable of keeping anyone in custody."

"It is settled, then. You will grant me the right to hunt these heretics as I see fit with no interference. Are we agreed?

Henri drew his sword.

"Hold." Reginald held up his hand to Henri. "Edward, I shall grant you the rights you seek but on the condition that Henri and I hunt with you."

"Let God's will be done." Edward smiled. He hadn't

even had to leverage the secret of who killed Wessex. That he could save for another time.

CHAPTER FIFTY-ONE

April 30, 1341

As Mila and her mother brought the horses around to the front of the Dover Dove, Lady Evelyn and Sir Raymond drove up in the carriage.

"Henri and his men will be along any moment." Lady Evelyn glanced back toward the castle. "We must hurry."

"We?" Mila was lost. She glanced at Raymond. He wore a blank expression as he climbed down. She guessed Lady Evelyn hadn't reprogrammed him yet.

"Evelyn and Raymond are coming with us," said Sandra.

Raymond came and took his horse's reins and began tying them to the back of the carriage.

John came out of the inn carrying the chest. "What did I miss?"

Lady Evelyn broke the silence. "Sandra and I have decided to pool our resources. We will help you, and you will help us."

"That's right." Sandra smiled.

Mila had no idea what deal her mother had made with this woman who couldn't be trusted, but she had no time. "Okay. Take my mother and father and head straight for the meadow. I'm not leaving without Margaret. I'll find her and meet you there."

"Not a chance," John said. "We have to stick together."

"John! We don't have a second to waste arguing." Mila mounted her horse and rode away.

———

EDWARD AND HIS MEN FOLLOWED REGINALD AND Henri down the keep stairs and across the inner bailey. A squire sat at the doors to the stable, cradling his head. Upon seeing Reginald and eight knights approaching, he jumped to his feet.

Henri pulled one of the young man's hands away from his head. It came away bloodied. "What happened?"

"I am sorry, sir. The Lady Evelyn took the carriage. I told her that I needed your word to release it." The squire bowed his head. "That is when she had Sir Raymond strike me."

Edward mounted his horse and noticed Reginald was smiling. "What have you found amusing in this poor man's plight?"

"Nothing, Your Grace." Reginald stopped smiling and climbed onto his mount.

Edward decided to let it go for the moment and led his men out the inner gate. When they reached the barbican gate, Edward reined in and addressed the knights. "I want each man to take one of the five roads that leads to the south end of the town. I will make my way to the cathedral square. When you have finished your patrols, meet me there. I pray one of you brings news of the witches. Do not engage them. You are only to find them and report back. God be with you. Now ride!"

———

Mila had no idea where Richard and Margaret might be, but Richard had asked where the cathedral was, so she started her search there. The side doors to the cathedral were unlocked, so she slowly pushed them open. Voices echoed from inside. She snuck a look into the candlelit interior and spotted three people near the altar. She stepped inside and hid behind a pillar. Richard stood watching behind the next pillar along the nave. She moved to him and whispered, "What are you doing?"

Richard's face was flushed, and his eyes were moist.

"What's wrong?"

"We were looking at the windows and all the pretty colors," Richard said slowly. But before he finished his explanation, a cry came from the altar. Mila snuck another look around the pillar. She recognized Margaret and some asshole holding her from behind. An even larger and uglier shithead was reaching inside the top of her dress.

"They took Margaret and told me to stay out of it," Richard continued.

Mila ducked back behind the pillar. "Why didn't you help her?"

"They said they were doing the bishop's work. It was God's will." Richard stomped his foot. "They told me to go away."

"All right, Richard, I get it." Mila didn't, really, but

she needed Richard calm if he was going to be of any use. "You know you don't have to do what they tell you, right?"

"Do I not?"

"Hell, no. If you think somebody is wrong, you just say no and do what you think is right." They clearly weren't teaching about stranger danger or that 'no' feeling here in the fourteenth century.

Margaret let out a scream. Mila peeked around the pillar. Things were about to get rough. Shithead had just ripped her dress down around her elbows.

Richard stood up and wiped his nose. His eyebrows lowered until his eyes were slits. He gritted his teeth and stomped out from behind the pillar toward the central aisle. The men at the altar heard him approach.

Mila crawled from pillar to pillar toward the front of the church.

"What are you doing?" Asshole asked.

Richard growled, ignoring them, and kept moving toward his ax.

"Go away," Shithead said. "You do not want to see this."

"Let him watch. Maybe he will learn something." Asshole laughed at his own joke.

"Stop it!" Richard's voice echoed through the church.

They laughed at him. He picked up his ax and stomped down the center aisle.

Shithead stopped laughing. "Idiot! Put that down and find a place to sit."

Richard kept coming.

"You do not listen very well." Shithead stepped away from Margaret and drew his sword.

Mila wondered what Richard would do when faced with an armed opponent, but he seemed fearless.

"Stop!" Asshole sounded scared.

Richard kept coming. Shithead swung his sword. Richard blocked the blow and drove the point of his ax into the big man's skull in one smooth motion. Richard could fight, and he was good.

Mila held her breath. She reached the back of the altar and stood up behind Asshole, who was still holding Margaret. "Let her go."

Asshole spun around to keep Margaret between himself and Mila. Richard took his head from behind. Margaret stumbled backwards as the corpse released her. Richard caught her easily and gently lowered her to a pew.

"I am sorry," Richard said.

"Why?" Margaret pulled up her dress.

"I am sorry that I did not help you right away."

Margaret finished repairing her dress as best she could. Mila knelt in front of her. "How are you?"

"I am well." Margaret smiled at her. There was no sign of the anguish she had displayed upon learning of Chad's death, or any acknowledgment that she had narrowly escaped a rape.

"Are you serious?"

"I am."

Mila was both shocked and impressed. Margaret gave new meaning to the term *survivor*.

The clomping of hooves on the stones outside the main cathedral door drew Mila's attention. She stood and offered Margaret a hand. "We have to go."

Margaret took her hand and stood. Mila led her toward the side door but felt Margaret pull away.

"What about Richard?" Margaret asked. Richard stood next to the corpses, wiping his ax on one of the dead men's chests. "We cannot leave him here. He will be blamed for the deaths of these men."

Mila had no time to consider alternatives. "Richard, come with us," she blurted.

"Where?"

Mila decided to start with the easy stuff. Explaining time travel to Richard seemed like a non-starter. "When was the last time you had a walk in the forest?"

"I cannot remember," Richard said, but he was already smiling.

"Well, come on, it'll be fun."

"Will there be food?" Richard licked his lips.

Mila stifled a laugh. "Yes. There will be food. Any other questions?"

"No." He put his ax over his shoulder and walked toward them.

She led them to the side door and out into the alley. "Put Margaret on the horse."

Richard lifted Margaret up and set her on Mila's horse. A rider came up the alley and stopped. Richard stepped between Margaret and the rider with his ax at the ready.

"Whoa, hold on there, big guy." Mila touched Richard's arm. "This is John. John, this is Richard."

"Hi, Richard. Nice to meet you." To Mila he said, "We need to go back out the alley the way I came in. Quickly—the village square is filling up with knights."

———

Mila switched places with John once they were safe in the forest. She needed to figure out if she could work the MCV, so she rode while he walked beside her, leading the horse. The device had a smooth face, and when Mila swiped her finger across it, a virtual app interface popped open. The first screen asked for a password. *Great.* After everything, she was going to fail because of a password. She was about to cuss when she heard the sound of approaching riders.

"Quickly. Into the forest." John led her horse off the road into the trees. Mila dismounted and hid.

Margaret passed them and rode her horse into a thick copse farther from the road. Richard followed her. He hadn't left her side since the cathedral. Margaret dismounted and urged him to come in behind the trees with her.

Eight riders in full armor rode past without incident.

This was good news and bad news. It meant that Sandra hadn't been captured yet. It probably also meant that Mom's group was ahead on the road. The bad news was that Henri had somehow figured out where they were going.

"They probably picked up the trail left by the carriage," said John.

"Oh, yeah." She smiled at him. "You're good at this stuff when you're not half-dead."

He frowned at her. "I'm sorry I haven't been much help lately."

"Better late than never," said Mila, returning her attention to the MCV as she remounted the horse.

Margaret and Richard joined them. They walked back out to the main road.

"Is there a faster way to the meadow?" John asked Margaret. "Can we go off road or something?"

"Off road?" Margaret repeated in her best Texan accent. "If you mean can we cut through the forest, then yes. We will arrive before dawn."

CHAPTER FIFTY-TWO

May 1, 1341

Mila sat in the shade behind the log where Sandra had pulled the bolt out of John's leg five days earlier. It seemed longer. There was less glare in the shade, and she could read the MCV's display more easily as she tried to guess Chad's password. John had wandered off with Richard and Margaret to explore the meadow. That was just as well. Mila didn't need them hovering while she tried to solve her problem. The jingle of horse tack caught her attention. The carriage drove out onto the meadow, rolled up past the single oak, and stopped. Raymond stood to climb down from the driver's bench.

A flight of crossbow bolts flew out of the forest. Three found their mark, and Raymond toppled off the seat.

Lady Evelyn stepped out of the door as Raymond fell past her and hit the ground. She screamed and dropped to his side. Sandra appeared in the door behind her.

A crossbow bolt thumped into the log near Mila. She ducked.

John came out of the forest and crouched by her side.

"Stay down," he whispered, then yelled toward the carriage. "Sandra! Get back inside and lie on the floor."

Lady Evelyn held Raymond in her arms, but his head hung limp. Sandra pulled her back toward the carriage. Farther down the slope, five knights walked out of the forest, holding crossbows at the ready. Three more knights appeared on horseback behind them. The mounted knights lowered their face plates: it was Baron Reginald, Bishop Edward, and Captain Henri. The little force walked up the slope. Sandra and Lady Evelyn disappeared inside the carriage.

Mila put away the MCV and picked up her crossbow.

"Can you hit those crossbow knights from here?" John said.

"I can try, but won't they shoot at me while I'm aiming?"

"They might. But we're in the shadows here, and they're looking through slits in those helmets. The other side of this log is in bright sunlight. The contrast here in the shadows should make us almost invisible. Just move slowly. They'll notice you if you move quickly." John smiled at her. "You've got this."

Mila's eyes widened. "Really?"

"I'll do it if you want me to." He reached for the crossbow.

"Hell, no." Mila pulled it back. "I've got it."

"Okay." John took a deep breath. "You get ready and wait for my go. Tell me when you're ready. Once you shoot, you duck and reload, then get ready again. Clear?"

"Clear." Mila loaded the crossbow. She slowly brought it up to her shoulder as she sat back on her heels. She aimed at the lead knight. "Ready."

"Reginald!" John shouted from the shadows. "Can you hear me?"

"Yes." Reginald's yell traveled back across the field.

"Heretic!" Edward interrupted. "Pay no attention to the baron. Today, you deal with me."

So the balance of power had shifted. Mila wondered what had brought that about.

"If you stop where you are," said John, "you can still leave with the silver."

Edward laughed. "I have no interest in your silver." He continued to advance behind the walking knights, but Reginald held up a hand, and he and Henri stopped their horses, letting Edward advance alone.

"Go," John whispered.

Mila squeezed the release. The bolt leapt across the meadow and punched a hole in the lead knight's cuirass. The knight went down clutching the bolt.

"Hold," Edward said.

The knights stopped. Edward glanced behind him at Reginald. They were too far away to hear their conversation, but it was clear that Reginald was distancing himself from whatever Edward had in mind.

Mila finished reloading and shouldered her weapon. "Ready."

"Go."

Mila let fly.

Another knight grabbed his stomach and fell to the ground.

"Coward!" Edward shook a gauntlet-covered fist. "Stop shooting the noblemen."

"Nice job," John whispered.

Edward and Reginald had a heated exchange.

"Ready," Mila whispered.

"Go."

Another knight fell.

The two remaining knights charged up the hill toward them. Edward dropped his faceplate and spurred his horse. The giant animal passed the running knights and raced up the hill alone.

"Will you shoot the horse?" John glanced at Mila.

"Not a chance." She finished reloading.

"Didn't think so. Take out those other two knights as fast as you can. I'll take the bishop."

At a full gallop, Edward tipped his sword forward. The mighty warhorse thundered toward them. John crawled to the right, away from Mila. He stood slowly and stepped into the sun.

Mila popped up and shot another knight. His companion got a return shot off in her direction. The bolt sliced off the bottom of her earlobe as it sailed past her head. It didn't hurt as much as she thought it would. *Weird.* She ducked and reloaded while her blood ran down her neck.

John held his sword with two hands like a bat as the bishop's horse galloped toward him.

Richard charged out of the forest. He had the battle-ax held high as he took up a position next to John. Edward reined in the horse and almost toppled forward out of the saddle.

The last knight finished reloading his crossbow. He brought the weapon to his shoulder and Mila shot him. The bolt penetrated his helmet and his head snapped back.

"Come on, you son of a bitch!" John yelled.

But Edward pulled his horse around and trotted back down the slope. His helmet was glued in John's direction, and Mila could only imagine the look of pure hatred hidden beneath it.

"Damn you." Edward spurred his horse and galloped back down the slope.

———

EDWARD RODE DOWN TOWARD THE COWARD REGINALD and his useless captain. They were responsible for his humiliating defeat. If they had only charged with him, he would surely have taken the day by sheer force of numbers. Perhaps he could convince them to charge again? No. They had made their position clear. Now that Edward had lost his force of knights, he had no leverage over Reginald. Even though it was God's will, Reginald would not respond to that line of reasoning. He never did.

Edward was the only one left to stop these heretics from spreading their sin throughout the kingdom. *Lord, help me to find a way to defeat this wretched evil.*

A scream came from the carriage. He had forgotten the women cowered within. Edward spurred his mount. God's righteous justice would be done after all. If he could kill even one more heretic, it would be enough. Stories would be told throughout the land of St. Edward who slew the heretics that threatened his flock. Edward smiled behind his helm.

Thank you, Lord. He spurred his mount toward the carriage.

———

MILA, JOHN, AND RICHARD RACED DOWN THE

meadow as the bishop's intentions became clear. The lumbering Richard was not built for speed, and John still limped from his injury. Mila quickly found herself in front of the other two, alone.

The bishop dismounted next to the carriage.

Mila had no time to reload her crossbow.

The bishop held his sword at the ready while he reached for the door handle with his free hand.

The inside of the carriage was in shadow, and the bishop paused to open his face plate.

Mila ran past the bishop's mount. Raymond's ornate sword belt glinted in the sun where he lay. She slowed just enough to grab the weapon and slide it out of its scabbard.

The bishop leaned into the dark of the carriage, leading with his sword.

Mila spotted the gap opening up between his back plate and his shoulder piece. Two-handed, she stuck the sword into the space like a pole vaulter launching herself into the air. All of her momentum and weight transferred to the tip of the sword. It was enough to defeat the links of chainmail, and the sword slid through, biting the bishop's flesh.

The bishop screamed and twisted backwards to see what was attacking him.

His own movements provided the additional force necessary for Mila to drive her sword into his heart. Mila held his astonished gaze as he died. This bastard would know he had been killed by a woman.

She was still holding the sword with both hands when she heard the approach of horses.

Sandra and Lady Evelyn climbed down from the

carriage. Lady Evelyn knelt next to Raymond's corpse and placed a hand on his chest.

Reginald and Henri walked their horses around the back of the carriage. Mila bent and loaded her crossbow as John and Richard arrived behind her with their weapons at the ready.

Reginald and Henri made no move to attack.

"I only came for the silver," said Reginald.

"You stupid boy." Lady Evelyn kept her palm on Raymond. "Look what you have done."

"Evelyn, I am sorry. I did not intend harm to Raymond, but when you abandoned your family—"

"You have no idea what a family is." She pointed at Mila and her parents. "These people are a family. Reflect on how they have acted not against one another, but together. This would never have happened if Father were alive. You have surely disappointed him here today."

"Reg." Mila pointed to the track with her crossbow. "You should go."

"But what about my silver?" Reginald said, as though that made his actions all right.

Mila shifted her aim to Reginald's head and took a step toward him.

Henri stepped between Reginald and the bolt, but Reginald put a hand on his shoulder and pulled him back. He climbed into his saddle and rode away with Henri following.

"You." John pointed a finger at Mila.

"What?"

"You were awesome." He walked over to her and pulled her into a hug. It was uncomfortable at first, but then her hands tentatively circled his back. Her hands tightened slightly, and he said, "I love you."

"I know." Mila pulled away. "I love you too." She was not surprised to see Sandra standing beside them, crying.

"What?" Sandra smiled through her tears and sniffed.

———

MILA STOOD AT THE TOP OF THE MEADOW WITH JOHN and Sandra. Richard had begun to dig a grave for Raymond near the carriage, and Margaret sat quietly with Lady Evelyn.

"I've been thinking about this time travel idea of yours," said John. "I want to make sure you both know what you're getting into before we commit to it."

"We're doing it," said Sandra.

"We're going," said Mila.

"Hang on, guys. Let me say this out loud and see if it makes sense to you." He paused. When neither of them spoke, he said, "If we go back—"

"*When* we go back," interrupted Sandra.

"Fine. When we go back, let's say all of that stuff works. We save the guide and meet ourselves as we arrive. Think about that moment. There will be another one of each of us standing there with Jess. Have you guys thought about the significance of that?"

"Yes," said Mila.

"What are you talking about?" said Sandra. "Just spit it out."

"We aren't going home with Jess," Mila said. She watched Sandra process it.

"We aren't going home at all," said John.

Sandra seemed to understand for the first time.

"If we do this," John continued, "It will only be to say goodbye to Jess. Once we've done that, she will go home with the other versions of us. And we will stay here, forever. Is that what you want?"

Mila held Sandra's hands tightly.

"The other option is to go home right now." John had to swallow before he could continue. "We'll have a funeral for Jess, pick up the pieces, and try to get through without her. What do you want to do?"

Without a word exchanged between Mila and her mother, they both said, "We want to see Jess."

"Okay then." John put his hands up in surrender. "I just thought it needed to be said."

"There is one problem," said Mila.

"What?" He and Sandra focused on Mila.

She held up the MCV. "I haven't figured out what the password is."

Without missing a beat, Sandra said, "Ask Margaret."

Mila's jaw dropped open. She grabbed Sandra in a hug. "Mom, you're a genius."

CHAPTER FIFTY-THREE

May 1, 1341

M "Last chance to back out," Mila said. "My family and I are about to activate this device. If it works, we'll go back in time seven days. It may not work. If it doesn't, we could all be killed." She put her arms around Sandra and John. "We think it's worth the risk. You have to decide for yourselves."

Margaret spoke first. "There's nothing left for us here. With the baron angry with us, we cannot stay."

"Okay." Margaret had a reasonable grasp of what was about to happen, and Mila doubted that she'd tried to explain it to Richard.

Lady Evelyn's eyes wandered to the fresh grave in the bluebells. "I will get to see Raymond again, yes?"

Mila nodded. "Anything's possible."

Lady Evelyn stood up straight and stated firmly, "I will come with you."

They walked up the narrow path in the bluebells to the arrival point. Mila pulled the MCV out of her breeches. She swiped the surface, and the holographic display appeared.

Margaret had said the password was *thealamo* but that the screen would be "veer ball." She said Chad had made her memorize the word in case she ever had to explain it to a guest. Mila had had no idea what "veer ball" could possibly mean. She'd run it over and over in her head like she was playing Mad Gab until the words ran together, and there it was. *Verbal.* You had to say the password out loud. That's what Bob had been doing when he said "little big horn" for no reason, back in the SSTTC control room.

Mila said, "The Alamo." The sub-menu system appeared. She typed in the date they had arrived, minus two days.

"Everybody ready?" asked Mila.

They all nodded.

"Okay, come closer." She waved them toward her. "Everybody has to be touching it at the same time."

They all shuffled in and put a hand on the MCV.

"Here goes." Mila swiped a finger across the surface of the sphere.

The meadow began to glow around them. The wind kicked up. Mila had to close her eyes against the intense light. The last thing she remembered was feeling a lump under her foot. She knew instantly what it must be, rolled it between her ankles, and held it as tightly as she could.

————

April 25, 1341

This time the nausea never came. When the air

pressure on her clothes subsided, Mila opened her eyes. They were all standing in the meadow, exactly as they had been just moments before. The only proof they had moved was the absence of the carriage and the dead knights.

Mila still held the MCV between her forefinger and thumb—she had determined not to drop it when they arrived. She placed it back inside the folds of her chainmail then bent and fished around in the bluebells for the lump she had found. She came across a green striped ball that matched the bluebell stems perfectly. When she picked it up, it became the color of her hand. It was their original MCV, the one they'd travelled back with seven days earlier. None of her family had known enough to look around for it when they arrived. They had just assumed it stayed in the present. How different would their trip have been if they had known it was lying here in the meadow the whole time? Mila placed it inside her chain mail with the other one.

"Okay, Margaret," said John. "Take us to Chad's, the fastest way you know."

Margaret led them straight off the meadow into the forest. It wasn't a trail, really, but the undergrowth was sparse and they were able to follow easily. They made good time, and Mila was hopeful the next step in the plan would go well. Then Lady Evelyn began to lag behind.

They all stopped and waited as John walked back to where she was slowly following the group. "Is something the matter?"

"Why must we travel through the woods?" With an expression of disgust, Lady Evelyn lifted one ornate boot at a time and held the hem of her dress out of the dirt with both hands.

"There is no choice," said John in an unusually diplomatic voice. Mila thought he would normally have just thrown her over his shoulder to make up time. "We have to get to the guide's cottage before dawn."

"I am sorry, but I am going as fast as I can."

"Would it help if I shortened your dress?"

"You will do no such thing." Lady Evelyn stopped walking and stared, wide-eyed, at John.

John smiled at Mila and Sandra, mouth open, palms to the sky.

"But perhaps I can suggest a solution," said Lady Evelyn.

"Let's hear it," said John.

"I will return to the meadow and make my way to the inn, on the road. I can await your return there, in comfort." Lady Evelyn smiled. "Perhaps Sandra would like to join me?"

"I like your idea, but Sandra is staying with us," John said. "There is absolutely no chance our family is splitting up."

Mila rolled her eyes. John hadn't changed that much, but she was okay with it. She thought they should stay together too.

"But you shouldn't be alone either." John pointed. "Richard will go with you."

"And Margaret," said Richard.

It would be hard to part Richard from Margaret, but they needed her to lead them to Chad's. Mila tried to think of a way to convince Richard but soon realized Margaret could do it easily. She stepped over to Margaret, but she was interrupted before she could speak.

"I do not need a babysitter." Lady Evelyn started back toward the meadow as if the matter was settled.

Mila smiled. Lady Evelyn had no idea how stubborn John was. Mila touched Margaret's arm and nodded toward Richard.

"Richard," said Margaret. "Look after Lady Evelyn, you big baby. I'll see you soon."

Richard's mouth dropped open. Margaret kept walking in the direction they had been going.

"Thanks, Richard." Mila smiled at him and followed Margaret. She forced herself not to look back, knowing that John wouldn't follow until he knew Richard was on task. A few minutes later, John and Sandra caught up to her and Margaret.

———

Lady Evelyn rushed toward Annie's inn. Richard followed behind her with his head drooping like a petulant child's, still sulking about not being allowed to stay with Margaret. When they reached the inn, it was still dark. "Richard, you will wait outside while I go in and see if Annie is about."

"Yes, Lady Evelyn." He bowed his head and stood to the side of the inn.

Evelyn stepped to the door and hesitated. The next few moments could well change her life forever, but she had come so far and sacrificed too much to turn away now. Inside the inn, just a few steps away, lay proof of whether this strange magic was real. If it *was* real, then Raymond De Falaise would come for her on the morrow and take her in his arms. Evelyn's hand drifted to her secret pocket. She always carried her dagger regardless of how she was dressed. She felt its weight, sucked in a breath, and stepped inside the darkened inn. She had to know.

Evelyn climbed the stairs one at a time, pausing to listen for any change in Annie's snores as they drifted in from the kitchen below. When she reached the door to the only upstairs room, she lifted the latch and stepped inside. A candle burned on a small table by the window, throwing enough light across the room to reveal a woman dressed in the white robes of the Sisters of St. Mary's lying on the bed.

The woman sat up. "I've been expecting you."

Evelyn stopped breathing. The woman sounded just like her. Evelyn crossed to the table and lifted the candle with her free hand. The other still held firmly to her dagger, hidden in her dress. "Do you know me?"

The woman stood and walked into the light. Tears rolled down her cheeks. "Better than anyone."

Evelyn stood frozen, staring at the abbess, who stood in front of her with one hand hidden beneath her white robes. "How did you know to expect me?"

The abbess raised an eyebrow. "At first, I thought I was dreaming, but as I awoke, it became clear that it was a memory. Strange that I should have memories of things that have not yet come to pass."

"What was the memory?" Evelyn asked, but she already knew.

"Raymond's death," said the abbess.

"It was so horrible." Evelyn's words caught in her throat. "You cannot imagine."

"I do not have to." The abbess sniffled. "I thought my heart would break from the pain of it."

"Then you know why I am here?" Evelyn asked.

"You would see Raymond again. Tomorrow when he comes for me, it will be you he finds." The abbess took out her dagger and dropped it quietly on the bed.

"Thank you," said Evelyn. "Let us take a short walk in the forest."

CHAPTER FIFTY-FOUR

April 26, 1341

Chad heard the crash of splintering wood and knew they'd found him. He rolled off the bed and crossed to the chest in the corner of the room. He grabbed the MCV and hissed, "Margaret!"

She rolled over slowly. "What is it, Chaddy?"

Another crash from downstairs.

"They've found me. Come here. Quickly."

She stumbled out of the bed and rushed naked to his side. He hugged her for a moment and handed her the device. "Do you remember what I told you?"

She was still half-asleep, but she nodded. He held the chest open as she folded herself inside.

Boots rumbled up the stairs.

He closed the lid and rushed to the bed.

———

JOHN BURST INTO THE BEDROOM. "DON'T BOTHER getting into bed, Chad. We have to go."

"Who are you?" Chad sat up.

John called toward the chest. "Margaret, get dressed. We have to leave."

"Hey, man, just tell me what this is about." Chad reached under his pillow.

John had his sword out and under Chad's chin before Chad pulled out whatever he was after. "That would be a mistake, Chad. Trust me."

Chad slowly took his hand away from the pillow. A piece of white cloth dangled from his hand. "I was just getting my hanky." Chad blew his nose.

"Margaret, please come out of the chest. I won't hurt you."

The lid lifted, and Margaret poked her head out and stood up. "Chad, darling, can you throw me my frock?"

John had never seen Margaret clean before. She was a beauty, and apparently uninhibited. He gave her the privacy of his back. "Chad, I'm from the future."

"Yeah, I got that from your accent. What's this all about?" Chad found Margaret's dress and tossed it to her.

"I'll tell you after we're on the road. You're going to be taken prisoner at dawn and tortured unless we leave now."

"Why?" Chad grabbed his pants. He was moving with purpose now.

John figured *torture* must have been the motivating word. "All in good time. My family is outside harnessing your horses to the carriage. Bring everything you want to keep. You're not coming back."

Margaret slipped her dress over her head and shrieked.

John spun around. The girl was pointing to the stairway. He followed her gaze. Old Margaret stood at the top of the stairs. *Not good.* "Margaret! I told you to wait downstairs."

"I'm sorry, John." Margaret sniffed. "I had to see for myself," she said, but her eyes never left Chad. "Hello, Chaddy." She smiled and went back down the stairs.

"Chaddy!" yelled new Margaret. "Why does that woman look and sound like me?"

John didn't let him answer. "You'll have all day to explain it to her once we're on the road. Let's go."

Chad threw on a tunic and grabbed his boots.

"I'm not going anywhere until you tell me what's going on." She crossed her arms and stood in the chest.

"Okay, Chad, time's up. Does this thing lock?" John pointed at the chest.

"Yeah, but..."

John crossed to the chest and pushed down on Margaret's head.

"Chad!" She gave way at the knees and folded herself back into it. "Why are you just standing there?"

John slammed the lid and sat on it. He held out his hand. "Key."

Margaret's muffled shouting was still audible. "Chad. Let me out!"

Chad handed John the key. He locked it and took an end of the chest. Chad grabbed the other end, and they carried the chest down the stairs and out the door.

———

AT CHAD'S COTTAGE, MILA AND SANDRA HELPED Margaret attach the horses to the carriage while John went inside to find Chad. Margaret showed them what to do, then drifted away. Mila assumed she had to relieve herself, but a few minutes later she came out of the cottage with a weird look on her face. John and Chad followed her out, carrying the coin chest between them. They struggled more than Mila and Jess had. "Why's it so heavy?" Mila said.

John ignored her and looked at Chad. "Anything else you want to bring?"

"Nope." Chad shrugged. "My MCV and my money are in here with Margaret."

That explained Margaret's look. Mila had forgotten there would be two of them. Why was new Margaret in the box? Mila wanted to ask, but John and Chad were struggling to get the chest up on the roof of the carriage.

"All right, let's go," said John when they'd succeeded. "Chad, you ride with me." He pointed to the driver's bench as he climbed up.

Sandra, Mila, and old Margaret climbed inside. The carriage was out of the glen and well down the road toward Annie's inn when the light of dawn began to filter through the leaves overhead. Mila was almost asleep, despite the constant bumping of the carriage and new Margaret's muffled protests. That's when John and Chad started talking. Now there would be no sleep.

"Can we let Margaret out now?" Chad said.

"Well, here's the thing. I don't know anything about the science of it all, but what if the two Margarets touch?" John asked. "You've heard the stories about matter and antimatter being in the same place at the same time, right? Is this like that?"

Chad took too long to answer.

"You don't know, do you?" said John.

"I gotta say no," Chad said. "No, I don't."

"She stays in the box, then."

"Yup."

"Chad!" The chest muffled new Margaret's shouts. "I heard you!"

"Can you tell me what happened yet?" asked Chad.

"Our Margaret knows more of the details than I do, but long story short, you got sloppy. You were captured. They used Margaret to get a confession out of you."

"No." Chad sounded surprised.

"You sold out your next set of visitors—us—to save her."

"Really?"

Did Chad really think John had made it up? Why would anybody do that? Was Chad that much of an idiot? Mila waited for a biting response from John, but when it came it was more tempered than she had expected.

"You know what, Chad?" said John. "Don't talk."

"Sorry."

"As soon as we arrived, they hunted us like animals. One of my daughters"— John had to pause, and Mila felt his anguish—was burned at the stake. We managed to escape. My other daughter figured out that we could travel back in time and stop it from happening."

"Clever girl."

"Yeah, she is. Are you done?"

"Sorry."

That made Mila smile. It was nice to hear her father on her side. She could totally get used to that.

"So, we're going to meet ourselves on arrival," continued John. "You're going to take us—*them*— immediately back to the future, and our daughter who died will get to live. Clear?"

"Yeah, but there's one thing."

"What?"

"If the other *you* goes back to the future, you have to stay here," Chad said.

"We know. You got a solution for that? I'm all ears."

Chad said nothing.

Great. They had clung to the hope that Chad would know the science or the software and come up with a solution. Now that hope was gone. "So that's the plan," said John, sounding as disappointed as Mila felt.

"What about the two Margarets?" said Chad.

"Your problem," said John.

CHAPTER FIFTY-FIVE

A*pril 26, 1341*
Captain Henri led his guards out of the fog at the forest's edge. He stopped his horse where the village path met the Roman road. The moist air sapped the heat from his body, and he pulled at the neck of his chain mail to ease the rings away from his chin. Across the valley, the castle seemed to float in a sea of fog, and he pictured the baron's dogs sleeping on the warm hearthstones of the great hall. The dogs had it better than the men. But here they were, out in the brisk air just after lauds. Best get to it.

"Jean-Pierre."

"*Oui, capitaine?*" His tracker hurried over to stand near Henri's horse.

The man could speak a little English, but Henri preferred to stick to French so that nuance was not lost and the English guards were not privy to their conversations. "Can we still see the trail?"

"The tracks are clear until they reach the main road. Then the carriage is lifted up out of the mud, and they are gone." Jean-Pierre indicated the point where the tracks disappeared.

"It sounds like we just need to follow the road until we see the tracks leave it. Yes?"

"Yes, but if we miss them, we could wind up in Canterbury."

"Please do not miss them. I have no desire to go to Canterbury today or any day."

Henri signaled his squad to follow Jean-Pierre and waited as they marched past him. He dismounted and led his horse up onto the road. Warmer now that he was moving, he settled into the slow but steady pace his men had set.

Around prime, Jean-Pierre left the road and disappeared behind a copse of oaks.

"Hold." The squad stopped at Henri's command.

When Jean-Pierre reappeared, he smiled. "We will not be going to Canterbury today."

———

"Perhaps we *will* be going to Canterbury after all." Jean-Pierre followed the squad as it marched back out of the glen.

Henri smiled and remounted. They had searched the cottage, the barn, and the surrounding fields, but there was no sign of the heretic. Henri squeezed his horse, and it caught up to Jean-Pierre. "The barn door was open when we arrived, was it not?"

"*Oui.*"

It was still too cold for the door to be left open at night, yet there was no one tending to the livestock, and the carriage was missing. Something was not right. "They must be close. Quickly now."

Jean-Pierre ran to the front of the squad.

They climbed up onto the Roman road and followed Jean-Pierre as he picked up fresh tracks that led away from the castle and deeper into the forest.

CHAPTER FIFTY-SIX

April 26, 1341

A   Mila woke up to the sound of Richard's voice.

"Where is Margaret?"

When John steered the carriage down the path in front of Annie's inn, Richard was there to meet them. He hurried along beside the carriage, looking up at John and trying to peek inside the gaps in the curtains.

"She's fine, Richard. Don't worry," said John. "She's in the carriage."

"Who's the freak?" Chad said.

"Don't be an asshole, Chad. He already killed you once."

"Killed me? What? You never said that."

"Well, now you know, so be nice."

The carriage stopped near the front of the inn. Mila, Margaret, and Sandra stepped out of the vehicle and stretched after the long ride.

John climbed down and pointed out the chest to Richard. "Can you help me lift this down?"

"Yes." Richard grabbed it by himself and hoisted it off the carriage.

"Carefully. It has precious cargo."

Richard placed it on the ground between them.

Margaret went over to Richard. "How are you, big man?"

"I am well." He smiled. "I am happy that you are back."

Chad wandered over and tried to pull Margaret into a hug. "It's good to see you."

Richard lowered his brows and clenched his fists, and Mila thought there might be a fight. But Margaret placed a palm on Chad's chest and pushed him off.

"No, Chaddy. Do you not see? You were dead."

"But Margaret... I thought you were my girl."

Richard loomed closer and stood between Chad and Margaret.

Sandra touched John's back, gently pushing him toward the trio and nodding not so subtly at Richard.

"All right," John said. "Margaret, can you teach Richard how to feed and water the horses?" Margaret nodded. "Thank you. We need to leave again as soon as you're finished."

She led the animals, still pulling the carriage, around to the stable behind the inn. Richard glared at Chad then followed Margaret.

"Mila, I need you to make sure Richard stays by the stable. I don't think he could handle seeing two Margarets."

"I think you're right." Mila followed Richard and Margaret toward the stable. She stopped at the corner of the inn, where she could see the stables but still hear John and Chad. There was no way she was going to miss this.

"You can't leave her in there all day." Sandra pointed at the chest.

"I know. I'm getting to it," said John. "Hey, Chad, you need to start thinking about boxed Margaret. She *is* still your girl."

"Yeah," said Chad, sounding almost disappointed. "I guess you're right. This is confusing, man."

"I don't doubt it." John leaned over the chest and took the key out of his pocket. "You have to keep boxed Margaret under control. Can you?"

"I think so, dude."

"Can or can't, Chad. Otherwise she stays in the box."

"Can, can. Why are you such a hard-ass, man? You sound like a drill sergeant or something."

Mila smiled. Chad was learning, albeit slowly.

John knocked on the lid of the chest. "Margaret, can you hear me?"

"Yes!" New Margaret offered a muffled yell.

"I'm going to let you out now."

"Well it's about bloody time!"

"We're going to explain why we've been keeping you in the box."

"I don't care. I just want out."

"You have to listen to me once I open the box. If you can't listen to me, I can't open the box."

"What do you mean, you can't open the box? You've got the bloody key!"

"Margaret, are you going to listen to me?"

There was silence from the box. "How about this? You open this box right bloody now or I'll start playing with this wee ball."

John stuck the key in the lock, turned it, and whipped the lid open. He reached in and tried to grab the MCV out of her hands. She bit his forearm. He yanked his arm back.

Margaret clutched the MCV to her bosom. "Start talking."

"Chad, you tell her." John held the gash on his arm. Blood showed through his fingers.

"Here, let me see it." Sandra lifted John's hand up. "Let's wash it and dress it." She gestured toward the inn. John hesitated, then followed her toward the door.

CHAPTER FIFTY-SEVEN

April 27, 1341
Somebody knocked on the roof of the carriage as it came to a stop. Mila opened her eyes. They had stopped at the turnoff to the bluebell meadow. The plan was to leave Lady Evelyn, Margaret, and Richard there while they went to the meadow to say goodbye to Jess.

Mila, Sandra, and Lady Evelyn stepped out of the carriage.

"This is the place," said Chad as he and John climbed down from the driver's bench.

New Margaret slid toward the door, but John shut it before she could come out.

"Chaddy!" new Margaret yelled from inside the carriage. "I want to come out."

"You're up, Chad," said John.

Chad huffed then climbed inside next to her. "Let me keep you company. It will only be a little while longer."

Mila closed the door behind Chad. The carriage only had room for four, plus two on the driver's bench, so they had had to choose who would walk and who would ride.

Old Margaret and Richard were the logical choice to walk. It helped keep the Margarets apart and kept Richard from discovering that there were, in fact, two of them. As she watched the road, old Margaret and Richard rounded the last bend and walked toward the carriage. There was about a minute left before they arrived.

John said to Lady Evelyn, "Chad figures we'll be gone most of the morning. We'll try to be as quick as we can."

Lady Evelyn nodded. "I suggest you hurry. When Henri does not find Chad at his cottage, he will continue his search—first to Annie's and then along this very road."

"Ladies." John nodded Mila and Sandra toward the carriage, and they climbed in. He banged the side of the carriage with his palm. "Chad, you stay put. I'll drive."

————

THE CARRIAGE WAS PARKED UNDER THE SOLITARY oak. Chad stood in the bluebells nearby, while a gust whipped the flowers into an angry sea. He slipped his hood over his head and pulled Margaret's face to his chest to shield her eyes. The meadow ignited in a plasma flash, and when the light dissipated, he removed his hood.

Just up the slope, four people had arrived. He saw John bend over and hold Sandra's hair while she threw up. Mila sank to her knees and held her stomach. A gorgeous woman he didn't recognize stretched and tried to fix her hair. She had to be Jess. Chad took Margaret by the hand and walked toward them. "Welcome to the fourteenth century. I'm Chad, your tour guide. This is my friend Margaret."

"Hi, Chad. Margaret," John said. "This is my wife Sandra, and our daughters Jess and Mila."

"Hello." Chad nodded toward them.

Margaret reached toward Jess's head. "Ah luv yer hair." She tried the Texan accent he'd been teaching her.

Chad brushed his foot through the bluebells between them. He felt the fallen MCV before he saw it. Marking the spot with his toe, he bent and scooped it up. It did not become visible until he held it up to the light. Only then did the auto-camo response shut off. A ball of bluebells reverted to just a ball.

"I'm afraid I have some bad news." Chad pocketed the device. "We're going to have to cut short your trip."

"What?" John glanced around the meadow. "Why?"

"This is going to sound strange, but it will be easier for Jess to explain it to you once she has spoken with the people in the carriage." Chad pointed down the slope.

"That's not happening." John stepped in front of Jess. "She isn't going anywhere near that carriage until I get some answers."

"He said you'd say that."

"Who?"

"Nothing," Chad said under his breath. "How about this: you escort her to the carriage. Once she looks inside, she'll tell you herself that she's safe to enter."

"Will everybody stop talking about me as though I'm not here?" Jess stepped around John and started walking toward the carriage. John hurried after her.

"Please wait here." Chad left Margaret standing with Sandra and Mila and rushed after John.

Jess reached the carriage and waited for him. "Now what?"

"Just open the door and take a peek inside. Once your eyes have adjusted to the dark, take a good look at the occupants."

John grabbed her elbow. "You don't have to do this."

"Dad. I'm a big girl." She opened the door and stuck her head in. She whipped her head out and stared wide-eyed at John. Her mouth dropped open. She glanced up the slope toward Sandra and Mila and shoved her head back in through the door. "Holy shit!"

"What is it?" John took a step toward her.

Jess pulled her head out of the door to stop her dad. She put a hand on his chest. "I'll be fine. I'll see you in a minute."

"I'll be right here. You just have to shout, and I'm in the door."

"It's not like that. There is no danger in the carriage. Please go back up and keep Mom and Mila company. They're probably getting a little freaked out."

"*They* are?"

"Dad. Please." Jess tilted her head to the side. John stood there a moment. "Go." Jess crossed her arms and stood blocking the door.

"All right." He walked back up the slope toward his family.

Chad handed Jess the MCV from his pocket. "Please give this to your other dad." He nodded to the carriage. "He might need it."

"Um, okay." Jess accepted the sphere and climbed into the carriage.

Chad walked up the slope toward Margaret. He wasn't quite sure what she might say, and he didn't want to leave her alone with the new arrivals for long.

———

"HI, BABY." SANDRA REACHED OUT TO JESS AND TOOK

her hands. They were warm and strong, like her smile. Sandra squeezed them gently and tried to forget that this was the last time she would ever hold her daughter. She let her eyes study every curve of Jess's beautiful face, every nuance of light in her hair. These memories had to last a lifetime, and she was starting to realize just how long that might be. Suddenly, she grabbed Jess into a hug. The tears flowed freely down her cheeks and dripped onto Jess's shoulder, but she didn't care. Her baby was in her arms again, and that was all that mattered. She wanted to hold her and squeeze her until they were one. She needed to imprint this moment on her soul.

"Will somebody please tell me what's going on?" Jess said over Sandra's shoulder.

"I'm sorry." Sandra loosened her grip. "We're here to say..." Her fingers flew to her lips as her throat tightened in a knot. If she said the word, it would become real. This moment would end, and she couldn't bear the thought of it. She shook her head and squeezed her eyes shut. She just had to hold Jess for as long as she possibly could.

———

Mila held Jess's gaze over Sandra's shoulder. After a while, Sandra let her pull away.

"Hey, Jess." Mila gave her a hug.

"Hey, Mi." Jess released her and sat back. "What happened to your ear?"

"Oh, this is nothing." Mila touched her missing lobe. "The trip doesn't go all that well, especially for you. It pretty much goes tits up from the moment we arrive and ends with you dying."

"What?" Jess's eyes flipped to John and Sandra.

"Yup. In our timeline, you're dead." Mila raised her eyebrows for effect. "We had to watch you..." The image snuck up on her. She'd promised herself she'd keep it light, but the pain in her chest had other plans. She took a breath and choked it back. "So, through the magic of time travel, we're here to send you home before that happens... and say goodbye."

"Goodbye?" Jess glanced at Sandra and John. "You guys can't come home?"

"What would we do with our other selves?" Mila smirked. "Keep them in the closet?"

"Okay, that's enough." Sandra put a hand on Mila's knee. "Give her a minute to process it."

―――――

JOHN WATCHED HIS DAUGHTER COME TO GRIPS WITH what Mila had told her. She was a smart kid. She'd work it out.

She watched him too. He opened his arms, and she climbed in. He squeezed her hard. He didn't want to lose it, but he could feel it in his throat like a grapefruit. "I... wanted," he said, taking a deep breath and blowing it out slowly, "you to know... that I love you."

"I love you too, Daddy." Jess smiled and held his face.

That just about did him in. He took a quick breath to head off the lump in his throat and *growled* it out on the exhale. When he had reined in his voice, he said, "Now you go home and have an awesome life. Follow your heart and do all the things you can dream of. Just not time travel." He paused. "Promise me!" he barked.

"I promise." Her eyes were tearing up.

The grapefruit jumped back in his throat with a

vengeance. "There's something else I need to say, not to you but to Mila." He looked into Mila's eyes. "I'm sorry."

The tears attacked him, and his chest heaved with sobs. "I'm so sorry... I couldn't save Jess." Through the blur of salt and fluid on his face, he managed to spit out, "You deserved to have her in your life."

———

"Excuse me." Mila tapped Jess on the shoulder and waited for her to lean out of John's arms. Mila hugged John and then raised his tearstained face with both hands. "*We* couldn't save her." He took a beat to process it as he stared into her eyes. "You weren't alone. We all failed. Together."

He sniffed and smiled at her. "How did you get to be so smart?"

"I'm your daughter... and you're my father."

"You bet your ass you are." He hugged her.

Mila couldn't remember the last time he'd hugged her like that. She hugged him back.

"Wow." Jess sniffed and wiped her nose on her sleeve. "I've never seen you guys get along like this. I kind of want to stay here with you."

"No. This is my family." Mila pointed up the hill. "Yours is out there."

Jess pulled Mila into her arms and gave her a hug. "I love you."

Mila patted Jess on the back and gently pushed her away, wiping a tear from her cheek. "Now you need to go before we all lose it and your family comes down the hill to see why there's water pouring out of the carriage."

Jess laughed as she backed out of the carriage. She paused at the door and mouthed, "Bye."

When Mila could no longer hear Jess walking back up the slope, she opened the door a crack and peeked at their doppelgangers up the hill. "I have to look."

Chad took his MCV out of his pocket and held it up. They all placed their hands on it.

"You should shut your eyes," said Dad.

"Why?" Couldn't he stop being a dad for one second? The sphere erupted in pure light. The inside of the carriage lit up as Mila fell away from the door, grasping at her face. "Shit! I forgot about that part."

Her dad chuckled as she blinked helplessly.

———

**The McLeods are back in the next Split-Second Time Travel Story, BACK IN TIME.
Read on for a preview.**

If you enjoyed this book, please leave a review wherever you bought this book to help other readers discover the series!

April 5, 2018

Jess squeezed her eyes shut. The unbearable light bled away, and she felt the hard metal grate poke through her soft leather slippers. When she opened her eyes, Chad stood next to her in the SSTTC launch room.

Alone.

"Where are they?" Jess grabbed Chad by the shoulders and shook him. "Open your eyes. The light's faded."

"Hey, take it easy." Chad opened his eyes.

"What happened? Where is the rest of my family?" Dread fell on her chest like an engine block.

Chad walked to the tinted glass door and slid it open. A wall of computer noise assaulted their ears and he had to yell above it. "Hey, Bob. Jess has some questions for you."

Bob, the same guy who had launched her whole family twenty minutes before, stepped past Chad into the launch room. "Please come with me, Miss McLeod." He stood to the side, eyes downcast, and held his arm out, indicating the door.

Jess watched Chad wander away between the rows of computer racks. To Bob she said, "You can call me Constable. And I'm not going anywhere until I get answers."

"I can answer all of your questions if you'll just step out of the launch room and follow me."

"Where is my family?"

"Please." Bob pointed at the door again.

Jess folded her arms across her chest. "I'm not moving."

"We need the room, Bob." A red-bearded man in chain mail filled the doorway behind Bob. He had a longbow and quiver of arrows across his back and a sword and dagger at his waist. He stepped into the tiny room, pulling his chain mail coif up over his head. "Let's go, buddy."

"Derek! I told you to stay in holding until I had the room prepped." Bob darted his eyes between Jess and Derek.

Three more men dressed and armed like Derek edged their way around Bob and walked into the launch room. They took up positions around the MCV, and Derek began punching in a date on the touch-screen interface.

"Guys!" Bob looked like he was going to pop a vein. "You're breaking protocol here."

"You know how time sensitive these SR missions are." Derek's focus swiveled to Jess. "Just tell her the truth."

"Somebody, tell me something." Jess waited for Bob or Derek to address her directly.

"Will you leave the launch room if I tell you?" Derek asked her quietly.

"Don't do it," Bob said like a threatening parent. "This has to be contained."

Jess ignored Bob and focused on Derek. "Absolutely."

"The APR kicked in. My team got tagged for the SR mission. We're going back to get the rest of your family. But the longer we stand around here talking about it, the farther away from the arrival point they'll be."

"You know you're getting fired, right, Derek?" Bob pointed a bony finger at the larger man.

"Don't threaten me, Bob," Derek said calmly. "It won't go well for you."

"I want to come with you." Jess took a step toward the group of men at the MCV.

"Rolly." Derek nodded slightly to the guy with his back to Jess.

"No can do, sweetie." Rolly put a hand on Jess's shoulder and pushed her toward the door.

Jess grabbed his hand and whipped it behind him, driving his face into the door frame and pinning him in place. "Did you just call me *sweetie?*"

Derek laughed at his buddy struggling against Jess's hold. "What is your name, ma'am?"

"Constable McLeod." Jess glanced at Derek, keeping upward pressure on Rolly's arm.

"Constable, I understand emotions are running high here. But right now, I have a job to do, and you're not helping. In fact, you're delaying me, and that'll only make it more difficult for me to find your parents."

Jess sighed. She needed to let the professionals do what they were trained to do. How many times had she given civilians the same speech? "You're right." She released Rolly and stepped from the room.

Rolly rubbed his shoulder and glared at her like he

might retaliate. Jess met his gaze and took a half step back, bending slightly at the knees.

"Rolly!" Derek's voice was like a whip. Rolly slumped at the shoulders and walked back to the MCV.

Bob stared in wonder. "Holy shit, Rolly. I've never seen a woman take you like that."

Rolly flipped the bird at Bob without looking back.

"Bob." Derek pointed. "Out."

Bob exited the room and slid the door closed just in time to contain the light emissions. He stepped over to the console and checked the readouts. When the light died away, the men were gone.

"What does APR mean?" Jess still had questions, and Bob was going to answer them.

"I can't tell you." Bob turned from the console. "It's proprietary."

"Are you kidding me?"

"No, ma'am. You should never have heard those terms."

"So give me the official version. What were you going to tell me if I had *stepped from the room* like you asked?"

"I can't tell you anything. I would have taken you to the change room and given you your locker key so you could shower and change back into your own clothes. Then when you came out, one of our PR people would have met you and explained what we were doing about your family."

PR people. Seriously? "Does this happen a lot?"

"No." Bob shook his head.

"But Derek said he was tagged with this mission, and it didn't look like it was his first time."

Bob turned back to his console. "Derek and his team have some experience in survivor recovery missions."

"So that's what SR stands for?"

"No. Yes. Shit. That's proprietary—you can't repeat it."

"Fine." Jess took a breath. "You said it hadn't happened before, and then you said Derek had some experience. Which is it?"

"It's never happened before... on the Canterbury tour."

"So this is Derek's first mission in that time period." That wasn't good.

In an instant, Jess jammed her eyes shut. Her left breast screamed inside her dress. She clutched her chest.

"What's the matter?"

"I don't know." Jess opened her eyes. Why was she clutching her chest? "That was weird."

"Are you sure you're all right?"

"I'm fine. How long until Derek gets back with my family?"

"Hard to say."

"Bullshit."

"It depends how quickly he finds them." Bob looked away before meeting Jess's eyes again. "There is no way to guess at that."

"Wow." Jess sighed. It wasn't a shining moment for the SSTTC. First Rolly insulted her, and now Bob was flat-out lying to her. Not to mention fucking up their holiday. "Does your company train you in asshole behavior, or is it a prerequisite to get hired?"

Bob's jaw dropped open. "I beg your pardon?"

Jess poked his chest. "A minute ago, you were talking about protocols, and now suddenly it's guesswork? It's time travel, Bob. You expect me to believe that Derek can't punch in a predetermined return time, regardless of how long the mission takes?"

Bob looked at his watch. "I'm sorry. I can't tell you. I'll get fired."

Jess rolled her eyes. "Jeez, Bob, grow a pair. I just want to know whether I should go get changed or wait here in the control room."

"You have time to change. Afterwards you can wait in the cafeteria. I'll send the PR guys to meet you there." Bob grabbed a key hanging on a pegboard next to Jessica's name and handed it to her.

He led her through the racks of computers to the hall. He even went so far as to point at the door with the sticker of a woman's silhouette on it. "Right through there."

"Dude, really?" Jess shook her head as she walked into the change room that she had used with her mom and sister less than half an hour before.

———

Jess walked along the row of lockers looking for the one she'd used that morning. Inside her locker she found her jeans and hoodie along with her underwear and Nikes. She couldn't wait to get into her own comfy clothes.

She stripped off the scratchy JumpGear dress. Something clunked when she dropped it down on the bench. She rummaged through the garment and found the MCV. Chad had given it to her in the meadow back in 1341. *"Give this to your dad. He might need it,"* Chad had said. Then she'd climbed into the carriage and met a devastated second version of her family. They'd said the second version of her was dead and they were going to have to stay in the past so she could come home with the version she'd arrived with.

She'd forgotten all about the MCV with the shock of it all. Could Chad blame her? That was a lot to take in. Now add to that, the version of her family she was traveling with had not arrived home with her, and the SSTTC had sent an SR team to find the devastated one. And why hadn't Chad known that would happen? Shouldn't the SSTTC have trained their guide to know the protocols for these situations? This wasn't the first time, was it?

She needed to find Chad. She could give him back the MCV and get some answers.

But first the shower called to her.

ABOUT THE AUTHOR

Ken Johns spent twenty-five years working in film and television postproduction. Now he writes commercial fiction from his home on the west coast of British Columbia. Visit Ken online at www.kenjohnsauthor.com for more information.

ACKNOWLEDGMENTS

Thanks to my mentor, Eileen Cook, and my ongoing cohort at TWSO Speculative Fiction at SFU: Lisa Voisin, Nick Clewley, Cynthia Sharp, and Jocelyne Gregory. Your feedback on this journey is both inspirational and indispensable. To my first beta readers, Ken Hayward, Bill Hammond, Dave Jennings, Daryl Smith, and Greg Brown, your input was invaluable. To my publishing consultant, Crystal Stranaghan, and my editor, Amanda Bidnall, your expertise has saved me a million headaches.

And thank you to my family, Collette, Adelle, and Penny, for your infinite patience.